Ten Days
of
Perfect

Andrea Randall

Ten Days of Perfect

November Blue Series, Book One
Copyright © 2012 by Andrea Randall
Cover Photo and Design by Evan Spinosa
Permission for use of song lyrics to *"Heaven When We're Home"*
given by Ruth Moody

ISBN-10: 147937296X
ISBN-13: 978-1479372966

DEDICATION

To Western Massachusetts, for fostering creativity, independent thinking, and being the place I still call home—even when I live hundreds of miles away. Thank you for giving me the best teachers I could have asked for.

Always love with reckless abandon

xo

THE KISS

"There is the kiss of welcome and of parting, the long, lingering, loving, present one; the stolen, or the mutual one; the kiss of love, of joy, and of sorrow; the seal of promise and receipt of fulfillment."
~ *Thomas C. Haliburton.*

A tear splashes on the crisp page, blurring the delicate lines, as I trace Haliburton's words with my thumb. How wise he was. Ten days ago, I had no way of appreciating the true meaning of these words. The anticipation of the first kiss simmers with more passion than the kiss itself; filled with possibility, it can be anything you want it to be. Time stands still inside its magic. Your heart races as eagerness takes the reins. Swollen lips pulse with lustful expectation while the space between you begs for closure; the connection that follows met with equal parts relief and exploration.

Yes, the first kiss is intense, and this one was no different. Who am I kidding? It was completely different; passion sprang from places in my soul that had previously sat undrilled. I've been kissed before, that much my brain remembers; but his kisses linger in my bones, leaving me with a weight my soul can't bear to lift.

The first time I laid eyes on Bo, I knew he was different; all internal dialogue stopped and my soul nudged my eyes to meet his. Each time his fingers strummed across the strings of his guitar, the sound reverberated in my soul as if it was receiving a message my ears couldn't hear.

All things considered, that was the second time I saw him. But, it was the first time my soul wept at his beauty while being dipped backwards, holding on to her pillbox hat, and kicking up a heel. Most notably, it was the first time my soul whispered to me, in words so clear, *Oh, November, this is it.* I can still hear them...

CHAPTER ONE

Ten days ago...

I worked late that Tuesday to finish up some lingering projects before dropping my car off at the local garage. Two blocks from my apartment, the garage stood vacant. I parked my car and left the keys in the glove compartment, as instructed. I turned to walk home, enjoying the pinks and purples that brushed through the May sunset on Cape Cod.

The sound of a car door slamming next to the garage made me jump. I decided I'd poke my head around the corner and see if someone was there so I could hand my keys to them. My head only made it far enough around the corner to see the tailgate of a large, rusty blue pickup truck, and two sets of feet hit the ground. Something, perhaps my intuition, set off warning bells in my head, and I decided to turn around and go home instead. I'd taken two steps away from my car before I heard their sneering voices. Voices can sneer, I learned in that instant, and I immediately froze.

"Well... where the hell is he? This is bullshit." A young man, I guessed, coughed as he addressed his truck mate. "I'm gonna kick the shit out of him after we get his money and *still* make Ray pay for it."

I begged my feet to move. *Please, please go. You're alone, these guys are clearly bad news, and you really have no way of defending yourself other than running; they have a car, they'd catch you eventually.* Still, my feet were anchored in morbid curiosity,

1

forcing me to listen longer.

"He'll be here, Bill, take it easy. Christ, he's never stiffed us before, and he won't start now—it's for Ray, after all."

Once I heard their names, fear convinced me that I now knew too much. The one with the simmering temper was Bill. He was as tall as the cab of his truck, if not taller, and his voice sounded like pain personified. It was a voice I never wanted to hear directed toward me; it churned my stomach and sent chills racing off my spine. Thankfully, the more levelheaded, albeit smaller, guy was there to calm him down.

Realizing how irresponsible I was being with my safety, I forced myself to move. It would be dark soon and talk of ass-kicking and getting money from someone was more than I needed to hear. As my feet hit the sidewalk at the edge of the small parking lot, another car pulled up from the street behind the garage. I slowed when I reached a large oak tree at the corner of the lot. Curiosity stopped me with her hand; made me listen as I tried to catch my anxious breath. *Why do you care? Didn't curiosity kill the cat?* Thankfully I'm no cat. I could see just the backs of the men as I used a giant tree as my camouflage.

"Gentlemen, you're early." A young-sounding male with a confident voice emerged from vehicle number two.

"Cut the shit, Spike. You're late and you know it. We didn't come all the way down here to fuck around. This is a favor, remember?" Bill's anger tore through the quiet lot.

Spike? Seriously?

"No need to swear, Buddy, I have it right here. And I appreciate the *favor.*" I noted the sarcasm in Spike's voice.

"Hand it over so we can go home, Asshole. You've *got* all the money; I don't know why we're still doing these little exchanges." Bill's unnamed friend sounded curt and bored at the same time.

"You're a real prick, you know... "

Suddenly, I heard a thump followed by a low grunt when Bill punched Spike square in the stomach. I had to cover my mouth to suffocate the scream that was trying to use my throat as an emergency exit. Terror flooded all five of my senses. One side of my brain told me to run away while the other told me to wait to see if Spike was OK. That side held its blue ribbon as I rooted my feet next to the oak tree.

"Bill! Son of a bitch, what'd you—ugh—what the hell?!" Spike, folded in half at the waist, stumbled back for a second before righting himself, one arm still clenched around his stomach.

"Seriously Bill... " his friend cut in, trying to step between him and Spike.

"Shut the hell up Max! We're doing this bastard and Ray a favor and he strings us along like he's the one in charge. Sometimes, those of us *in* charge need to remind those of us who *aren't*."

OK, so the calm one was Max. This was little consolation given the tension hanging like fog around them; I begged the tree to swallow me.

"Don't *ever* talk to me about Ray, you prick!" Spike threw a hook that drove Bill to the ground. I counted this as astoundingly impressive given that Spike was probably two inches shorter, and 50 pounds lighter, than Bill.

Suddenly, arms and legs were everywhere as night poured in around the brawl that erupted between the three men. My eyelids rose, taking in what little light was available as my eardrums pounded with the sounds of battle.

"I'll talk about who and what I want, douchebag; especially about lying, trashy—ahh! Asshole!" Bill recoiled to the fetal position on the pavement when Spike kicked him.

"Bill, I'm *fucking* warning you," Spike's voice was calculating and calm, purring like a panther ready to pounce, "*never* say Ray's name in front of me again. Got it?" I knew if I was Bill that I'd make damn sure never to say it again.

"Come on, Bill, let's get the hell out of here before someone calls the cops," Max interjected, adrenaline ringing in his voice. He'd spent more time trying to break up the fight than participating, so he was still thinking clearly.

The cops, why didn't I think of that?

"Max, just get in the truck if you're going to be a useless pussy." Bill's body was sure to match his clearly bruised ego. Max didn't listen; he stood cross-armed, probably waiting for Bill to back the hell down.

Bill threw his colossal body forward for one final punch, followed by a string of garbled cussing and the shutting of two truck doors. I jumped again as the engine roared to life, driving Bill and Max away. Luckily they went out the back driveway as I remained glued to the tree.

Looking around, I realized that despite being only two blocks from my heavily populated neighborhood, I was in the middle of a business district that was closed and locked up for the night. Those guys were no fools; they knew no one would be around. I had every right to freeze earlier—no one would have heard my screams if I'd gotten into trouble.

Relief escorted air away from my lungs as I heard the truck motor further into the distance, but a thought in the back of my nosey head made the blood leave my face. The rusty truck carrying Bill and Max had left, but the other vehicle was still here. Spike was still hanging around the garage, and I didn't know if he was OK.

The remaining street lights flickered on as sunset whispered its goodbye. I figured I should call 911 if the guy was still lying on the side of the garage; I could no longer see him in the shadows from where I was standing. Even if he was gone, I thought I should still call. I walked cautiously across the top of the parking lot, looking for Spike. A shadowed figure slowly stood up, and my breath was slammed beneath the trap door of my throat.

"H-hey! Are you OK sir?" I managed. For all he knew, I had *just* walked over.

"I'm fine," he clutched his ribs as he coughed, "thanks." Well, *that* was convincing.

"You don't look too good," I said as I leaned in close enough to

4

see him moving with a strained and painful effort. I remained far enough away to leave room between us should I need to run. "Can I call an ambulance for you, or something?"

"Look, you need to get out of here. It's dark, you're alone, and those guys might circle back." He didn't look up. Speaking through clenched teeth, he had his hands on his knees, regulating his breathing.

Why did he say "those guys?" How did he know I'd just witnesssed the fight?

"What guys." It wasn't a question, really, since I didn't need an answer.

"I saw you dropping off your car when I came down the front street, there, earlier." He pointed to the front of the lot and took a deep breath before he straightened himself all the way upright. He stood maybe 6'0", 6'1"; it was hard to tell given the distance I kept.

"Those idiots were sitting in their truck waiting for me. I didn't want you to get caught up in the middle if I had shown up right on time. They must have had music on and didn't hear you pull in."

"I... uh... I'm really sorry..." I stood there like a deer in the headlights. He'd just suggested that he planned on being on time for whatever the hell that was all about. He saw a woman alone in a garage parking lot and circled the block, effectively making him late. He was beat up, in part, for protecting some woman he didn't even know. *Me.*

"Sorry? For dropping off your car? Look...just... we both better get out of here. I'm fine, no need for medics. Get home, or wherever you're going." His words were even. He sounded like a man who rarely took "no" for an answer, and expected me to follow his orders. He turned without bravado and headed for his car.

"I... OK..." I just stood there as the ice-cold wave of the last half hour crashed violently over me. Spike turned around and stared in my direction for a minute before speaking. He couldn't see my face, of that I was sure, due to the darkness that swept in without invitation.

"Shit. I'm sorry. Are you OK? I don't know what you heard or saw and it's probably best if you don't think too much about it. Are you OK to get home?" He sounded genuinely concerned.

I suddenly had no words; my throat was tight under the noose of panic. If I'd blinked, I would have started crying right there in the parking lot, so I kept my eyes wide and slowly turned to go home.

"Hey, you alright?" he repeated, his voice up an octave. He took a step forward, landing just under the streetlight to the side of the parking lot.

He was standing much closer to me now, but still about 20 feet away. Despite the haunting shadows cast by the street light, I could make out more than his height. He was broad, tight but not a muscle-head, with a narrow waist that held up his dark blue jeans. A snug red t-shirt clung to his shoulders and rested just on top of his belt. He was pretty hot and that thought annoyed me, given the circum-stances. I couldn't make out his face, but could tell he had dark hair and a fair complexion.

"No, yea, it's fine. Glad you're OK." My emotions bound an unforgiving fist around my vocal chords. I had to get out of there.

He nodded as he touched his hand to his bloodied lip, cursing as he pulled it away.

I turned and ran. He didn't call after me, didn't follow me, and I didn't look back. I ran all the way to my apartment, locked all the doors and windows, and tossed through a sleepless night.

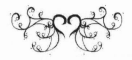

Tick-tock. Tick-tock. The clock marched time through my ears on Friday as the work day neared its end. Usually up to my neck in paperwork, today had been graciously light, and I was ready to go home and get ready for girls night. I thought I might wear my black pants and a tank; not too conservative and not too slutty. Never too slutty.

"You want a ride tonight, Ember, or you gonna meet us there?" Monica, my best friend and co-worker, startled me away from my gaze out of the window.

"Geez Mon! You scared the hell out of me!" I huffed, realizing I startled her, too, and continued. "Sorry, yea I'll meet you there— nine o'clock, right?"

"You sure? I mean, after what happened the other night you don't want us to come get you?" She tilted her head to the side.

"Monica, it didn't happen *to me*, remember? Besides, I have my car and I'll meet you there at nine. You can't imagine how much I'm looking forward to it."

"I guess you're right. See you at nine." She turned and headed out of my office.

"See ya!"

I still hadn't shaken off the events from the garage a few nights before; the emotional trauma loitered in my gut days later. Tonight, I declared to myself, I would get over it.

CHAPTER TWO

I took stock of myself in my full-length mirror while I touched up my make-up. *Looking good, November.* My height of 5'8" seemed to work in my favor; people typically didn't mistake me for younger than my 26 years, and guys usually didn't try to mess with me the way they might a 5'1" counterpart. My thick auburn hair fell in soft waves to just below my shoulder blades, and my green eyes set in my pale face made people think I'd won the DNA lottery.

I rarely struggled with self-esteem issues growing up, save for the acne debacle of freshman year high school. I liked how I looked, so I took good care of myself. I was an athlete in high school, continued working out through college, and maintained a healthy relationship with the local gym.

My friends assume my lack of boyfriend means I have some serious issues since *clearly,* according to them, my looks don't have anything to do with it. They are the kind of friends that fuss over their looks more than I do, and they insist I don't *have* to care what I look like. Why do women do this to themselves? Anyway, my lack of boyfriend didn't have anything to do with my looks or my personality. It had to do with the men. They're idiots. Not all of them, of course; just the ones that are single, 25-29 (my preferred age range), and trolling for a meaningful relationship in a bar with Jose, Jack, and Jim as chaperones. Please.

Even though my parents raised me with an appreciation for all things *love*, I'm a realist. I was born on the warmest day of that

November in New England, under the bluest sky they'd ever seen. My name, November Blue Harris, exemplifies everything my parents loved about that day. Despite my mother's encouragement to always love with reckless abandon, I grew up slightly guarded and suspicious. To her, spontaneity was as easy as breathing. To me, it seemed like skydiving without checking to see if you had a backpack or a parachute.

Either way, I was going out with my friends for fun. Although, in general, I disagreed with their hopes of finding a future husband and father of their children at a bar, I was supportive in the kind of way that every girlfriend needs to be. I learned to do this in college.

I worked hard to get in to Princeton University and remained focused on my studies so as not to blow my parents money. Monica and I found each other there. We were the same major, and had most classes together. We formed an instant friendship over our comfort in hard work and penchant for sarcasm. I had my fun, but I just wanted to get through school in one piece and find a job. I *really* didn't have an interest in a boyfriend. Not after Adrian anyway. Adrian and I dated for a year, but it was purely physical and when I wanted more he backed off. That was that. Well, that wasn't really all there was. I loved him. It was the first time I had truly felt like *this* was love. I shook thoughts of Adrian out of my head as I flipped my hair and checked the time.

"Shit, 8:55!" I yelled at my clock. I jammed my feet into a pair of not-too-tall heels and ran out the door.

Finnegan's, the Irish Pub, is only about a five minute drive from my apartment, which allowed me to show up at 9:00 on the dot. I liked Finnegan's; they often have live music, and the bartenders know me by name. In the four years that Barnstable had been our home, Finnegan's served our drinks.

I'm from Connecticut—for all intents and purposes—and Monica is from Rhode Island. We both wanted to move to Cape Cod, Massachusetts so we found a non-profit agency on the Cape that helped at-risk teens and families, and set our sights there. I got a job as a grant writer for the agency, and she secured one as a community educator; we agreed to have separate apartments so we wouldn't get sick of each other.

Finnegan's is the kind of place that has a hometown feel, appealing to both locals and tourists. It's always busy on Fridays; I had to use a little extra muscle to make my way past the people drinking out on the patio and find my friends who would be waiting for me at the bar.

"HEY! EEEMMMBEERR! Miss November!" Monica screeched like an idiot. Her milk chocolate hair was twisted in to a cute up-do.

When Monica is giddy, drunk, excited, or a combination of the three, she likes to shout out 'Miss November' as if I'm pictured on a calendar somewhere in my bra and panties. My friends typically just call me Ember, which is equally as counter-culture, but somehow "cooler".

As I headed toward the bar, I noted a stack of CDs by the bouncer signaling who was playing tonight. The name 'Bo Cavanaugh' graced the CD, and his smoky hot face sat above it. Steely blue eyes were set masterfully in his pale face against a black background. There may have been a guitar on the cover, but who could be sure—and who really cares—with a face like that? *What is it about a bar, and a guitar, that makes me so tingly?* I shook my head at the carnal thought and met Monica, Callie and Sarah at the bar.

"Ay caramba!" Callie rolled off her tongue like the sexy Venez-uelan goddess she is.

"Thank *God* you wore a heel, Em." Sarah slid in, "As much fun as it is always watching you wear flip flops…" Sarah's about 5-foot-nothing and is constantly tip-toeing around in impossible heels, God bless her. She pulls it off, though, and is nearly more graceful in her heels than out of them.

"Thanks guys, you're all *so* sweet," I gushed sarcastically. "Who's the new guy singing tonight?

"Don't know," Monica entered, "Josh said he's not from here, but has performed for years."

Josh is Finnegan's manager, and Monica's boyfriend of 2 years. We've known him since we moved here. He is boyishly rugged with sandy hair, olive skin, and a killer smile. He helps bring in the music at Finnegan's, so we always share our likes and dislikes, which he promptly ignores. Josh and I share musical taste so actually, I do have *some* input.

Artists that played at Finnegan's were warned well in advance that the patrons enjoyed live karaoke and they were expected to facilitate that. It's amazingly fun. My parents' affinity for music served me well on these nights. While I never took to an instrument myself, I was able to sing along with those who could play. I rarely had anyone to sing with at Finnegan's, since my folk-rock taste isn't shared by a majority of the musicians that turn up. However, since Josh took over the bookings, I found myself on stage more and more.

Over the next several minutes we drank beer, talked about our week, and I reassured everyone that I'd recovered from the frightening scene at the garage; when I picked up my car on Wednesday, everything seemed in place and no one mentioned a disturbance. Josh left us, hopped up on stage, and tapped the microphone.

"Ladies and *gentlemen*," Josh cleared his throat into the mic and emphasized "gentlemen" in an effort to encourage his species to rise above and act as such, "Finnegan's is excited to introduce the talented Bo Cavanaugh!" Josh clapped, and we all followed.

"Wow, he's hot," Sara whispered to us as Bo walked on stage.

He was wearing dark, worn jeans and a thin, loose fitting long-sleeved shirt that looked blue under the lights of the stage. His guitar was slung over his shoulder.

"Yea, I saw the CD at the door, now shush." I was always interested in the musical talent that Finnegan's was able to wrangle in, and I wanted to see if this guy had chops.

Bo adjusted the microphone, and pushed his sleeves to his

elbows as he took a seat on the stool. His dark hair and pale complexion suited the stage. It appeared to be just Bo and his guitar and I loved that.

"Thank you all for having me. Enjoy," Bo's voice was the perfect kind of husky that made my heart skip a beat; my heart hadn't skipped in a long time. He took a deep breath and began.

His strumming took more of my heartbeats with him; he was playing one of my favorite songs. I stared at his beautiful silhouette as he began "All Over Now" by Eric Hutchinson. It's a fairly upbeat tune that requires strumming and tapping the guitar; the acoustic version is absolute heaven.

He sang with such fluidity and passion you'd have thought he wrote the song himself and, knowing most of the people in this bar, they probably thought he *did*. Without removing my eyes from the stage, I backed up to the table that held his CDs. I flipped it over to check out his play list and nearly fainted. While he had some original tracks on there, the list of covers was stunning; Eric Hutchinson, Gregory Alan Isakov, Mumford and Sons, and Indigo Girls. Indigo Girls!

I walked back to my friends and mouthed a grateful, "Thank you," to Josh for this breath of fresh air. Josh beamed a proud smile like a little boy. He knew he had nailed it.

Inexplicably, Bo's eyes caught mine as my jaw hung open and I looked between the CD and him. He half-smiled, seemingly acknow-ledging my reaction, as he finished his first song. My cheeks felt flushed.

The clapping began as I stood wide-eyed like I'd never heard music before in my life. I joined in before anyone noticed. For the rest of his set he held me captive through the covers I recognized on his CD, as well as some songs he identified as his own. It was heaven; the few times we made eye contact, his gaze ignited some-thing in me, and heat spread through my body. The way his mouth turned up in a grin was nearly enough to send me running for the fire exit. I sang loudly along to all of the songs, and Monica joined in.

"Thank you all for letting me share some music with you tonight," Bo said, shifting on his stool. "It's my understanding that you all enjoy a little live karaoke? I had a request placed at the beginning of the night, so I suppose I ought to honor that. Could Monica and... Ember join me?"

Josh wrapped his arms around Monica and me, giving a slight squeeze before saying, "You're welcome."

You're welcome indeed. When Bo started the intro, I thought I'd crossed into a different dimension. He began *The Wailin' Jenny's* song, "Heaven When We're Home." Monica and I squealed like the college girls we were when we saw them perform this song on campus during our junior, post boyfriends, year. *The Wailin' Jenny's* were one thing Monica and I had always agreed on and no one at Finnegan's had *ever* played them.

Nervousness took over as I got up on stage; I had never felt nervous on stage before but I froze under Bo's striking masculinity. While his shoulders didn't overpower his guitar, I flippantly thought about them overpowering me. He stopped playing to shake our hands.

"Bo Cavanaugh." He stuck out his hand.

"Monica, nice to meet you. I can't believe you know this song!" I was glad she spoke first because my eyes were the only thing working in that moment. *He is really something to look at.*

"You must be Ember? I like it." He gave my hand a gentle squeeze.

The second our hands touched I felt *it* run up my arm, through my veins, and land square in my gut. A ribbon of instant desire tightened around my insides at the sight of his half smile just a few short inches from my face. I managed a small grin in return, and let my eyes linger on his as our hands parted.

"Yea, Thank you. I'm thrilled you know this song." I silently thanked my voice for making a gracious return.

"Are you kidding? Judging by the crowd here tonight I'm thrilled *you* know the song," he chuckled.

Bo started strumming the intro again, and I swear I could feel his soul through the music. Thankfully, Monica broke my uneasy stare at this beautiful guitar-playing god by tossing me the microphone. Bo cocked his head to the side, indicating he wanted us to sit on the stools on either side of him, so we obliged.

Bo sang the first verse with us and the crowd went wild. Josh, Sarah, and Callie were beaming, air toasting us with their drinks as we sang,

"Don't know what time it is, I've been up for way too long
And I'm too tired to sleep
I call my mother on the phone, she wasn't home,

And now I'm wondering the street
I've been a fool, I've been cruel to myself
I've been hanging onto nothing

When nothing could be worse than hanging on
And something tells me there must be something better than all
this..."

It only took until the end of the first line for our voices to harmonize. I'd never heard a guy sing this song before, let alone with two women, but it was hot. His low register pulled the soul of the song from deep within my body and cast its spell over the crowd. Everyone was staring, like they were all wondering if we'd cooked this up ahead of time.

Electricity amplified on the side of my body closest to Bo, and I liked it. I held the microphone in my right hand, causing my elbow to brush against his left arm as we both moved to the music. Each note he strummed found its way into my body, leaving it thirsting for more. He let Monica and I carry the next two verses as he guided his skilled hands across the neck of the guitar.

The fourth verse of the song is my absolute tattoo-worthy

favorite. I was so lost in the music and watching Bo's hands that I got carried away. I stood up from the stool, placed the microphone in the holder, and really went for it. Monica stopped singing and Bo grinned behind his microphone.

"There's no such thing as perfect
And if there is we'll find it when we're good and dead
Trust me I've been looking
But tonight I think I'll go and take a bath instead..."

The guitar stopped as I sang the word "instead," and I turned as I held the note. Bo tilted his chin toward me to tell me to keep singing, only this time he stood up, put his hands on the microphone and joined in—a cappella. As his lips brushed the microphone, he placed his index finger under my chin, lifting my gaze to his. His dark eyes held a stare that ripped through me; a stare that said something I couldn't read, but begged me to learn its language. We were singing this incredible song to each other, for the crowd, as if we'd written it ourselves. My soul wept with excitement and pleaded for more. If there was such a thing as song sex, I reached my climax as we sang,

"And then maybe I'll walk a while
And feel the earth beneath me
They say if you stop looking
It doesn't matter if you find it
And who's to say that even if I did
It's what I'm really looking for..."

I thought for sure I was sweating through everything I wore, but that was just my soul panting in the background. Keeping in time with the music, he sat back down and continued playing into the next verse, amidst hoots and claps from the people in the bar. The three of us finished the song together and when the final note was plucked,

Finnegan's erupted like a stadium full of crazed Sox fans.

I was breathless and invigorated; my insides screamed in delight and made note to do that again very soon. Monica lunged in front of Bo and gave me the tightest hug.

"That was *so* beautiful... and hot!" She half-whispered in my ear. *Did she see the song sex, or was that in my head?*

I turned to Bo and smiled. "Thanks for letting us share that with you. It's kind of our song."

"Ladies, the pleasure was all mine. That was excellent." Bo grabbed each of our hands, gave Monica a kiss on the cheek, and followed up with a kiss on mine.

"Really beautiful," he reinforced how fantastic I sounded with one more soft kiss on my cheek before he dropped my hand. I cocked an eyebrow, let a grin reach my eyes, and headed back to my friends, who were anxiously waiting with shots in hand at the bar.

"Chicas!" Callie squealed as she handed Monica and I our shots. We clinked our glasses together and downed the shots.

"Guys, that was unbelievable!" Sarah jumped up and down as if she'd just seen *The Wailin' Jenny's* perform.

"I thought you guys would like it," Josh shrugged coyly. I could tell he was just as thrilled as the rest of them, and us.

"Josh, give us a warning before you bring the Indie Rock God in here next time, eh?" I smiled, still dazed.

Monica gushed about what a rush that whole scene had been. I smiled and nodded, but I found my eyes drifting toward the stage as Bo Cavanaugh finished his closing number. He met my eyes and smiled as he slipped off the stage and out of sight.

CHAPTER THREE

Still on a high from my now-favorite singing performance at Finnegan's, I floated out to the deck by myself, beer in hand. I sank into the chair, taking a long sip of my beer, and sighed out to the ocean. *I am definitely attracted to Bo.* I shook my head at the thought. I hadn't felt that instantly attracted to anyone since Adrian, and we were both lucky to come out of that relationship with any hope stitched to our hearts. I briefly considered accepting an invitation to another heart battle if it meant spending a few minutes with Bo Cavanaugh.

I greedily took another serving of salty air into my lungs, but something was different. I peered over my shoulder, and there he was.

"Ember, right?" Bo motioned to the empty wooden Adirondack chair next to me with his pint. "Can I sit?"

"Of course." I straightened myself and turned toward his chair. The chatter of the jukebox purred from inside Finnegan's. I caught Monica's eye near the door and she shot a thumbs-up. I gave her a quick nod, acknowledging her encouragement.

"Ember," he continued, "is an interesting name."

I took the bait.

"It's November, like the month, November Blue, actually. I know, I know. My parents," I looked up at the sky with my hands raised, "hippies."

He chuckled as he settled into his chair, "No, that's great, I like it." He paused to take a sip of his beer. "You were really great up there tonight."

He raised his glass and I accepted his toast. I kept my glass up against his a second longer than was standard, but he didn't pull his away first either. The wind carried his cologne through my senses. He smelled like sandalwood and sex—why hadn't I noticed that on stage? Also, points for him that he didn't want to base an hours-long conversation on the origins of my name.

"Thank you, though I should be the one paying *you* the compliment. That was a killer set; I'd lost all hope of Finnegan's bringing in someone like you," my voice was sincere, if not a tad overeager, as I searched his eyes.

"Thanks," he replied, "Josh saw me play a show in New Hampshire a few months ago. He said he liked my sound and would love to have me play here if I was ever in town. Here I am." He faced me as he spoke. "Where'd you learn to sing like that?"

"My hippie parents that I mentioned before? They instilled a lot of things in me, but my favorite is their love of music. My mom calls my voice 'my instrument'. It thrilled them that I could hum and sing along to the melodies they played on their guitars, banjos, and fiddles…" I trailed off with a smile, thinking that despite moving around a lot when I was a child, music had always been my home.

"That's awesome," Bo replied.

"How long have you been playing? And, where did *you* learn to sing like that?" I let the smile paint my face.

Bo shrugged with humility, "I started with the piano, when I was little. My parents wanted me to try it, so I did. I got pretty good, but then I found the guitar attracted loads more women." He smiled cautiously behind his glass and I let out a full-bodied laugh.

"Fair enough, Mr. Cavanaugh, I'll toast to that." We clinked glasses again and returned our gaze to the ocean.

"Seriously, though. Your voice comes from deep in here," I patted my stomach to try to illustrate the soul, "It's captivating." I didn't tear my eyes from the water.

"Well, life happens, you know?" I saw him give his head a faint shake out of the corner of my eye, "You take what you get and you use it for what you want."

I shot him an imploring look and noted that he was staring absently at the sand. *Tortured artist?*

"So, Bo, is that short for something?" I quickly shifted gears. I wanted to reach out and touch him because he was so damned attractive but I feared that if I did, he'd scatter into the ocean breeze like the seeds of a long-gone dandelion.

"Bowan, actually."

"Oh, is Bo just for CD covers, or do you prefer it all the time?" I had loosened up in the last three quarters of my pint and decided to turn up the flirt.

"Ha, well, no one's ever really asked me that. Is Ember just for friends or do *you* prefer it all the time?" he chided, nudging my shoulder with his.

"Ah, I see. Bo it is." I winked as I finished my pint and stood up.

"You heading out?" Bo asked, and stood up a second after me.

"No," I giggled, "but my friends are inside. I only came out for a little air and to bask in the afterglow of your set."

I wrapped my hand around his forearm for a second, half-congratulatory and half "let me feel you." His arms were tight from years spent with his guitar. I dropped my hand as soon as I realized what I was doing, but he caught it mid-fall and held it there, in the charged space between our bodies. My face heated as electricity transferred from his fingers to mine. That split-second of silence felt like an eternity, and I forgot to breathe.

"Can I join you guys for a drink?" He lifted his empty glass as proof that he needed more.

He let go and stuffed his hand into his pocket. *Why'd he do that?*

"Absolutely, they'll love it." I exhaled as I turned toward the door.

He held the door for me, guiding me by the small of my back with his free hand. I wanted to grab his face and explore it with my lips, but pushed down the thought in favor of a more responsible one.

"There you guys are. How's the air outside?" Josh raised an eyebrow in my direction, causing me to subtly shake my head to erase whatever inappropriate thoughts he may have had.

"Great breeze right now," Bo replied.

"Another perfect May day," I interjected, "Where are Callie and Sarah?"

"They headed home. It's just us four. Let's grab that open table." Monica headed to the back of the pub where a lone booth sat waiting for us. She slid in and patted her hand on the cushion next to her, looking at me. I slid in, which gave me full-view of Bo Cavanaugh.

Over the next two hours we sat and talked about music and beer. Josh told Monica and I about the first set he saw Bo play; he had nearly fist-pumped the air when Bo played an Indigo Girls song, because he knew Monica and I would *love* him. Josh bragged about Monica and I to Bo, telling him about Princeton, while we rolled our eyes in unison. Bo told us he grew up in central New Hampshire and played in a local bar at home nearly every weekend. All the while, our feet were intertwined under the table and I caught him stealing lingering glances at me as he spoke.

At closing time, Monica decided she was going to stick around and wait for Josh to lock up. I hugged them both and thanked Josh again for the awesomeness that was Bo Cavanaugh.

"Can I walk you to your car, Ember?" Bo climbed out of the booth and raised his arms overhead as he stretched his neck side to side.

"That'd be great," Monica cut in, "Em saw some brawl near her house the other day..."

"*Monica!* It was nothing, and it was nearly a week ago. Would you let it go?" I drew my eyebrows together. Monica had been overly curious about the 'handsome stranger', as she named him, and spent the entire week pushing me for details that I didn't have.

Bo stiffened and his eyes curtained with darkness, "What do you mean brawl? Did you get hurt?" The way his voice hung on "hurt" ignited something in me. His husky incantation beckoned my primal senses, and the hair on the back of my neck stood at attention.

"God, please, don't worry about it. It was too dark to see anything—I was just in the neighborhood. And it wasn't really *near* my house." I forced a smile and put my hand on his lower back as I glared at Monica. "Night Josh, night Mon."

Josh waved goodbye while Monica held her pinky and thumb to her face, indicating that she wanted details about Bo Cavanaugh. As we exited Finnegan's, Bo once again held the door for me. When I walked by him, I instinctually hooked my arm around his waist and liked the fit. He paused for a second and looked at me with an unreadable expression. He turned and continued walking beside me, wrapping his arm comfortably around my shoulders.

"I didn't think this was a violent town. Where did this brawl happen exactly?" Bo said, scanning the parking lot.

"It's not. It just happened a couple blocks from where I live and it's *really* not a big deal. I think Monica's jealous she missed out on some action." I'd tried to lighten the mood but he didn't bite.

The moment was sliding through my fingers and I decided to take action. When we got to my car, I leaned my shoulder against it, and he copied my stance. Our hips were almost touching as I ran my thumb across the collar of his leather jacket.

"I had a great time tonight," I said, "listening to you play, singing with you, talking with you..." I trailed off as I breathed in closer to him; *now* our hips were touching. His height forced me to tilt my chin up to meet his eyes. Our lips were closer now, and I felt my heart beating in mine.

"The pleasure was all mine, November." Wow, *November* slid off of his tongue like nectar. He studied my eyes carefully as his hand cradled the back of my neck.

21

I tugged with little subtlety, telling him it was OK. I wanted his beautifully talented lips to touch mine, but he seemed to hesitate. Bo glided his hand away from my neck, down my arm, and paused at the hand I had on his collar. He interlaced his fingers with mine, and a ghost of a grin laced his lips before he slid my arm down his body, resting it on the top of his hips. He released my hand and held my face, staring at me in what can only be described as baffled wonder.

"You're incredibly beautiful, November Blue. And so talented..." his voice trailed off as he brushed an errant strand of hair away from my eyes.

No guy—or really anyone besides my parents—ever called me November Blue and it sounded so passionate coming from his mouth.

I swallowed so hard I was sure he could hear it. The moment swayed between us, asking who would go first. The current he sent through me was visible in his eyes. I couldn't take any more. I stole his hands from my face and forced them to my hips as I hungrily pulled his mouth to mine. Every thought and feeling I had about him over the last several hours exploded through my mouth and tongue as I searched his. This was no ordinary first kiss—it was deeper than any first kiss had ever been in the history of kisses.

His music, his guitar, his singing, his eyes—it was all burning through me as I moaned between his parted lips and tightened my fingers through his hair. He released hot, lust-filled air into my mouth as his fingertips slipped inside my back pockets. My anxious hands raked down his sides; when my thumbs found his belt loops, they held on for dear life. The world was vacant outside of us in that moment. His heart drummed through his thin shirt, its cadence matching mine.

I forced myself to take a deep breath before pulling my mouth from his. I placed one final soft kiss on his lips.

"Wh-why'd you stop?" he stuttered, searching my face for answers.

Because you completely disarmed me.

"Will you be here tomorrow?" I coyly smiled. I knew he would be; I'd already asked Josh.

"Uh...yea, I'll be playing a set tomorrow." He seemed shaken, and I liked that.

His hands remained on my hips, my thumbs in his belt loops.

"K, I'll see you here tomorrow," I said as I removed my thumbs and grazed them across his tight stomach, "you better get back inside to get your stuff."

He let out a chuckle as he gave my hips a tight squeeze and placed a kiss just under my ear lobe. *Why, yes, dessert sounds great...*

"See you tomorrow, Ember." He turned and shuffled back to Finnegan's with his hands in his pockets as I balanced myself against my car.

I listened to "Heaven When We're Home" twice on the way home from Finnegan's, and once in front of my apartment. Each time the intro filled my car, my body craved Bo Cavanaugh. I floated up the stairs and poured myself into bed, where I drifted off to the most relaxing sleep I'd had in nights. I woke with a smile on my face and the lingering memory of his kiss on my lips.

CHAPTER FOUR

I'd forgotten to text Monica when I got home. That was a mistake. My post-first-kiss-smile faded as I saw roughly fifteen "Are you OK?!" texts from her on my phone. I called her immediately, lest she send the police knocking.

"Mon, I'm fine. More than fine, his kiss..."

"November! You may *not* kiss strange men in a parking lot and not let me know you got home safe!" Her tone was the only reminder I needed that I broke the best friend safety pact.

Oops.

"Not strange men, Monica, God. Not even strange, it was Bo..." his name fluttered in the air for a second before Monica continued her verbal chastising.

"Well, anyway, spill it!" Monica's desire for details outweighed her anger.

"On the deck, we just talked. When we walked to my car..." I trailed off as the memory temporarily satisfied my still-hungry lips.

"What?" Monica squealed.

"It was just amazing, Monica. I haven't felt that way *ever*. When I pulled his lips to mine..."

Monica cut me off, "You initiated it? That's so aggressive, Ember!" Her pitch was window shattering.

"And *that's* so fifties, Monica. Anyway, we were alive in it, like we'd done it a million times before. Don't worry, I'm the one that pulled away first; wanted to leave a little appetite for tonight. I didn't even give him my phone number." I was proud that my parents taught me to love passionately, with responsibility.

"Well, at least we know he won't stalk you on Facebook," Monica said snidely.

"Fucking *Facebook*," I snarled cynically and hung up the phone.

After our college graduation, Adrian updated me on Facebook about life at Harvard a few times in private messages, and wanted to know if we could "catch up" on the Cape sometime (he was less than 2 hours away). I found my mind wandering to a place that had us being a hot little power couple, he as an attorney for those less fortunate, and myself managing his office and all. Adrian and I always made sense "on paper" in that way; our brains, our looks, and our determination. I quickly pushed those daydreams aside and told him that I thought it best that we got on with our lives and I deactivated my account.

Maybe it broke his heart; I didn't ask and he didn't tell. I do know that we would have hurt each other in the end because, judging by all of his cute little *Facebook* albums, he was after girls that were pretty enough to make an impression, but dumb enough not to challenge him. *Screw that.*

I spent all day cleaning and organizing my kitchen in an effort to pass the time until I would get to see Bo again. Of course, it wasn't just the singing I was looking forward to, but I needed to keep my good-girl side appeased. I arrived at Finnegan's by 8:00—an hour earlier than usual—hoping to catch him before he went on stage.

"You're early." Josh grinned from behind the bar.

"Yea, thought I'd try to get a beer and a good seat if it's supposed to be busier than last night."

Josh shook his head as he dried glasses; he knew I was lying.

"Shut up, Josh. Is Monica here yet?" I laughed. I was speaking to Josh, but looking for Bo.

"Hey, I didn't say anything," Josh put up his hands in defense, "it was just awesome seeing you up there last night, that's all.

Monica should be here in a few."

"It felt so good being up there. I want to do it again."

"You should think about singing here regularly." Josh slid my pint across the bar.

"You're kidding," I panned as I welcomed the cold brew into my mouth.

"I'm not shitting you, Em. You've got something special goin' on." Josh playfully smacked my arm with the bar towel.

"Where the hell is your girlfriend, anyway?" I teased.

Almost on cue, Monica glided next to me and lifted herself up on the bar. She gave Josh the kind of kiss one gives to someone they'd been separated from for months. Once again (and this was a pattern a girl could get used to), I felt and smelled Bo before I saw him.

"Hey guys!" Bo Cavanaugh looked every bit as striking as he had the night before on stage, and in my dreams. The dark jeans from last night returned, but tonight he was wearing a fitted black sleeveless shirt in response to the heat. His shoulders sat with such prominence, it was like they were guarding the rest of his body. His taught masculinity made my mouth run dry.

"Hey, Bro. Here's a pint on the house." Josh was certainly a class-act. He knew he wanted Bo to play here regularly, and what better way is there to butter a guy up than with some hometown brew?

"Thanks, Bro, I appreciate it. Ember, you wanna sing something with me tonight?" Bo touched the small of my back, but it rather lacked that little something extra that I was hoping for. He seemed a little casual after last night's kiss. I wondered if I offered too much, too soon.

Hell no! That was hot.

"Sure. Did you have something in mind?" I smiled and cocked an eyebrow as I turned to face him. I ignored Josh's snickering.

"I'll surprise you. Just come up when I give you the nod." He mimicked his nod and I giggled. Giggled. *God help me.*

The four of us spent the next hour sipping a beer, or two, and talked about music. I raved about Ani Difranco, Goo Goo Dolls, Patty Griffin, and the list went on. I had certainly found my musical soul mate—one who rivaled my parents even—and I could have lived on that conversation alone. Well, I could have lived on a music conversation alone, had I not kissed him. No, now that I knew what his mouth was capable of away from a microphone, I needed more.

"K, I'm headed up," Bo said a second after Josh tapped the mic. "See you in a few," he whispered in my ear so closely that I thought it was meant to be a kiss, as well; his electricity overrode my system once again. As he walked away, I saw what appeared to be the top of a tattoo at the base of his neck, and made a mental note to check that out later.

Bo started his set with some of his original work, which blew me away; Monica kept elbowing me during his songs to raise her eyebrows and widen her eyes. Josh had a proud smile on his face, shaking his head back and forth like he couldn't believe we hadn't heard of him until now. My insides sashayed with each note.

My soul has always felt music deeper than my ears could ever hear it; I was involuntarily swaying to his beats. Occasionally, he'd glance up at me during his songs; it felt like musical foreplay. I always returned his smile, sometimes while casually biting my lower lip. Two could play at this game. Then he nodded in my direction, which lead me up on stage.

"Those of you who were here last night were treated to the voice of this talented woman, November Harris." His hand embraced my knee as he spoke, which sent me into the stratosphere. *I need to get ahold of myself.*

The crowd clapped. Even if they weren't there last night, most of them had likely heard me sing at least once before. Monica hollered and Josh whistled.

"Thank you, Bo, but, the pleasure was all mine. How talented is he?" I asked the crowd as I clapped in to the air. They followed graciously.

I whipped my head toward him and narrowed my eyes at his guitar while he plucked the intro to the song he wanted me to sing. My heart plummeted head-first into the wicked sea of my stomach.

"Shit, what are you doing?!" I whisper-yelled in his ear as I covered the microphone, " I haven't sung Ani Difranco anywhere in public!"

He smiled his hot half-smile and continued the intro to "Both Hands", leaving me panicked at the thought of the unique register I'd need to reach to pull it off. What the hell was he doing?! He started the intro again since I missed my cue. His knee knocked into mine and he mouthed, "Go." I cleared my throat and begged for feeling to return to my face.

As I finished the first verse I reveled in how great it felt. I wondered how he knew that I would recognize that song. *I guess I did mention that I liked Ani...* He was song-flirting with me all over again. I rolled with it and had to refrain from jumping him right there on the stage when his voice joined mine. He brought a husky rock undertone to the harmony that shook my insides.

When we finished, I exhaled with such force that it felt like I'd been holding my breath the entire song.

"Meet me outside when you finish your set," I breathed into his ear as the crowd applauded. And, just so he was sure, I grazed my lips across his earlobe before I headed back to the bar. I heard his breath hitch just before he cleared his throat, and a seductive smile of satisfaction concealed itself behind his microphone.

Bo finished the rest of his set with a shade of crimson on his cheeks that suited me just fine.

"That boy has it bad for you, Ember. What'd you do to him last night?" Josh elbowed my side.

"Josh!" Monica slapped his arm.

"You'd like to know, wouldn't you Josh. I'm heading outside. Bo's gonna meet me out there when he's done-don't hassle him, Josh." I grabbed two pints and, with a wink, I headed out to sit in a chair facing the door. I wanted to see him first this time.

The familiar applause that comes at the end of the set erupted, and within two minutes Bo was walking through the door and straight toward me with a mile-wide grin. I stood up and handed him his beer.

"Walk with me." I stepped through the dry grass on to the sandy beach that hugged the ocean.

"Can you take your beer out here?" Bo asked, faking concern for the law.

"We're just going right here, Officer." I plunked down in the sand and kicked off my sandals, digging my toes into the cool earth. This effort, I'd hoped, would keep me somewhat grounded from his electrical output.

Bo sat next to me and spilled a bit of his beer when I playfully punched him in the shoulder.

"What kind of a dick move was that? Pulling out an Ani Difranco song, assuming I'd know it?" I tried to sound playful as I relived the initial terror of hearing him strum the song that, up until then, I'd only sung in the shower or when drunk.

"Hey," he said as he rocked his shoulder in to mine, "that was crazy good. I've never sung that song live before either."

Bo's shoulder paused on mine as he placed his elbows on bent knees, dangling his pint from his long fingers. He slipped off his black Sperry's and dragged his toes through the sand. *Even his feet are sexy.*

"Still, you're an asshole. I nearly fainted!"

My scalp tingled as he brushed my hair aside, dancing his fingers across the back of my neck. His hands were tight, like guitar strings, and just as delicate. Despite the callused fingertips that come from years of plucking, their graze was soft and inviting.

"Forgive me," he chuckled as he pressed his thick, soft lips on the spot where my neck meets my shoulders.

"K," I sighed as I turned my lips to his.

He grabbed my chin and turned my face away as he worked his lips from the base of my neck to my ear. Nothing inside me had recovered from the night before, but I was nearly panting for more. I felt utterly helpless as his lips grazed my ear a second time. All I could do was kiss the top of his head, which caused him to right himself and look me straight in the eyes. I leaned forward and pressed my lips into his sharp jaw line. His breath stopped for a moment as I pulled my lips away and returned them to his neck. Our pint glasses hit the sand, and he placed both hands behind my head. Once again, his eyes held mine captive.

"I don't usually do this," he said more to himself than me, "you're just so beautiful, so talented…"

I silenced him with a crushing kiss and we had to steady ourselves.

"Neither do I." My body shook as my free hand rode up the outside of his thigh.

He exhaled sharply as he slowly brought his free hand to the base of my shirt; disregarding the soft cotton in favor of my skin. I pulled it in tighter, making my desire clear. The tip of my fingernail drew a line of goose bumps on the skin just inside his belt line.

"Ahh," he sighed as he lunged forward and laid me down in the sand, cradling my head in one hand.

Our lips found their homes in each other, and we picked up where we left off the night before. If square had a taste, it was his jaw. If clouds had a touch, they were his lips. Every pore on my body drank him in with such eagerness that I could hear their cries of gratitude. My body had wandered the desert for too long; Bo was my oasis.

His full weight wasn't on me, as his legs were still on the ground to my side, but it was enough for me to crave more. I released my hands from his waistband and surged them through the back of his thick, loose hair. I forced our lips tighter together. A faint groan of relief escaped my throat as we worked our tongues together in familiar rhythm. I wanted all of him, badly, but it couldn't happen here. Not in the sand behind Finnegan's.

"God... November." It seemed to be all he could manage when

he lifted his mouth from mine.

Each time he spoke my name, I was recharged with a need I'd never felt before. It was unsettling, but only in the way drinking half a bottle of wine is unsettling. My quenched thirst had turned to emotional drunkenness; I had to sober up.

I anchored one hand to the sand, and slowly pushed myself to a seated position. He didn't fight it, but our mouths never parted. When we were both seated again we heard the back door to the bar open; the second act for the night had finished, and everyone else in Finnegan's wanted to enjoy the ocean breeze. Their interruption forced a quick space between us. *Damn them.*

"Shit!" I giggled as I returned my gaze to the ocean, my face hot with a desire I'd yet to feel in my 26 years.

"Yea, shit." His voice was clipped and his body seemed a bit wobbly as he wrapped his arm around my waist and pulled me in to him, "Next time I hope we're not interrupted." Once again an unidentifiable feeling ran through me at the sound of his voice. When he was on stage, it was one thing. This was different, it was confusing.

"Get a room!" Monica teased like the teenager inside of her that I loved.

"Mon, really?" Josh tried to pacify the situation.

"Like you're any better, *Joshua*," I jested.

Bo laughed as we turned our bodies so they could join us in the sand. Josh and Monica congratulated Bo on another great performance and Josh asked if he'd be back any weekend in the near future. Realization grounded my live nerves; he was from New Hampshire, just here for the weekend. He owed nothing to me, we just happened into this and now he had to go home. Monica must have seen me turn white through my thought process because she shot me a sympathetic smile. She understood. In that same moment, Bo found my hand.

"I'd love to come back and play." He didn't release his grip. "I've actually got to stay in town this week for business. I've got plans Friday night, but I'd love to play Saturday."

The color returned to my face and Monica's smile echoed; no longer sympathetic, it was excited—devilish even. My eyes told her to "shut up," and she took a long look at Bo before flinging a cheeky smile my way.

"Bo, let's get you settled up inside." Josh flashed me a sweet and knowing look. He knew Monica and I needed to talk; he was more emotionally tuned in than I was sometimes.

"Wait for me?" Bo tilted his head, eyeing me when he stood up.

"Of course." I smiled back as I watched Josh and Bo head back inside.

"Ember! I've never seen you like this. What's gotten in to you? He is so *freaking* hot," Monica squealed.

"You just answered your own question, my friend."

"Are you going to go home with him tonight?" Her seriousness drew laughter out of me.

"Geez Mon, I don't know. I don't really *know* anything about him. He's hot, he plays music, and he sings. Oh, and he's from New Hampshire, we have the same taste in music and we sing well together. That's all I know." My responsible side came up for air for the first time after 24 hours of swimming in desire.

"You two have serious chemistry. I haven't seen *that* look on your face since Adrian." She winced a little as she said his name.

"You can bring up Adrian, Monica, we broke up like five years ago. We dated and had great sex. I fell in love but he didn't fall in after me. That's all."

Monica also knew that wasn't *all* there was—she was there. She held me as I cried. When Monica and I first met Josh at Finnegan's, I saw sparks between them immediately. Still, she nearly asked my permission to date him. She treated what happened with Adrian with great care, even though it was years old. Maybe she knew more than I did how much it hurt. The dissolution of that relationship didn't dissolve my belief in love, though. What I was feeling for Bo was completely soul-shifting.

I had to tread carefully, even though my bones ached and my soul thirsted for everything he had to offer. I'd spent the last day trying to think spontaneously, to remind myself that I didn't care he would have to go home. After just a second kiss, however, I was starting to care.

Josh and Bo came back outside as Monica and I were dusting the sand off of ourselves.

"You guys want to come back to my place?" I asked, noting Monica's gaping mouth.

They all agreed, and off we went. I knew it was risky to have someone I barely knew over to my house, but my friends would be there. And, if something should happen when we were alone, I'd know how to get out; an advantage you don't have when you're in unfamiliar territory. We each got in to our respective cars and I used the drive home to gather the nerve I'd need to ask Bo to stay the night with me.

By the time we got to my apartment, I was riddled with indecision. I wanted to spend more time with Bo, but I didn't want to play the Sex Card too early as a means to get him to want to spend more time with *me*. I wanted him badly, but the memories of what happened with Adrian reminded me to proceed with caution. I was already feeling things beyond physical desire for Bo, and I didn't want to ruin that.

I gripped my steering wheel with the frustration that I couldn't deny myself the physical satisfaction of this beautiful man because I was afraid of endangering a relationship we didn't even have. *Ugh!* Still, it would be *no* for tonight.

The four of us headed into my apartment and opened up a bottle of wine in the living room. Monica and Josh settled for different chairs, which allowed Bo and me to sit together on the couch. I loved watching Josh and Monica look at each other. Her intense personality matched her dark eyes, and Josh looked like he was carved from the earth; he grounded her. They were truly fire and earth.

Josh is the type of man that my parents would love to see me with. He strums a guitar well enough, has the type of relaxed personality my parents thrived on, and he is nice to look at. I'd never really been physically attracted to Josh; almost as long as I'd known him he'd been with Monica. But I appreciated those qualities in him, which is why we hit it off as friends. The heat of the man sitting next to me was enough to break my view of "The Josh and Monica Love Show."

"Hey, where'd you go?" Bo shook me out of my daydream with a warm hand on my knee.

"Ah, you know, young love." I gestured dramatically at Josh and Monica, which caused Josh to chuck a pillow at my head.

Over the next couple of hours I learned a lot about Bo. He was in town on business for the foundation he works for. He said he didn't want to bore us with details, but his trip had to do with fundraising. He graduated from UNH six years ago, placing him only two years older than me. Perfect. He had one younger sister, Rachel, whom he hadn't seen in a couple of years, but his voice softened when he spoke of her. The big brother role looked good on him.

"What about your parents? Do they still live in New Hampshire?" I stroked the back of his hand, my other arm on the back of the couch.

"Uh, well, they died four years ago. Car accident." The words staggered their way out of this throat.

"I'm so sorry." My hand rested on top of his and gave a little squeeze.

"It's OK," he exhaled, "I was out of college and on my own as it was. Physically it was more of an adjustment for Rachel. She was a senior in high school and had to grow up too quickly." His eyes focused on something that wasn't in the room. I decided to drop it.

"OK," Josh interrupted, "Monica and I are heading out. I'll be in touch this week Bo."

"K, Man, thanks. Talk to you later." Bo got up and shook Josh's hand.

"Ember, call me tomorrow, K?" Monica asked as innocently as possible.

"Sure, talk to you tomorrow."

"Be careful," she whispered as she gave me a goodbye hug. I nodded and shut the door behind them.

Bo gathered the wine glasses and walked them to the kitchen. I followed behind him.

"Thanks." My hand brushed his when I reached for the dishtowel to dry the glasses.

He faced me and playfully grabbed my butt, pulling me to him for a quick, but passionate, kiss. I giggled like a fool and he laughed against my lips. Suddenly there was no giggling; we started to give in to the passion again. Bo spun me around and pressed my back against the refrigerator; my goosebumps punched the frigid stainless steel. He pinned both of my hands above my head as he leaned into me. *Yes.* His hips met mine, kneading in to me as his lips parted my own. The hurricane of passion that flew through his kiss rocked the boat holding my resolve.

"Shit," I breathed into his open mouth.

He groaned in agreement. I nudged my wrists forward, and he released them. I searched the deep muscles in his back and shoulders with my tense, longing hands.

"Mmmm..." he hummed as I ran my hands up his back on the inside of his shirt. His skin was soft, but the heat nearly burned my hands. I couldn't tell if that was real, or in my head; regardless, I wanted more of it on me.

I stepped forward, urging my back off of the fridge. Bo gracefully stepped back without leaving my lips for a second. I turned him toward the counter, backing him slowly into it. This was the hottest dance session I'd ever had. We moved together, to the same rhythm, which I was beginning to think was my heartbeat since that's all I could hear.

Actually, I *could* hear music; the music we sang together, and the music he played. Another song sang along to the beat of my heart; I couldn't place it, but I could feel it. My soul felt like it was singing to him, about him. Whatever it was, it took with it the last grain of my resolve, and I led him to the living room. We sat down in silence, but Bo stared so intensely in to my eyes that I thought I would melt right there. He tucked a hair behind my ear and left his hand there, redirecting the goosebumps down my neck.

Bo closed his eyes tight for a moment and reopened them at me, seeming to search for an answer to a question I hadn't asked—at least out loud. He exhaled, "November…"

My only response was tug on his shirt—my eyes never leaving his—as I pulled him onto my reclined body. My long-gone resolve was swept under my 'Welcome' mat. The softness of his lips surprised me, given the sharpness of his jaw. But, the softer his kiss, the more I wanted. He let out a throaty approval as my hands slipped between us and found his yearning. I massaged the outside of his jeans, and as his pulse increased, mine followed. Swiftly he sat up, pulling me with him, and in one motion I was straddling him. His commanding hands held my hips in place as he grinded into me.

My pulse was frantic with need as I met his rhythm. I grasped one of his hands and guided it up the inside of my shirt, placing it on my breast. He worked me with firm hands that caused a faint whisper of ecstasy to flee my throat. He drew his hand greedily down my side and placed both palms on my back. The heat radiating from his long fingers was unreal. *God, I want him.* Our lips hadn't left each other's since we sat on the couch; it was as if they were making up for a lifetime's worth of missed kisses.

I let out one low groan into his mouth, and the sound of my own voice startled my resolution into action from under the 'Welcome' mat. It dutifully hammered its way back through my veins and grounded the live wire whipping erratically inside me. If what I thought I was feeling for Bo was real, I couldn't give it all away tonight.

I slowed my breathing and my motions, nervous for a moment

that he would think I was a cock-tease; but my concerns about his opinion of me bowed to my opinion of myself. Bo didn't resist; he relaxed his hands as I slid off his legs, but our mouths weren't finished with each other.

Still kissing in this less provocative position, I felt a small smile cross his lips as he planted soft kisses on my lips, nose, and forehead. Stopped, with our foreheads touching, our breathing was too erratic to allow words. We sat, panting for a minute, before moving. He stretched his back against the couch, put his arm around my shoulders and kissed the top of my head before leading it to his shoulder. I responded with a kiss under his chin.

"Hey," I looked up at him with apologetic eyes, "I..."

I began to apologize for putting on the breaks; my experience with men taught me that a move like that often warrants an apology of some sort—no matter how half-hearted.

"Don't, November." Tenderness glistened in his eyes as he combed his thumb down the side of my face. "This has been one of the best nights of my life." I kissed his thumb when it met my lips.

Speechless, I laid my head back on his shoulder.

Several minutes later we were back in the kitchen.

"Hey," I said as I put the last wine glass away, and slid my hand in to his back pocket to retrieve his cell phone, "let me give you my number."

I tapped my number into his phone, entered my name as *November Blue*, and slid the phone back in to his pocket.

"Awesome," he beamed, "I'll call you to get together sometime this week?"

"Sounds great. I typically work 8 to 4, but you can text me during work if you want to set something up." My attempt at not sounding desperate wasn't going quite as I'd hoped.

Bo walked over to the door and took a long, slow breath. "Thank you for having me over, Ember." His tone was sweet, carrying through my apartment like an aria. "This night was..."

"Yea," I tipped my head up and kissed him, "it really was, Bo.

I'll talk to you later, K?"

I met him at my door and gripped my fingers around the edges of his jeans pockets.

"Absolutely." He pulled me in to him and gave me one hard, demanding kiss. "Later."

I shut the door behind him and thumped my forehead against it, letting out a small hum of sexual frustration. His sensitivity and understanding when I didn't want things to go any further flooded me with relief, and respect for him. When I got into bed five minutes later, my cell phone dinged with a text. The number wasn't one I recognized, so I took it to be Bo's. I opened the message, smiling.

603-259-6398: *Hey, it's Bowan, now you have my number*

Me: *Excellent :) Bowan, is it?*

Bo: *It's only fair, November Blue :)*

Me: *Fair's fair. Good night.*

Bo: *Hey I hope to see you during the week, but in case work gets ahead of me, I definitely want to see you on Friday*

Me: *Great! But I thought you told Josh you had plans Friday?*

Bo: *You are my plans on Friday*
Horray!

Me: *Presumptuous, don't you think?*

Bo: *Sorry. Would you like to get together on Friday?*

Me: *Better :) I'd love to. Talk to you this week I hope.*

Bo: *Night*

Me: *Night :-**

Crap, I kissy-faced in a text. I rolled on to my belly, threw my pillow over my head and endured the most angst-filled sleep I'd had in years.

CHAPTER FIVE

"We had the decency to duck out early and you mean to tell me *nothing* happened?" Monica sat, exasperated, on my couch.

Her early morning texts didn't wake me—since I hadn't slept much—but she made up for her dramatic entrance by bringing me a latte.

"*You* are a bad influence. He was a perfect gentleman, Monica. So..." My face heated as I recounted the details of our kiss and his request for a date on Friday.

"I thought he told Josh he *had* plans on Friday." She raised an eyebrow as if she knew what I was about to say.

"Evidently I *am* the plans he had for Friday night."

"Hell yes!" Monica cheered.

"Hell yes, indeed." I let seduction paint my smile as we toasted our coffee cups.

When I went back to my bedroom after Monica left, I saw I had two missed texts from Bo.

Bo: *Good morning.*

Bo: *I had a great time last night, thank you.*

Even in his absence, my body reacted to him. I couldn't form anything intelligent, or witty, but I didn't want to be rude and not reply.

Me: *You're welcome—I had a great time too.*

I needed to go for a run. I put on my shorts, tank, and shoes and headed out the door.

As I ran past *the* garage, which was closed on Sundays, I instinctively turned to the left to look. I nearly tripped and fell as I saw the exact pick-up truck in the same spot, engine running. Two bodies were inside, and one was as broad as I remembered Bill to be. I ran like hell and didn't double-back; I took the long route, which allowed me to avoid the garage completely on my way back to my apartment. *Why the garage? Why in the daylight?* These were quest-ions I shook from my head as I rounded the corner to my apartment and flew up the stairs. I wouldn't tell Monica about this tomorrow at work because she might lose her head and call the police herself. I was exhausted by the time nightfall arrived, since my raging libido prevented a sound sleep the night before, so I drifted off early.

I shot out of bed with my alarm on Monday; I had dreamt of *Adrian*, and woke up feeling flustered. Monica had talked about Adrian Saturday night. My feelings for Bo were mixed with my relationship with Adrian, and it led to a weird mash-up of Finn-egan's, Princeton, and Adrian Turner inside my subconscious.

I hadn't had a serious boyfriend since Adrian. In the four years since I had graduated college (five since I broke up with Adrian), I'd gone on dates and had sex, but never committed myself to anyone. There were never any strings attached. My parents would be *so* proud, which is funny, because they actually would be. They're all about "free love", despite the fact that they've been together since their freshman year of college. I suspect they have a rather open relationship but I've never asked.

The Monday morning routine came with its usual lackluster appeal. I loved my job, but I was beginning to think I loved hanging out at Finnegan's with Bo even more. One week of distracted thinking couldn't hurt. I headed into the office, grateful that it was

Monica's turn to pick up our lattes. Part of her job included speaking at fancy parties, with fancy people, to help garner donations for our non-profit. As a grant writer, I was in charge of securing large sums of money from private organizations, rich people, and the government. We were thrilled that, when we were seeking out new donors or partners, our work intersected.

Such was the case today. We were meeting with a representative from a New Hampshire-based drug prevention/ education group called DROP. The group's name is "Drug Resistance Opportunity Program," and seeks to empower children and adults facing drug abuse and addiction issues. While this was also a non-profit, and we wouldn't actually be receiving donations from them, the purpose of the meeting today was to see if we could develop them as an alliance. The long-term goal was a community center that could serve the interests of both organizations.

Further, we wanted The Hope Foundation to set up offices up and down the New England seaboard; DROP had the same objective. An alliance would mean a larger resource base, both intellectual and financial—something no non-profit can afford to turn down.

Monica didn't actually tell me about this meeting until Friday because I had been slammed all week with a new secured funding initiative, meaning I felt uncharacteristically unprepared to speak in public. She said all she knew was that DROP was two years old, they didn't have a website (meaning our established internet presence would be a huge benefit for them), but they had at least two multi-million dollar backers (enter the main reason they'd be a huge asset to us). Our meeting today was intended for each side to present their strengths. It was meant to be casual, not competitive, and the goal was to see if our organizations would make a good fit for collaboration.

"Hey Mon." I poked my head into her office, knowing she'd be there early to prepare for her presentation. Luckily, when I was working on the secured funding initiative last week, I had refreshed all the information I would need for today. My public speaking nerves were fully charged, however.

"Morning, Ember. Here's your latte, Lady!" The perfect community educator, she's incessantly bubbly and wonderful.

"You're the best. By the way, asshole, thanks for talking about Adrian on Saturday. I dreamt about him last night."

Monica's skeptical eyebrow forced more explanation from me. "Nothing happened, he was just—there." I flipped her the middle finger as I sipped my latte. "Anyway, what's the name of the woman from DROP we're meeting today?"

"Actually, it's a man. We were supposed to meet with a David Bryson, but I had a message waiting for me this AM that one of his partners, Spencer Cavanaugh, will be joining us. He's one of the founders, so I'm officially freaking out. He's going to come in for a meet-and-greet before the official meeting. And, yes, I know his last name must have you all hot and bothered, but keep your head on, will ya?" I'd smiled at the last name—she knew me too well.

I sat in the chair across from Monica's desk just as she picked up her ringing phone.

"K, send him in." She hung up the phone and looked at me. "Spencer's on his way down."

"I'll say hi, introduce myself, and then let you two discuss whatever you need to before the meeting." I started to stand.

There was a polite knock on Monica's door frame. Before I turned to greet Spencer, I saw Monica's eyes widen in a mix of confusion and shock. I turned around hastily, and was immediately face-to-face with Bo Cavanaugh.

"Bo?" I managed.

Inexplicably, I was standing in front of Bo Cavanaugh. Hair gel manicured the tousled look that had graced Finnegan's stage—and my fingers—all weekend. Gray suit pants, a pale yellow button down shirt, and a blue silk tie that matched his eyes stood in place of the jeans and sleeveless ensemble that walked out of my apartment two nights before. His eyes were a deeper blue than I observed at night; they were the most beautiful color of ocean blue I'd ever seen. My smile faded as his eyes fell from me to the floor, then to the wall, and back to the floor.

"N-ember? Uhh." He looked increasingly uncomfortable and his fair skin seemed to pale even further.

"Ooooo-kaaayy..." Monica uncomfortably attempted to organize the papers on her desk.

I just stood there while a thousand thoughts scattered to the floor of my brain. In the split second before Monica spoke again, I reasoned maybe his brother's name was Spencer and Bo was standing in—even though he didn't mention a brother the other night—or this must be some sort of mistake. Judging by his complexion, and his inability to say my name without stuttering, I gathered it was neither of these reasons.

Monica swept papers off her desk with little regard to their order. "So, I'll let you two talk. Anything *I* have to say can wait 'till the meeting." She said this with such professionalism that anyone walking by wouldn't have noticed the five-ton elephant in the room.

"Excuse me." Monica slid past Bo (or Spencer), forcing him in to the room a little ways and placing us in a close proximity. Not more than 48 hours ago, being this close to him had tantalized me. Right now, it made my muscles twitch with anxiety. Monica shut the door.

I walked around my chair and stood behind Monica's desk, deliberately distancing myself from "Bo" so I could think clearly. It occurred to me that this was the first time I'd seen him in the daylight, rather than under the stage glow at Finnegan's. He was slightly less fair-skinned than I'd previously assessed, but just as dreamy. *Dreamy, November? Figure out what he's doing here.* I cleared my throat and stared directly at him, handcuffing his eyes to mine.

"November, you work here?" He looked as if he was really trying to work it out in his head.

Seriously? That's the statement you're opening with?

"Yeeees." There was a slight inquisition in my voice, imploring him to feed the elephant in the room. "Spencer, is it?"

"November, it's my first name. It was my father's name. My full name is Spencer Bowan Cavanaugh. David Bryson was supposed to handle the meeting here today, but he had a personal emergency, so he called me *this morning* to ask me to come here. The only information I was given was to come to The Hope Foundation and ask for Monica. What are the odds?" He spoke faster than normal—faster than necessary. I assumed he was anticipating any follow up questions I might have, which is why he offered up so much right away.

"Wait a minute, Monica said that Spencer Cavanaugh is one of the *founders* of DROP. You never told me you *founded* a non-profit agency." I felt an annoying itch of betrayal.

Bo chuckled, "I'll counter *your* wait-a-minute with my own. You never told me you were *the* grant writer for a very successful and stable non-profit." My inner academic cheered a bit at his accentuation of "the" as if I was a prize to be sought. *Damn straight.*

Then, I was forced to address the issue of his ever changing name.

"So, Bo, that's just for music?" I was no stranger to people using stage names, I just felt pissed about this one for reasons beyond my in-the-moment analysis.

For the first time since Monica shut the door, Bo took a step toward me. He sat in the chair I previously occupied. He rested his elbows on the desk, peering at me from his smoldering ocean blue eyes.

"Bowan, or Bo, is typically all the time, except for at the foundation—they call me Spencer. I use it there as homage to my father. I've been "Bo" my whole life. My parents were working on developing this organization when they died. Two years after their death, I gathered enough strength to continue what they started." His tone was littered with something just slight of irritation as he sat back in the chair and finally met my stare.

"I'm sorry, Bo I was just taken by surprise." My relieved exhale was louder than I'd intended, "I guess we didn't really squeeze in time to discuss our jobs." I grinned at the memory of all the things we *did* have time for. "Shit. The meeting. So, double agent, I'll call you Spencer for the meeting?" I raised an eyebrow and he smiled.

"Knock knock!" Monica exaggerated as she carefully opened the door. Bo and I rose to greet her. "All set in here...or whatever?" Professional Monica was replaced by nosy Monica.

"Monica, this is Spencer *Bowan* Cavanaugh. Non-profit founder by day, musician by night."

"Nice to meet you, Monica." Bo stuck out his hand and Monica rolled her eyes.

"Shut up. I'll get the details later. Right now we have a room full of people that need to meet you... Mr. Cavanaugh." Her to-the-point humor made fast friends with my cynicism early in our friendship. It came in handy in times like these.

As we headed to the meeting room, I was eager to hear what he had to present. How had a man, like Bo, decided to pick up the pieces of his deceased parents' dream? As soon as he started speaking, I was fighting tears.

"My little sister, Rachel, was in a drug rehab facility by the time she was fifteen." Bo didn't make eye contact with me, which my glistening tear ducts appreciated. "She had been doing drugs for about six months when she nearly overdosed on cocaine and alcohol. She was in the ICU for a week before she was sent to rehab. My parents' eyes were opened to the rampant drug and alcohol use among her friends and in our community. The issue crossed class lines, it didn't discriminate. Pills, alcohol, and cocaine seemed to be the easiest thing for my sister and her friends to come by; it nearly killed her." He inhaled deeply and continued.

"Rachel was in the rehab facility for almost six months. She was very depressed, and expressed several times that she wasn't ready to go home for fear of using again, but she *was* home in time to start her junior year of high school. I had already been out of college for a year, so I was able to help Rachel stay out of trouble by spending a lot of time with both her and her friends. The summer before Rachel's senior year, my parents started working on DROP. Their vision was a community action organization which provided realistic opportunities for young people to engage in, alternatives to drug use, and a place to seek help when needed. At the end of the first year my parents—Spencer and Vivian—were busy lining up donors and spaces, when they were killed in a car accident." His voice clipped at the memory.

"Two years after their death I was ready, and able, to reignite DROP. I've spent the past two years securing financial backing, and developing a solid program with David Bryson. In our hometown, DROP has been fully operational for a year, and has successfully set up both a community center and a mentoring program. Now, we're ready to expand. The problem isn't just in our hometown—it's everywhere. We'd like to align with an organization that focuses on domestic violence, as we've seen drug use in our teens is often paired with violence at home or violence in their relationships. Thank you for letting me share our story."

I blinked for what felt like the first time since he started speaking, thankful my tears had burrowed back into their hole. I caught Monica's eye, and she seemed to be thinking the same thing. *Wow.*

Monica rose and shared The Hope Foundation's mission statement, and her work with community education. She noted that while our foundation didn't have its own centers outside of offices, we did work in conjunction with domestic violence shelters. She concluded that, from her standpoint, being able to have our own center(s) would ultimately work in the favor of the community by providing a non-threatening place for young people or families to spend time, and not just seek us when they're in crisis. All through Monica's speech, Bo listened attentively. He continually shot me side glances and *always* caught me staring at him—I blushed every time.

Whatever hotness level I thought he attained in Finnegan's was blown to smithereens when I saw him in business attire. I spent my whole life balancing the free lifestyle I grew up in, with the structured life I craved. Sitting across from me seemed to be another human being balancing conflicting lifestyles. And, I happened to know what his tongue could do outside of the boardroom.

When it was my turn to speak, I presented a resume-style list of the grants I was able to secure during the past four years. I lauded myself on my ability to maintain consistent and respectful contacts with people in both the public and private sectors. Most of our success had come from outstanding government grant programs, but I'd spent the last year researching private funding options due to the financial mess of the government.

"Mr. Cavanaugh, Monica tells me that DROP has two, multi-million dollar backers. While we wouldn't want to piggy-back off of those donors, would your grant writer be willing to teach me a little bit more about securing large funds from the private sector? My specialty is in public money, which is tight these days."

"Yes, Ms. Harris. In fact, I know at least one of our backers would be open to financially supporting whichever organization DROP teams up with." A boyish grin crossed his face.

"Oh? Do you mind sharing which one, so I can research them a bit?"

"Me, Ms. Harris. My parents were wealthy business people. When their estate was settled, I decided to use most of their money to fund their dream. My sister also puts her inheritance into the organization. I can't speak for her, but I know I would be interested."

Oh, so he and his sister are the two multi-million dollar backers. Neat. I kept my game face on while our boss, Carrie, called the meeting to end.

"Thank you, Mr. Cavanaugh. Ember, I'd like it if you and Monica could set up some more meetings with Mr. Cavanaugh, his community educator, and financial person to see if this is a collaboration that would work on the nuts and bolts level. It all seems very promising, so I'm leaving this project to the two of you." She left, followed by her secretary, and Don, our IT guy. Monica, Bo, and I were left in the empty meeting room to discuss a time for our "next meeting."

When the door shut, Monica spoke, "Bo, what the *hell?*"

"Monica," I interrupted, "did any of us talk about our jobs over the last two days?" I knew what she was thinking.

"Well, no. But this is weird... and great!"

Bo cleared his throat, "This *is* weird. We'll figure it out, I'm sure. For now, though, do you all want to go for lunch?" The question wasn't directed toward Monica.

"I can't," she retorted, "I have to go pester your community educator via email. You two have fun." Reason number two why we're best friends; the girl knows when to make an exit.

Over lunch, Bo and I managed to discuss the business that my boss intended us to talk about. I told him about my work at Hope, and that I was really pleased with the role I've had in the growth of the organization. He admitted that while he found my list of accomplishments impressive on a business level, he also found it *very* attractive.

"Well, I have to tell you that you look mighty fine in your day job couture, Mr. Cavanaugh." I reached out across the table and grabbed his hand. It was the first physical contact we'd had since Saturday night, and just as electrifying.

"Ms. Harris, I don't know if this is appropriate," he joked. He pulled his hand away when he saw my smile vanish. "What?"

"This *isn't* appropriate. Shit." My pulse raced as I ran through the list of implications.

"November, it's fine." Nervousness colored his eyes.

"It's actually *not* so fine. The grant writer for one NPO and the millionaire founder and backer for another..."

This sounds worse by the minute.

"Listen, just relax. We'll just play it safe until we know what sort of collaboration, if any, our organizations will have. Then we'll sort it out from there.

"Damn, does this mean our plans for Friday night will have to wait?" I wanted to slam my fists on the table in protest.

"I don't think so, but I'd like to get together for dinner tonight, if you're free." He did little to mask the undercurrent of urgency in his voice.

"That sounds good. Let's do it at my place—I'll cook." I wanted to soak up as much time with him as possible before it might be shortened due to ethical obligations.

"Sounds great," he said as he claimed my hand in his, "I'll see you tonight."

He kissed my hand, paid for our lunch, and we went back to The Hope Foundation. He spoke with my boss, and I didn't say one word about tonight's dinner plans to Monica—and she didn't ask.

CHAPTER SIX

I finished chopping the vegetables just as I heard a knock on my door. The butterflies that hibernated in my stomach all day flew to life. I opened the door and found Bo standing there in light khakis and a grey t-shirt that stretched across his chest.

"Hey," I breathed out, barely above a whisper.

"Hey."

He walked in, shut the door, and pulled me in to a hard, exploding kiss. "God, I've wanted to do that *all* day," he said when he finally pulled away from me.

"Good, me too," I admitted as I staggered back to the kitchen.

"What's for dinner?"

"Stir-fried veggies. Chicken for you, tempeh for me. And, Riesling."

"Tempeh, huh? What if *I'm* vegetarian?" He casually placed his hands in his pockets as he walked toward me.

"You're not. You had the steak sandwich at lunch. Take a seat in the living room; I'll bring your food in." I did my best to hide my grin.

"You're good, Harris. OK, hand me the corkscrew." He grabbed two wine glasses, the wine, the corkscrew, and headed to the living room.

Over dinner we talked about singing, food, wine, and the music he wanted to play on Saturday. I told him I'd love to hear more of his original work before I brought up the meeting.

"I'm really sorry about your sister and your parents, Bo. I can't imagine what a stressful few years it's been for you." I looked into my wine and shook my head.

"Thank you, really, but I'm OK. Rachel struggled more after they died than I did. I went into protection mode and she fell back into drugs for a while."

"But she's okay now?"

"She is. She's studying at UNH and devotes as much free time as she can to DROP. She was really a mess the year after our parents died." He took a deep breath and grabbed my hand. "If I can help *one* family to not go through what we went through with Rachel, I've succeeded."

He kissed my hand gently, then stood up and began gathering our dinner dishes.

"You don't have to do that." I started to stand.

"Sit." He pointed at the couch. "You made this delicious food. Helping to clean up is the least I can do."

He took everything into the kitchen and I heard the faucet run. I waited exactly one minute before heading in after him.

"You don't have to rush out, do you?" I asked, pausing in the doorway.

"Not if you don't want me to." He set the wine glasses down and turned toward me.

"I don't want you to." I padded toward him, a feline grin pulling at the corners of my suddenly dry mouth.

My blood raced faster as the space between us closed. He leaned back with his palms behind him on the edge of the sink, his knuckles white against the counter. He watched me with intense eyes. When I reached him he wrapped his arms around my waist, and I wrapped mine around his neck.

"How do you do this to me?" I asked as our noses touched.

He shrugged and smiled, carefully placing a kiss on the tip of my nose.

"*We* are doing this," he interjected between thick kisses down my neck, "and I don't know how either."

"This is so wrong..." I wanted to be wrong about that, but I wasn't.

"Do you want to stop?" He *did* stop, waiting for my answer.

The little voice in my head that tried to remind me *why* this was wrong choked on the current that hummed between us. In that moment, all reason and responsibility vanished.

"I don't want to stop." I tightened my grip around him and our lips fell into each other.

Bo pulled away and twirled me around. My back was thankful for the cool release of the granite countertop. He ran his hands down the back of my shorts, stopping where the shorts stopped. His firm hands lifted me to a seated position on the edge of my sink. I instinctively wrapped my legs around his waist, but started to pull them away at the risk of seeming too forward. He countered by grabbing my calves and twisting my legs back to where they'd been before. His body pressed in closer.

We were silent, staring at each other, searching each other for answers to unasked questions. I sighed as my heart tried to keep pace with the intensity my soul felt. As heat radiated from his body, I craved him more. This time, when his lips met mine, a high pitched sound released from somewhere in the back of my throat; as if I were taken by surprise. My hands wrapped around the bottom of his shirt and I guided it up his chest. He conceded, releasing his arms from around my waist and over his head, dropping the shirt to the floor. He scooped me off of the counter with my legs still around his waist.

"That way," I panted as I pointed down the short hallway that held my bedroom.

"You sure?" He barely pulled his mouth from mine.

"M-hmm," was all I could manage as I tried to hold myself together.

He skillfully opened my bedroom door with one hand, while still holding and kissing me. In that instant I was relieved that I had cleaned my house *and* made my bed. My deep purple comforter cushioned my back as he lay me down and backed away. I slinked up to the head of the bed and stared at him, but he seemed frozen. I rose to my knees and made my way back to him. My fingers curled around the waistband of his pants and I urged him onto the bed. He pulled back and put his hands on mine.

"Are you really sure?" His question was infused with rasping want.

"Are you?"

"November, I've been sure since you caught my eye when I played my first song at Finnegan's. I wanted you then, and I want you now."

I pulled my hands away and took off my shirt.

Those were the last words we spoke. He cupped one hand under my breast as I pulled him onto my bed. I began grinding my hips into his as my body absorbed his weight; neither one of us bothered coming up for air. I shifted my weight to one side and rolled him over, my knees straddled his waist. He was rock hard beneath me. I tossed my bra to the floor and reached for his belt. He moaned beneath my touch, causing my hands to fumble for a second. With his belt on the floor, he slipped out of his pants and rolled me over to take off my shorts. When our underwear found their way to the floor, he reached down for his jeans, searching the pocket.

I reached blindly to my bedside stand drawer and pulled out a condom. "No, I got it."

I was always prepared in the bedroom, but all at once I hoped he didn't think I made a habit out of this. He smirked as he took the foil from my hands, but ignored my confused look as he set it on the pillow next to me.

Bo adjusted his position. His torso was on mine and his lower half was off to the side of my body, resting on the bed. His hands were like silk as they massaged my breasts, quickening my breath. I reached for him; I could feel him on the outside of my thigh, but he took my hand and placed it authoritatively on his back as he kissed each one of my nipples. My hips were rising involuntarily against his touch. He traced a line of supple kisses from my breasts to my navel. He did this for an eternity before he rose to meet my mouth. His tongue danced across my lips and I parted them, welcoming him in. *This all feels so right.* He hooked one arm under my hips, leaving his body over me. I was gloriously pinned to my bed.

Our tongues got reacquainted as I tried again to reach for him; he stopped my hand for a minute before he gave in, and his tongue quickened its search of mine as I gripped him tightly.

I want him so badly.

"Damn." Bo pulled away from my mouth, biting his lip with his eyes closed tightly while I glided my hand up and down. He buried his forehead into my shoulder, and tried to control his breathing as I worked faster.

"I'm not in a hurry," he breathed as his hand rode up my inner thigh. All the air left my lungs as he expertly manipulated his fingers. I released him and dug my hands into his shoulder blades. He didn't protest. He didn't stop. I dragged my fingers across his expansive back and up his neck. My sighs of pleasure were punctuated by the tightening of my fingers through his damp hair.

Every inch of me bowed in wonder at his attention. He wasn't in my room for anything quick and meaningless. No, he made that clear as he moved his hands up the length of my body and interlaced his fingers behind my head. I shifted my hips a little so he was positioned between my slightly bent knees. His kiss was enough— more than enough—to make my soul weep in jubilation.

Any other sexual experience I had up until this point was focused on the intercourse itself, getting there and hurtling through it until a climax on *his* part, and acting on mine. It was hard to omit a comparison to Adrian, when everything about Bo, and his touch, and his kiss, was so staggeringly different. *I mattered* to Bo; it wasn't just my body he was trying to please—it was my spirit, my soul, my *core.*

"Bo..." I turned my face just enough to speak. He pulled his head back and looked at me.

"Are you OK?" His thumb crossed my lips.

"Perfect. God... Bo...I want you." My body was trembling under him, begging me for a release.

Bo's lips turned up at the corners as he reached for the condom that was lying in wait on my other pillow.

"Are you sure, November?"

"A hundred percent." I wound my arm through his and gripped the back of his head, pulling his mouth to mine for a reassuring kiss.

Bo sat up to roll the condom on. He replanted his hands on either side of my shoulders. My knees rose higher as he kissed me from my ear to my navel once more. I shifted restlessly beneath him, anxious to feel him inside me.

We moaned simultaneously as he slowly and carefully entered the deepest part of me I could physically offer. It took no time at all to find a rhythm, as if we were made to do this with each other only. I lifted my hips to meet his movement, and he hummed through clenched teeth as he increased his speed and pressure. I braced myself on my headboard as I arched my back.

"Bo," I panted as my breath ran out of control.

He slowed for a minute, studying my face carefully.

"No. Don't stop." I hitched my knees up as I spoke, forcing him deeper in to me.

"Ahh... Ember, Jesus!" He cried out in ecstasy as sweat rained from his forehead, splashing gratuitously across my breasts.

We resumed our rhythm, and our rise to perfection. He offered all of himself as he kissed my neck and chest. He slowed almost to a stop, forcing me to open my eyes; when I did, I saw him staring back at me. His pupils swallowed my form as they worked over me and spoke with ocean blue words. His regard pulled me out from inside myself. He seemed to drink me in—it was invigorating.

Oh my God. November, you love him.

My climax began its swell from deep in my body; I released the headboard and dug my hands into his tight back once more. His pace

55

resumed, and I kept my hips moving beneath him until I felt all the muscles tense across his rock hard torso. He was close. I sat up, and with skillful expertise I rolled him beneath me. The surprised look on his face nearly sent me over the edge, but I maintained my grip on reality. I clasped his wrists above his head and slowly rode him as my tongue hunted through his mouth. I carried his hands to my hips and he responded dutifully, guiding me up and down. His fingers buried into my hips as he moved me faster. I wanted to bring him there. I drew my knees out as far as they would go, forcing him as deep inside me as he could be. I was there.

"Bowan!" I wailed as my insides tightened around him.

"Oh my god, Ember, I'm…*ahh*." He heaved beneath me.

My climax carried on to a foreign destination as I leaned back. Bo placed his hands on the front of my thighs, quickening his hips beneath me. He flipped me onto my back, and in another minute he was pulsing through me with audible satisfaction.

He carefully slid out of me and drew his forehead down my body as his heart jumped through his chest.

"Fuck," he said into my stomach, "I've never felt…"

"Yea," I tried to catch my breath, "me either."

You love him. You are holy-shit in love with him.

CHAPTER SEVEN

I'd slept so heavy, that the sunlight blazing through my window at 6:45am startled me. *Did I really sleep through the whole night, naked, with Bo in my bed? Or, worse, had I dreamt it all?*

I jumped up and took inventory of my surroundings. Bo's shoes were tucked under my bedside stand, and his jeans lay on the floor where I'd tossed them. I paused for a moment and breathed in the memory. Never had anyone looked at me with so much intention, or given me so much *attention*. My body held more memories. I felt him from head to toe; I had *never* felt this way before. Words I swore I wouldn't use carelessly again—not since Adrian—pushed against my gated teeth. Despite their silence, their presence tore through my veins. It was all too heavy to evaluate at such an early hour.

A clink of glass in my kitchen startled me back to reality and I suddenly smelled coffee. I hustled over to my dresser and threw on an oversized t-shirt. I was about to head out of the bedroom, when I heard feet cautiously approaching my room. I gasped internally as he entered my room. Morning did him justice; his "morning after" hair was a perfect mess of wild ebony set against his light skin, and he wore only his boxer briefs. It was the only cup o' Joe I needed.

"Did I wake you?" He seemed startled to see me standing there.

"No, not at all. For a minute, I thought you'd left." I swayed back to the bed and hitched myself against the headboard, drawing my knees to my chest.

"What made you think I'd leave?" He flashed concern as he handed me a warm mug of coffee.

"I'm just surprised I slept so heavily. I'm glad you didn't leave. How'd you know how to fix my coffee?"

"I saw the creamer in your fridge and took a guess." He smirked as he slid next to me and mimicked my position.

I sipped my perfectly made coffee, closed my eyes, and smiled again at the memory of last night. When I opened my eyes, he was smiling too. He turned slightly and, for the first time, I caught a glimpse of his perfectly sculpted back in the daylight—and that tattoo I'd meant to investigate. Between his shoulders, starting at the base of his neck and running to the bottom of his shoulder blades was a huge Celtic cross. It was intricately decorated, all in black, and read like a topographical map over each one of his muscles.

"Wow, that's gorgeous." I reached out and barely touched it, waiting for his approval.

"Thanks, I got it after my parents died. Their initials are in the center."

He shifted so his back was square to me, and stayed quiet as I traced my fingers up the cross and landed on the initials S.C. and V.C. I rested my hand there for a beat, trying to picture what it would be like if my parents were gone—taken from me at the same time. *These shoulders have carried so much...*

"Do you have any?" He turned back around.

"What, you didn't get a good enough look last night?" I joked.

"Ha. Well, not at your back." He winked as he leaned in for a kiss.

"Well, I don't—yet. I'll get one, but I'm waiting till something calls out to me." I smiled thinking of all the times my parents suggested I get a tattoo.

"I had a great time last night," I said, breaking the silence that draped comfortably between us.

"I did too. It was more than great, Ember..."

Jesus, my body was already responding to his voice. And,

Ember sounded just as great coming from his mouth as November did. He could probably call me "bar stool", I realized, and I wouldn't care. *He* just needed to be the one saying it.

"Listen, you should know I don't usually do this sort of thing. I just—it just felt so right with you." I found myself looking at him out of the corner of my eye, hiding behind my coffee.

"Hey, I don't think anything bad, Ember. I don't usually do this either." He set his coffee down.

"Look," he continued, "I feel a little nuts here. I mean, I'm here for business, I decided to play at Finnegan's to pass some time and, damn it, in you walk. When we sang together I felt like I knew all I needed to know about you, but I wanted more. Then you were at the meeting..." Tension made quick work of filling my room.

"Don't do that." I put my coffee down and faced him, my legs crossed. "I'm still here. You're still here. We've got this week. I felt the same things when we met, Bo. I had to force myself to pull away from you after our first kiss. I thought it was a dream; this couldn't be happening at some bar that I've been to every weekend for the last four years. But it did—you did."

I pressed my hand into his cheek. He leaned into it, kissing my wrist as I spoke. "Can we just enjoy this week and weekend and just see where it takes us? That's what you said yesterday, right? If our agencies end up working together, we'll sort out whatever needs to be at that time." I tried to sound positive, but the thought of only seven days left weighed heavily on my words. There would be no way we could carry on like this if we were coworkers.

"God, could you be any more perfect?" He whispered as he reached for my face.

"What do you mean?"

"I mean, *perfect*. You're smart, driven, you sing, and last night..." a grin overcame him, "last night was amazing." He looked up at me, his eyes still dancing with excitement.

"I've never felt anything like that before, Bo."

Suddenly my room felt like it'd been transported south of the

Equator. My palms began to sweat and I felt like my shirt was made of wool. I wanted him even more than I did last night.

Bo leaned forward, kissing me deeply with little regard for morning breath. Thankfully I'd at least sipped my coffee, but I realized I didn't notice at all—I just loved his taste. He pressed me back into the bed with kisses so soft it was as if he worried I would crack beneath his weight. So, naturally, the phone rang.

"Ugh, it's probably Monica," I said as I absentmindedly reached for my phone. I let out a grumble when I saw the number.

"What?" Bo laughed.

"It's her." I rolled my eyes. "We didn't talk about my plans for last night. This is as long as she could contain herself."

Bo's smile faded, but I waved it off.

"Hey Mon, what's up," I answered, maybe a little too blasé.

"What's up? Do you mean after the Spencer revelation yesterday you two *didn't* get together last night?" She sounded annoyed, and I pictured her arms folded with a tapping foot.

"Monica. It's fine. Look, we'll talk about it when I get to work, *okay?*" *She'll see right through it.*

"November Blue Harris, is Bo Cavanaugh in your apartment right now?" A fifteen-year-old girl took over her voice.

"Yes."

"Did he just get there or did he stay all night?"

I paused, not wanting to let Bo know that I was going to tell Monica about last night. Monica didn't miss a beat.

"Ember, did he stay last night?"

"Yes."

"Shit! Ember!" She exclaimed excitement and panic in one breath. "Can you be to work by 7:30 so we can talk about this before *Carrie* gets there?"

"Sure, Mon. See you soon." I hung up as Monica grumbled something unintelligible and I looked at Bo. He seemed frozen in the same position he was when I answered the phone.

"Does she know I stayed last night?" There was no inflection in his tone.

"She's a smart girl. She's also my best friend and *won't* say anything. I know we've only known each other a couple of days but you have to trust me on that."

Bo's sigh of relief took his shoulders down with it, "I just don't want to ruin anything for anyone." It was hard for me to determine if he was speaking about our jobs or *us.*

"It'll be fine. I do, however, have to get to work early. Crap, we're supposed to set up a meeting. What are your other commitments this week?" Discussing business in the bedroom only served to highlight the issues present.

"Today is the local high school, tomorrow I'm free after ten." He rested his head against my headboard.

"So how about we do a lunch meeting tomorrow, in our office? Just text me later to confirm that's OK."

"Sure thing. David Bryson will be there too."

A devious smile erased all concern from his face. He took our coffee mugs and placed them on the bedside stand.

"Hey, I need that!" I joked.

The scorching heat from his lips melted me into my bed. He pulled away as quickly as he came in, and swiftly dressed.

"And *I* needed that," he teased. "Talk to you later."

He kissed me on the head before moving out of my bedroom.

"Hey!" I called out. "Don't go trying to stalk me on Facebook or anything, I don't have an account!"

"Hey!" He called back, out of sight, "Neither do I. Looks like we're both out of luck!"

I hurried to my bedroom window when I heard the door shut. Bo reached the sidewalk, paused in front of my car a moment, and glanced up to my window. I waved and he grinned before getting in his car and driving away.

Monica and I got to work at the same time. She was already shaking her head at me as she put her car in to park.

"Morning, Mon," I said coolly as possible.

"Don't 'morning Mon' me, smartass, get inside so we can talk!" The grin didn't leave her face; even when we got into my office and shut the door.

"What do you want me to tell you? That just because we happened to have a meeting with Bo yesterday I would break whatever plans we had this week? Yesterday's meeting was informational, set up before we met him, and he wasn't even supposed to be here." *Why am I speaking so fast?*

"Ember, relax. I just want to know how he is in bed." She arched her eyebrow as she sipped coffee.

"Monica!"

"A hot man like that does *not* find himself at your apartment in the morning without having been there the night before. And, to the best of my knowledge, you don't make a habit of platonic sleep overs with the opposite sex." She could have been on CNN with the seriousness she used to deliver that line.

I caved. "It was intense. We had this rhythm—it wasn't awkward. I felt him on a different level I've ever felt anything, or anyone. He took his time, touched and kissed what seemed like every single part of my body, didn't rush. His eyes were on me the whole time, Mon... like he was at a museum, looking at art—or something. He was slow and sweet—holy shit. And this morning he brought me coffee in bed for Christ's sake!"

"Miss November, I do believe you're blushing," She exaggerated a southern drawl as she fanned herself.

"Seriously, seeing him in here yesterday only made me *more* attracted to him. Do we have *everything* in common? Jesus, I don't know what to do. By the way we're doing a lunch meeting tomorrow to further discuss the collaboration." I flopped down in my chair and sighed.

"Em..." Monica sat down across from me.

"I know. This could be a real nightmare."

Monica and I majored in Public Relations; sex "scandals" are both the easiest thing to avoid *and* the most damaging for an agency.

"We'll figure it out Ember. Just be cautious until all the cards are on the table and we know what we're dealing with." She seemed relaxed, which helped.

During the rest of the morning I researched what I could on DROP. I already knew their major benefactor, but it was clear that they needed internet assistance. I emailed their grant writer, William Holder, to get a read on him. William offered that he and "Spencer" had known each other since high school and he had a lot of emotional stake in the success of DROP. I seriously hoped Bo didn't share personal things with Will, at least about us.

Monica was able to connect with Tristan MacMillian, DROP's community educator, and start a rapport with him as well. The four of us agreed that we would need to meet sometime soon to see if we felt comfortable on a personnel level. Our boss was pleased.

"Ladies, you continue to amaze me," Carrie congratulated us in her office Tuesday afternoon. "Your professionalism is stupendous, especially considering that you two are friends; it doesn't always work out this well. I've spoken with David Bryson, and he said he would coordinate a time for the DROP team to come down and meet us. I suggested that we'd like a trip to New Hampshire, as well. We could see their community center, and you two could meet with William and Tristan. I'll be out of town for the rest of the week for that conference in D.C., but we can talk about this more when I get back."

I looked forward to seeing where Bo grew up, and it made me realize how far into him

I'd fallen. *Shit.* Ethically, I needed to rein things in with Bo.

Spiritually, I couldn't force myself to do it. Realistically, I shouldn't be excited to see the hometown of someone I was "just" having fun with, and might be working with in a professional capacity. *Double shit.*

We thanked Carrie, wished her well on her trip, and headed home for the day. I went to Monica's house for dinner. Josh was waiting for us; he'd spent most of the day hanging out and preparing dinner, since he didn't work on Tuesdays. As I headed up her stairs my phone dinged with a text message.

Bo: *Hey, sorry I didn't text all day-crazy busy. R we all still meeting 4 lunch tomorrow?*

I was both relieved and bummed by his casual sounding message.

Me: *It's OK—busy 4 me too. Boss will be out of town for the rest of the week. Tomorrow's still good—come by office at noon. At Mon's for dinner. Text you when I get home.*

As soon as I hit send, I wondered if I should have asked him to come to dinner—what with the amazing sex we had and all. But, I needed a minute to clear my head and talk with Monica, outside of the office, about the possible ramifications of all of this, work and soul.

"Ember! Good to see you—get your nose out of your damn phone!" Josh hugged me with the sincerity of a big brother.

"Shut up Josh, I text maybe once a day."

"Was that lover boy?" Josh elbowed me and I glowered at him just before Monica piped in.

"Shut it, Josh." She sounded as tense as I felt.

"What the hell?" Josh looked at both of us.

"Ugh. It's nothing, really," I lied.

Josh laughed dismissively, "Oh, you mean because lover boy isn't only rocker Bo Cavanaugh, but is *technically* the wealthy Spencer Cavanaugh—your future boss of sorts? You've gotten yourself into a real cock-up, haven't you?"

"Seriously Monica?!" My eyes widened in betrayal.

"Relax November. This is Josh, I tell him *everything*. Who is he going to tell? You had sex with a hot musician who happens to be seeking our mad knowledge."

"You guys had sex!" Josh half-cheered as Monica mumbled "oops" under her breath.

"You're 0-for-2. Got anything else you'd like to spill?" My anger hissed inside as she continued to help with dinner.

I couldn't reconcile if my anger was from embarrassment at my sex life being in Josh's head, or at myself for knowingly entering into a sexual relationship with a potential boss. I'd never felt so torn. My practical, realist side—the side with whom I chose to align most frequently—reminded me that the responsible thing to do would be stop seeing Bo until this collaboration deal was finalized. My free-love side told me to ride the wave with Bo; soak up his intellect, share music, share passion—have sex with the boy. I liked *her* more and more.

"Guys," I broke the awkward silence, "I'm sorry for being all weird. I just feel disoriented, disjointed, all sorts of dis." It felt weird being this vulnerable in front of Josh.

"Ember, it's fine. I just can't believe how shitty this is. This is the first guy I've seen you fall uninhibitedly for since Adrian, and this *thing* could get in the way." Monica walked toward me and gave me a little squeeze.

"Hey, ladies, isn't your boss out of town through the week and weekend?" Josh asked, and we nodded.

"Well, since *she's* the one you're worried will find out..." He looked at us with wide eyes and raised brows.

"What, Josh?" I asked.

"Screw it! Enjoy the week with Bo and worry about it later—or not at all. Mazel Tov!" He raised his glass to cheer.

Monica and I laughed and toasted Josh. With the clink of our glasses I willingly entered into a week of spontaneity. The rest of dinner had a much lighter mood, for the most part.

"You OK, Josh?" I sipped my wine, waiting for an answer.

"Yea. Why?" His eyes surveyed the table, but never met mine.

"You seem a little off." I shrugged.

"Yea, babe. You OK?" Monica placed her hand on top of his.

"I just feel bad for Ember, is all." He looked at me and continued, "This guy's really done something to you. I don't know, you're happier. I've never heard you sing like that, either."

"Josh, you hear me sing almost once a week." I looked at Monica, who shifted her eyes side-to-side. She didn't know where Josh was going with this either.

"It was different last weekend, Ember. It was *all* of you up there. No one else has ever brought that out of you before." Josh bit the inside of his cheek and left the table.

"What the hell?" I whispered to Monica as Josh washed his dishes.

"He really wants you to be happy, you know. He doesn't want this to blow up in your face. He can see how good Bo is for you." Hopeful sadness was the show playing in Monica's eyes tonight.

I furrowed my brow as I headed toward Josh in the kitchen.

"Hey, Josh, it's going to be fine, OK? And, even if it's not— I've got great friends to help me out." I gave him a playful squeeze across his shoulders.

"I know, Ember. You're tough as hell. But what's between you and Bo is obvious. It's gotta work out."

I patted him firmly on the back and headed back through the living room to leave.

"He's being weird. Tell him it's fine, OK?" I whispered to Monica as I left her apartment.

Walking to my car, I texted Bo.

Me: *You around?*

Bo: *Of course, why what's up?*

Me: *Can I come see you?*

Bo: *I just left a dinner meeting, getting in my car. Can I come to your place? It's much nicer than a crappy motel.*

Me: *True. Just head to my place, we'll meet there. :)*

CHAPTER EIGHT

Moonlight beamed off the hood of my car as I parked it in front of my apartment, right behind Bo. He got out when I did and we walked to the stairs. I noted his tense movements; maybe he was fighting the same moral demons I'd wrestled all day.

"Where the hell have you been?" I laughed out. "Your hair's a mess!"

I roughed through his hair like he was a puppy before unlocking the building door.

He chuckled like a high school boy, grabbed my hand and kissed it with tight lips. Something was off, and I didn't like it. *Everyone is bizarre today.*

"Hey," I continued as we headed up the stairs to my apartment, "is everything OK? You're all weird." I dialed down the concern and took a more *get over it* tone so he wouldn't think I was getting crazy.

"Sorry. Everything's fine. Just a little tense about our meeting with you guys tomorrow." By *our meeting,* he meant himself and David Bryson. He was definitely fighting the same demons.

I opened the door to my apartment and headed right for the wine rack. Sobriety had taken up enough of my time today. Bo thumped heavily on the couch.

"Do you want beer or wine?" I hollered from the kitchen.

"God. Beer please," he exaggerated with a hint of a smile in his voice. He was staring to relax, but I could tell this would be a two-beer kind of conversation.

"You're in luck. I've got a 'Whale's Tale Pale Ale' from Cisco's, the brewery on Nantucket—it's awesome." I handed him his beer and sat down on the couch, facing him with my knees bent toward the back of the couch. I swallowed half of my wine in one gulp.

"That bad, huh?" Bo looked into my eyes. It wasn't just *at* my eyes; he really got in there and scrambled things around until I no longer knew if I was feeling him or me racing through my veins.

"Not bad. Just... a lot. I just want to get through this meeting with David Bryson tomorrow and have you all to myself for the rest of the week. Am I crazy? I feel a little crazy. You're in the house of a crazy person." I rushed to the kitchen to retrieve more beer and wine.

"You're not crazy, Ember. Don't you realize what you do to me? Ha! You know..." He smiled as I returned with our refreshed drinks, "the second we sang that verse of "Heaven When We're Home," it was all I could do to *not* hoist you over my shoulder, hightail it out of the bar, and just drive around the country singing with you."

The thought speared me in the knees and I could no longer stand, thankfully I arrived at the couch.

"Are you kidding? God, you're a lot more 'by-the-seat-of-your-pants' than I am." Guitar cases, hotel rooms, stages, and harmonizing with Bo filled all available space in my brain.

"Are you saying you'd object to taking that voice of yours and sharing it with all of humanity? You want to keep all of it for yourself?" He seemed comically flabbergasted.

"Well, myself and you." We wouldn't be talking about work anymore tonight, so I let my already weakening guard completely down.

"Ember I can't tell you how many times over the past four years I've wanted to just take my guitar and go..." His eyes were now clouded with a different stress.

"Bo, I hate to bring this up, but the first time you came here—

with Monica and Josh—you said you haven't seen your sister in years; then two days later I find out you started a non-profit with her." That detail nagged my brain for days.

"I was wondering when you'd call me on that. When I first met you guys it was easier, I didn't have to get into it. I didn't have to say that she was a recovering drug addict, and my parents died in the middle of founding an organization based on helping kids like her, and so on. She was really screwed up, Ember..." His eyes welled with tears as he looked to the floor.

Wordlessly, I wrapped my arms around his shoulders and gave him the tightest hug I'd ever given anyone. He slumped forward and pressed his forehead to my bare shoulder. I was overtaken by his vulnerability.

The wetness I felt on my shoulder was the only indication he was crying. *Crying.* Girls make a production out of this; we let the whole world know with wails, throwing things, and we even stare at ourselves in the mirror while doing it. In front of me sat a gorgeous, hurt man who felt comfortable crying in front of me, and I froze.

Why does having someone cry in front of you feel more intimate and revealing than having sex with them? He sat there for just a minute, and I gave him the silence I assumed he needed. I rested my chin on the top of his head and felt him breathe deeper. I didn't let on that I knew he was crying, because I wasn't sure how much of the Y-chromosome he carried with him at all times; I didn't want to embarrass him. Finally, he looked up with dry eyes and a puff-free face that eludes every woman on the planet. He looked in to my eyes, and when he opened his mouth to speak I closed it with a kiss.

"Jeeeeesuusss..." Bo exhaled when I released his lips from mine, "Sorry 'bout that. I've just had to tell Rachel's and my parents' story so much this week that I guess it finally caught up to me. Do you want to run and scream?" His sheepish grin sucked the heavy from the room.

"No, we're in *my* apartment—I'd have to kick you out first." I smiled back when he laughed.

Quietly, an idea tiptoed into my brain that was so specific, I looked over my shoulder to see if my parents snuck in and had whispered it into my ear. Noting my confused look, Bo sat up.

"What?" He asked.

"Um..." I couldn't believe the words that were about to come out of my mouth, "could you show me how to play something...on the guitar?" *What the hell?*

"Ha, are you serious Miss 'I never took to an instrument but my voice is my instrument'?" he mocked.

"Don't make fun of me!" I laughed as my face heated.

"I'm just kidding. Let me go get my guitar."

"No," I paused, "I... have one."

"November Blue, you *own* a guitar and this is the first I'm hearing about it? *That's* hot. Go get the damn thing!"

Operation "Crying Distraction" complete. *God, now I have to play in front of Lord Hotness of the Guitar.* I walked to my room and opened the closet door. I had to reach all the way to the back for it; it was a miracle I still had it at all. I carried the worn case to the living room and set it like a live bomb on the coffee table. When I opened it, a gasp of juvenile awe filled my ears.

"This is gorgeous. How long have you had it? Can I pick it up?" Bo reached slowly toward the acoustic guitar.

"Be my guest. My parents had it when they were in high school. They gave it to me when I went to college in the hopes that I'd find someone to teach me to play, or something..."

"Why the hell don't you ever play?"

"Don't have to with a voice like this," I joked, pointing to my throat and smiling.

"Lame point. K, where do you want to start?"

"The beginning?" I shrugged, all 'damsel-in-distress.'

Bo chuckled as he helped me position the guitar on my body. It felt slightly foreign, but he didn't. He showed me a couple of cords, laying his hands on mine, often causing me to lose focus. I had retained a fair bit of this basic information from my childhood, but I refused to tell him that; I just wanted him to keep touching me. After about a half hour of musical foreplay, he ran to his car and brought up his guitar. He'd strum something and have me follow. We laughed at my mistakes, or when he'd play something that was ridiculously expert and ask me to repeat it.

A seductive and frightening voice reappeared in the confines of my subconscious. *You love him. You love him so much that you're not even thinking about sex right now. You're "guitar-playing, run-away-and-join-a band" in love with him.*

"OK, we're done now. My fingers hurt," I abruptly chuckled, lifting the strap over my head and placing the guitar back in the case. The guitar, and the L-word, could stay right in that case—for now.

"Baby," he teased as he set his guitar in its case.

"I'll show you baby, Mr. Cavanaugh," I said in my most seductive voice possible sliding over his lap in a straddle.

"Ms. Harris," a laugh choked his voice, "I do believe this would be *highly* frowned upon." He smoothed his hands up the sides of my torso, underneath my shirt.

Unhurriedly, I pulled his shirt over his head and tossed it by his guitar.

"I don't care. I can't—and won't—say no to you until I absolutely have to." My lips grazed his ear as I spoke.

His goosebumps answered before his voice did. "I'm glad you have that willpower, because right now I don't know if I could ever say no to you." He drew my shirt up my body, and it joined his on the floor.

My phone rang, interrupting us for the second time in one day, and we both let out sighs of exasperation. I checked my phone and grumbled.

"What?" Bo said.

"My parents." I rolled my eyes. When I remembered his parents I decided to cut the attitude, hoping he didn't notice.

"Hello?"

"Hey, Baby Blue! We're in your neck of the woods and we're thinking of stopping over—is that OK?" My mom's voice sang through the phone, the octave raised Bo's eyebrows.

"What? When?"

"We'll we're pulling into town now..."

"Mom, come on! It's like 10:30 on a Tuesday night!" Each time they rolled into town, it was a fresh reminder that they really marched to the beat of their own bongo.

"Oh, give it a rest November Blue. We'll be there in fifteen." Suddenly, my mother calling me "November Blue" seemed odd, as if it belonged to Bo alone.

I pressed "end" and let out an overstated whimper into Bo's shoulder. My hormones would never forgive me for this.

"What?" Bo asked as he gripped my waist.

"My parents are going to be here in a fifteen minutes. Now, they would be thrilled to meet you, and wouldn't think anything weird about never hearing about you, and yadda, yadda but..." I waved my hands erratically to indicate the insanity I was feeling. For such peaceful people, they could certainly ignite something frantic in me.

"No big deal," he chuckled, "I'm not really 'meet-the-parents' ready right now," He said as he shagged his hair back and forth.

I petulantly stepped to the floor as he stood up. I tossed his shirt carelessly in his direction, admiring the view. He hugged me bare-chested before he put it on; when he pulled away I noticed a fairly large greenish bruise to the left of his navel.

"Jesus, what happened?" I asked, realizing that, by the color, it had been there for a few days. I'd been too involved in other parts of his body to notice.

"This? Nothing." He brushed my hand away. "I was helping my friend in his barn last week and I bumped into his tool bench— serious idiot." He shrugged into his shirt.

"Well, you better not damage anything else, I love this body." There. I said *love* in a completely innocent manner and the floor didn't swallow me whole.

Bo smirked, "And I love *this* body." He pulled me closer and ran his thumb under my eye. I let my head fall into his hand for a second.

"Damn straight you do. I don't go running for my own mental clarity—gotta keep it tight for the bedroom," I joked, flexing my muscles.

Bo let out a full-bellied laugh and kissed me goodnight.

"See you tomorrow at the office, Mr. Cavanaugh," I toned out derisively.

"It'll be good, I promise. Goodnight."

I left my hand on the door after he closed it, praying for a split second that it really *would* be all right.

At precisely 10:46pm, I heard the unmistakable sound of my parents 1980's station wagon in front of my apartment. Their laughter carried them up the stairs before they knocked. The fact that I trained them to knock seared me with pride. Growing up, Ashby and Raven didn't even have a door to whatever bedroom they lived in at the time. I braced myself and opened the door.

"Rae! Ash!" I cheered as they walked in. Calling them mom and dad was out of the question growing up. They said it forced an uncomfortable hierarchy in the household. *You mean like parent and child? Imagine that.*

"Bluebell!" My dad squeezed me around the waist tightly, his arm snuffing out any memory of Bo's hands.

"Ember, baby, how are you?" My mom wrapped her arms around me and my dad before they both stopped dead and dropped their arms.

I turned to see what happened, and saw them staring wide-eyed and open-mouthed at the coffee table. I didn't have time to put the guitar away, and now I was going to have to explain. I walked the long way around the coffee table and stood facing them on the other side. *Talk about a five-ton elephant.*

"November, what's this about?" A hint of a smile graced my mother's face.

"When did you take this out, Sweetie?" Dad had a "no judgment or expectations" air.

"I met this guy. He's a musician." My parents shot each other a look in the hopes I wouldn't see. I did.

"No," I continued, "I mean, Monica and I sang with him at Finnegan's last week when he played a set. He's from New Hampshire. He..."

My voice was gone. As I tried to put everything into words for my parents, the two people who had more love between them than anyone I had ever met, a heavy sob escaped my body. I crumpled to the couch with my elbows on my knees, crying into my hands.

"Sweetie!" My mom rushed to my side and wrapped her arm around my shoulder. My dad sat next to her and cocked his head in concern. He's the only dad I know that's not afraid of tears. *Thank you, hippies.*

For several minutes the tears fell. Each one I shed held reasons why I loved Bo, reasons why it was irresponsible, reasons why I didn't care. My parents maintained their protective stance, and when I finally stopped I told them *everything.* The singing, the, meeting him at work, about his sister, his parents and about his foundation— it was all on the table. I told them that we had sex and it was the best thing that'd ever happened to me, physically and emotionally. When I explained that if our organizations collaborated we'd have to stop seeing each other—for a while at the very least, and forever at the most, I spilled more tears onto my mom's shoulder.

"You are so perfectly amazing, November," were the first words my mother spoke, "you need to decide what's important right now." Her words sat me up.

"Isn't it all important? Didn't you spend my entire life teaching me to follow my heart, and the wind, and whatever else?" Her practicality irritated me for the first time in my life.

"November," my dad offered, "it *is* all important. *But* it all can't be first-place. For instance, remember when you begged us to stay in one place long enough for you to go to one high school? While

Raven and I valued our freedom as a family over everything else, the look in your eyes raised your desire for a home base to the number one spot on our list of things that were important."

My dad reached across my mom's lap and gave my knee a squeeze.

"What are you saying? That I need to give up this core-shaking love to focus on what could be one of the most important career moves I'll ever have?" I was thoroughly confused.

"You need to *really* take time to think it all through. These are tears of confusion, love, sorrow and betrayal. Self-betrayal. You're feeling like no matter what you choose—if you have to choose— you'll be betraying the other half of yourself. Your free spirit and your practical spirit have worked together beautifully your whole life, and this is the first time they're at odds with each other. It's a bitch." Mom nailed it.

They stayed for another hour, told me they were headed back on the road, but would be back through next weekend. I told them that I wanted them to meet Bo, but I wanted them to meet him only if we were meant to be together; I knew they'd love him instantly and I didn't want to give anyone false hope. I assured them that there would at least be a decision between the organizations by then.

My mom interrupted me, "Don't let your job decide this, Ember. *You* need to decide this. Work through it and commit with reckless abandon. Even if the decision happens before your organizations decide what their positions will be, commit."

Being with Bo for the week was no longer the issue; the mist hovering over my mom's eyes told me she knew this was about the "after." She knew me well enough to know I was planning to decide after our organizations did. She knew, too, that it wouldn't be my decision, and I could blame someone else for the rest of my life for whatever happened. She was good.

I kissed them good-bye and told them to call me when they got back into town. I scuffed to my bedroom and collapsed onto my bed, begging my pillow to absorb my tears. *Maybe I'll cry out a solution,*

I thought as I fell asleep with my clothes on.

CHAPTER NINE

Emptiness rose with the sun on Thursday. Not the emptiness that comes from heartbreak, but an emptiness that left me with a clear head; free of confusion. Evidently, my subconscious had worked it all out overnight, and today's meeting between me, Monica, Bo, and David Bryson would be one hundred percent professional. I would focus on the collaboration only, try to set my swelling feelings aside, and see how that felt.

I texted Bo before I headed to work.

Me: *Looking forward to meeting David today. Is noon still good?*

Bo: *Good morning, noon is perfect—see you then.*

Me: *Don't think I'm being weird today.*

Bo: *?*

Me: *I don't want to screw things up for either one of us. I'm going to play it safe around you. Wait—David doesn't know anything does he?*

It occurred to me he could very well have shared things with David as I had with Monica.

Bo: *Guys don't "do that." No worries, you'll make it up to me later.*

Me: *:)*

A smiley-face was all I could manage. What if I *couldn't* make it up to him later?

The absence of Monica's car erased thoughts of Bo. She was

usually at work before me. Once I settled in to my desk I heard the main door shut.

"Mon?" I wasn't used to being in the building alone.

"Yea, coming," she said rather weakly. When she entered my office and took off her sunglasses, I saw the puffy-eyed evidence of a night, and likely morning, spent crying.

I'd seen this look before; when she came back from break in college. Grant broke up with her then. They'd been together since high school, and he broke up with her just as Adrian and I started sleeping together regularly.

"Monica, what happened?" I leapt to my feet and flew around my desk to give her a hug. She resumed sobbing in to my shoulder.

"Josh..." she inhaled with that uncomfortable cry-stutter and continued, "*thinks* he wants to take a break!"

That was all she could manage before she silenced a wail into my shoulder.

"Jesus, Monica! What the hell? When did this happen? What did he say? I was just there last night..." I ceased my barrage and sat us down in adjoining chairs.

Monica grabbed a tissue off of my desk, sat back, and took a long, slow, breath.

"After you left last night," her eyes welled with tears as she struggled to continue, "we were cleaning up and he still seemed weird, like when you were there. I followed him to the living room and he plunked into the chair and just sort of sat there with his head in his hands." She closed her eyes tight, as if she was trying to wake herself from a dream.

"What'd he say, Mon?" I didn't want her to replay all the gory details as she sat broken in my office.

"Ember he couldn't even look me in my eyes! He said that he loves me 'so much' but he felt like there was some connection missing. He said that watching you talk about Bo and how you are when you're with Bo... "

"Me and Bo? He hasn't spent much time with me and Bo,

Mon."

"I know, Em, and that's what I told him."

"And what'd he say?"

"He said that when he talked to Bo last weekend it shook him up." Apprehension stole her tears.

"He talked to Bo? About us? When?"

"After the second night that he played at Finnegan's, when they went inside to settle up. Josh asked him to be careful because you'd been hurt before."

"Again, *five* years ago. I'm not a wounded love-vet, just someone who's been focused on other things." *Jesus, if Josh spoke about my heartbreak, maybe it was more visible than I thought.*

"Anyway, he said that Bo looked at him with complete seriousness and said that when he first sang with you, and looked in to your eyes, it was like he was able to feel everything you've ever felt. He said his soul thumped inside of him and it felt like he'd known you and loved you for a thousand lifetimes." She blinked, sending two tears to stain her cheek.

My mind went completely blank. The reservoir I thought I'd depleted in to my pillow was brimming with fresh tears. *A thousand lifetimes? Feeling everything I've ever felt by looking in my eyes?* I stared at Monica wide-eyed.

"I know, right?" She sensed my lack of words. "A thousand mother-fucking lifetimes this guy has loved you, and *you* find his ass strumming a guitar in a bar we've been going to for *four years!"* She cried and laughed at the same time. A beautiful mess.

"I...what the hell did Josh say to you after that?"

"He said that if that kind of love existed for everyone," her voice broke the dam of sorrow once more, "he wasn't sure it was with me."

"Holy shit. What did you say?" I scanned the room for an escape.

"I told him to go. I was pissed, I was crying, I had no coherent response. He kissed me on top of the *fucking head*, said he loved me, and left. So, I'm left to understand that he *loves* me, just maybe not a thousand lifetimes worth," her tone of sorrow shifted to one of anger.

"What a coward."

"Exactly!" She seemed revived by her anger.

"Um…OK…So I'm going to call David Bryson and see if we can reschedule our meeting until tomorrow. We can close up, go eat ice cream and drink wine for the rest of the day—my place." I refused to say Bo's name for a moment.

"No, we've got to get this meeting out of the way so we don't have to think about DROP again until Carrie sends us off to New Hampshire to meet with the whole damn group." She drew her shoulders back and took a deep breath, like she was about to shoot a free throw.

"OK, Champ, whatever you say. Now, go to the bathroom and freshen up—you look like hell," I said, forcing a smile as I pointed to the door.

Monica hugged me tightly.

"You're the absolute best, Em. I think I've even loved you for a thousand lifetimes." She left my office and shut the door.

I reached for my phone to text Bo. I wasn't going to tell him about what Josh said to Monica. I didn't want to betray Josh; I wanted to smack him, but not betray him.

Me: *Just a heads up. Josh broke up with Monica last night. She's a hot mess.*

Bo: *Shit really? That's too bad.*

Me: *Yea—it's not good. See you at noon.*

I slammed my forehead down on the desk and waited for 12:00 to come.

A thousand lifetimes…

Knock knock... I jumped violently from the sleep I'd clearly been enjoying. I rubbed my neck as the door opened.

"Em, you OK?" Monica looked refreshed as I searched for the time.

It was 9:00am. I'd slept with my head on my desk for about an hour.

"Oh, yea, in super classy move, I passed out. Must have been all the crying I did last night..." I hadn't gotten around to talking to Monica about my night.

"What happened?!" She was genuinely concerned.

"Oh, you know, Bo came over for a drink and cried in my shoulder. For fun, my parents showed up after he left. They asked all kinds of questions about the guitar—oh yea, Bo and I played the guitar—which caused me to start crying and so I told them everything. They shared their theories and left after midnight."

She stared at me straight-faced, "I'm going to need a little more information."

After I filled her in with actual details and words, she relaxed back into her chair.

"Raven's right, you know." Monica stared out the window.

"Right about what?" *Besides everything.*

"Don't let someone else hold the strings, November. I'm not saying quit your job and frolic in the sand all day with Bo, but I'm saying don't necessarily push him aside and focus solely on your work. You've done *that* for ever. But, if what Josh said is right, about a soul-love, a *thousand lifetimes* love, I don't really know that you have a choice anyway..." *Did my parents kidnap her last night and say to her all of the things I thought they were going to say to me?*

"Monica, stop. Josh is an asshole. He took something Bo *may* have said out of context and used it as an excuse for some insecure bullshit he was feeling."

"Ember, you didn't see the look on Josh's face. He was changed by that conversation with Bo. He couldn't have ever made something like that up. Bo Cavanaugh clearly has it as bad for you as you do for him, and *you* need to drink that in. He loves you, November." While her tone was somber, it was stern.

"Wow, this is some heavy shit. OK, neither one of us can cry any more today. We've got that meeting at noon. Let's go walk for a few minutes to get some fresh air and get our acts together," I resolved as I stood up and ushered us both outside.

We walked to our coffee place and came back to our building. We sat on the front steps

and killing time until about a half hour before our meeting. Our boss would be *so* proud.

"Monica?" I said as we headed inside, failing to break my stare into the distance.

"Yea?"

"That 'thousand lifetimes' thing…Do you think that's kind of…"

"The absolute most gut-wrenchingly romantic thing I've *ever* heard? Yea, I do." She had a half smile, maybe to encourage me.

"I was going to say intense." I half-laughed.

"Intense, yes. Romantic, *hell yes*." Monica opened the door while shaking her head.

As we walked inside she continued, "I'm really sorry I spilled that to you. I just couldn't *make up* another reason Josh wanted to break up with me. But, you should have heard that first from Bo."

"No, honestly, I'm glad I heard it from you."

"Why? So you had permission to sit there with that blank look on your face?" Monica elbowed me as we headed to the meeting room to set up.

"Yea, actually. I almost cried. I wanted to cry about the fact that someone who knew me for five minutes felt that way, but more I wanted to cry because…" I trailed off as the L-word fought its way through my throat.

"Because you absolutely feel the same way, Ember." No inquisition was needed as far as Monica was concerned.

"Yea..." I whispered.

"Look. What I said and what your mother said still stands. Feel it, think about it, do it. The "it" is up to you."

The creak of the main door and the sound of two male voices silenced the conversation that would need to take place later.

"Good afternoon gentlemen," Monica cheerfully greeted.

"Welcome. Mr. Bryson this is Monica Pierce, and I'm November Harris."

"Oh, please, call me David." The silver-haired man stuck out his hand while a warm smile reached his soft eyes.

"Spencer, good to see you again." *Damn he looks good today.*

"Oh," David interrupted, "I guess these young ladies don't yet know that you're the famous Bo Cavanaugh; rock star extraordinaire?" He elbowed Bo as he spoke. Bo's eyebrows nearly hit his hair line.

I looked wide-eyed between Monica, Bo, David, and the floor before stifling a laugh.

"Well, um, we *know*, but we also know that he uses 'Spencer' for business." Monica swept in like an angel of grace.

Bo finally spoke, "David, I hypnotized these fine women with my music nearly a week ago—see how anxious they are?" He grinned like a cat with a mouse in its mouth and raised an eyebrow in my direction.

The four of us broke in to a relieved laughter; more relieved than David could even know that this little itty bitty cat was out of the bag. We just had to keep the lion at bay a while longer.

During the hour-long meeting, we acquainted ourselves with David, and he with us. He promised to get in contact with our boss to arrange a trip to DROP headquarters in New Hampshire. I glanced quickly at Bo, for the first time during the whole meeting, and caught him looking back at me, smiling at the mention of going to New Hampshire. I was acting a little more distant than I'd planned, but I couldn't look at him directly in the eyes; not with the weight of a thousand lifetimes resting on my bones.

David's soft voice broke my stare, "Bo's father, *Spencer*, was a good friend of mine. I'm thrilled to help his boy carry out his vision. I'm looking forward to the meeting next week."

"We're looking forward to it, as well," Monica entered. "I do have to ask, though, there are thousands of non-profits up and down the New England coast; how did you stumble upon ours?" I shot Monica an interested look.

I had assumed that they researched articles on various organizations and saw that ours was often featured for Monica's outstanding efforts at outreach and education, and my ability to seek out and secure funds from various sources for large amounts of money. Maybe she knew this, too, but wanted to hear it.

"Good question," David answered, "We had our legal team do some research on successful non-profits, and yours was among them. While we have visited several in the area over the last week, yours came highly recommended by a member of the team. Adrian Turner."

Monica's gasp filled my ears, and competed with the sound of my pounding heart. I prayed the look on my face didn't match Monica's; she was as white as the paper she was holding. *Maybe you've cracked under Bo's hot gaze and gone crazy—and Monica has too.*

"Um," I cleared my throat with what little grace I could muster, "did you say *Adrian Turner*? Princeton University undergrad, and Harvard Law School?" I tried to will the still-unidentified feeling from my face. *Fear, anger, general nausea?*

"Yea, that's him. You know him?" Bo's tone told me he read my face just right.

Monica composed herself quicker than I could. "Yea, we both know him. He had a lot of public relations classes with us at Princeton; we were in the same study groups and whatnot. He's an incredible asset, you're lucky to have him. We'll have to thank him for the connection!"

She's good.

"OK," I continued, immediately needing this meeting to end so I could go scream into a pillow, "Thank you so much for squeezing us into your busy week. David, I'll have Carrie get in touch with you on Monday to arrange an overnight in New Hampshire."

"Sounds great. Thank you Ms. Harris, Ms. Pierce." David shook our hands and headed toward the door.

"I'll catch up with you later, David." Bo told him, slowing down while gathering materials.

Shit, does he want to talk to me about last night, this weekend, my reaction to Adrian, or all of it?

By the time the sound of David's car faded to the distance, the three of us hadn't moved from our seats.

"Bo, could you hang out here for a couple of minutes, I have to talk to Ember in my office." Monica attempted the most graceful exit possible under the circumstances.

"Sure." He shifted uncomfortably.

The searing neon blinking "Adrian" sign overtook my brain and I wanted to run and scream. We left the door to the meeting room open, but shut the door to Monica's office.

"Holy shit! What the hell?" Monica said in the loudest whisper known to man.

"Did you have *any* idea?" I was breathless, my eyes darted around the room.

I knew Monica was friends with Adrian on Facebook, but she never spoke of him. I also knew she'd tell me if he mentioned he was working with someone and referring us to them, but I was grasping for any explanation.

"Get a grip, Em. You *know* I'd say something to you if I knew." Monica rolled her eyes, annoyed.

"I guess it's totally possible he was just doing the fellow-graduate good deed thing by showing us preference in the search process." That really *was* the most likely explanation, had we not cried during break-up sex.

"Yea, let's go with that for now. At least until we have a chance to talk with him."

"Agreed, I guess we *will* have to talk to him. I suppose I should be the one to call him; he'd know I was avoiding him if you called." Uneasiness regained its footing in my gut.

"Smart. OK, I'll get his contact info, email Carrie about our meeting, and then stay here until you've finished talking with Bo," Monica said, motioning to the door.

"Oh shit!" I had completely forgotten he was waiting for me.

In the meeting room, Bo was leaning against the window with his hands in his pockets. The light sought out and illuminated his deep blue eyes as he turned to me.

"Hey, sorry about that. Today has been ridiculous." I shut the door behind me.

"It's OK." He smiled so sincerely I instantly felt my throat tighten. "How's Monica?"

"Ugh," I sat down in the closest chair and rested my elbows on the table while my hands held my head, "my heart is actually breaking for her, Bo."

I wanted him to tell me that I would never feel what Monica felt. I certainly didn't intend to make *him* ever feel that way. He, however, didn't know how I felt about him. I was at an unfair advantage with the information Monica had given me.

He left the window and sat in the chair next to me. "What happened?"

Leave out the thousand lifetime's thing, whatever you do. My eyes met his as I rested my chin on closed fists.

"He just…he told her that if there was a soul-shifting, core-quaking love for everyone…" my breath caught for a split second, "he wasn't sure she was his."

I broke his gaze and glanced out the window.

"He didn't even look her in the eyes when he told her, Bo. He couldn't even give her the respect of a little eye contact as he shredded her soul." My cheeks burned, fighting the tears working their way to the surface of my eyes.

"Damn," he said, closing his eyes briefly. I wondered if he was relieved that I didn't seem to know his part in that conversation. I wondered if he felt bad at all, even though it wasn't his fault.

"Do you believe him? Josh, I mean, about the soul-core thing?" he asked. I nodded and rubbed my forehead.

"I really do." I opened my eyes and found him studying my face.

"Does Adrian Turner have anything to do with that look on your face?" It was barely a question.

Well, that didn't take long.

"Yes, but not in the way you might think," I said softly.

This wasn't the place I wanted to talk about Adrian. I didn't really want to talk about Adrian at all, but my hand was forced in more ways than one.

"I saw the look in your eyes, Ember, when David said his name. It was like you saw a ghost." His concerned eyes teetered on hurt. *Yea, the Ghost of Sexcapades Past.*

"I haven't talked to Adrian in like three years. When he was at Harvard Law he Facebooked me a few times, but I was tired of seeing the pictures he posted with girls who were nothing like me. I know that sounds bad, and I don't mean it to. We haven't meant anything to each other in five years, Bo. And, even then—look, I want to talk to you about this, but not here and not now. Monica's coming over tonight so we can emotionally process what happened with Josh. Can we get together tomorrow night?" I wanted to tell Bo about Adrian, about my feelings for him, everything, but I couldn't do it at work.

"I have to head back to New Hampshire today for a quick meeting, but I should be back by tomorrow late afternoon. I'll call you when I get back to town, OK?" The distance in his voice sent tension searing through me.

"Bo," I reached out and gripped the top of his hand, not wanting him to slip away. Thankfully, he turned it over and interlaced his fingers with mine, "what happened with Adrian is ancient history."

"November, you don't owe me an explanation." He kissed my hand, "But, it can't be *that* ancient to Adrian if he used work to get in contact with you, without giving you some sort of heads up or 'how's it going' first…"

Gut punch.

He was right about Adrian, but he was oh-so-wrong about me owing him an explanation. *You owe one to Bo because you love him; he just doesn't know that yet.*

CHAPTER TEN

"Do you think Bo was right, about Adrian not being over you?" Monica asked as she plunked on my couch with an over-full glass of wine.

Before Bo headed back to New Hampshire, he kissed me with complete disregard for the workplace, and told me he'd text me later. The second Bo left our office, I told her about our conversation.

"He didn't say Adrian wasn't over me, Monica. He doesn't even know what happened with him; I told him I wanted to tell him about Adrian, but that everything was ancient history. Bo said it couldn't be that ancient since—"

"Since Adrian pulled the weasel-move of orchestrating a venture between our agency and one whose legal team he's on? I'd say ten points for Bo." It'd been a long day for everyone.

"What the hell am I supposed to tell Bo about him?" I really had no idea, so this was the perfect Josh-distraction technique.

"Start with the truth; you two were Princeton's most beautiful couple with the best sex life." She gave an impish smile.

"Oh, well, that seems easy enough," I laughed.

Monica's phone rang and she ignored it as soon she saw who it was.

"Josh again?" I asked sympathetically.

"Yea. Not sure what he could *possibly* have to say to me. He covered it pretty well last night." Her face blanched at the thought.

My phone began to ring. It was Josh.

"Mon, he's calling me. Let me answer so he doesn't track us down." I scurried to the bedroom and answered.

"Josh *what* do you want?"

"Ember, Jesus, thanks for answering. Is Monica with you?" He sounded calm, with just enough angst to keep me from hanging up.

"She is. She came here after work." I wasn't going to offer any of what Monica already filled me in on.

"Is she OK?"

Yea douchebag, she's perfect.

I caved a little. "Not really, Josh, what the hell?" I kept a firm edge to my voice.

"November, you have to understand. Just, like, when you *know* you feel something, you *know* when you don't..."

"You didn't *know* you didn't feel whatever it is you think you're supposed to feel until you chatted up Bo, *Joshua*." I hoped he could sense my arched eyebrow.

"Shit, I should have known she'd tell you about that." *Yes, you should have.* "Don't tell Bo, OK? I don't want him to think I'm a lame blabbermouth."

You are lame.

"Whatever Josh, look, she's here, she's with me and she's fine, no thanks to you. You need to leave her alone for a while. If she wants to talk to you again she'll call, and you better answer your damn phone." I'd given Josh all I could afford with my broken-hearted best friend in the next room.

Josh let out an exasperated sigh, "OK, Ember. Listen..."

"Josh, not tonight, I'll come by and see you at Finnegan's tomorrow after work, OK?" *Why the hell did I just offer that?*

"Really? Thanks, Ember."

"Yea, really. I meant what I said about answering any and all of Monica's future calls. And, if she gathers enough of herself together to see you face-to-face, don't be a douche—look her in the eyes this time." I hung up, feeling rather triumphant on behalf of Monica.

As I walked into the living room, tears in Monica's eyes were escorted away by curiosity.

"He was just checking that you were OK..." I shrugged.

"What'd you tell him?" A hint of a grin graced her face.

"Oh, you know that we finished the VooDoo doll in his likeness and were dancing around a fire on the beach drumming a death chant.

"Awe, thanks!"

"I told him to leave us alone, and you'd call him if you wanted to." She smiled. "But I told him I would meet him tomorrow at Finnegan's after I got out of work."

Monica's brow furrowed as I continued.

"He knows that I know what Bo said and, Monica, if I'm going to be spending any more time with him I need some more information on their discussion." It wasn't fair. Not to Josh, Monica, or Bo—especially Bo—that I was stalking out his feelings for me, *and via Josh, no less.*

"Why can't you just bring it up with Bo?"

"I will talk to him about it, when he's ready to talk to me about it. I'm sure he never intended for Josh to tell anything."

Before she could answer, my phone dinged with a text message.

Bo: *Wish I could see you now*

"Who's that?" Monica questioned

"Bo wishes he could see me." I tried to shrug off the Irish jig trampling my insides.

"Em, you don't need me here taking up your possibly limited time with Hottie Mc Guitar!" I flinched a little at 'limited', but quite enjoyed her nickname for him.

"Ha, thanks for your concern. But he's in New Hampshire tonight—we're going to get together tomorrow." I picked up my phone and texted him back.

Me: *I miss you too. Wish you were in town.*

Bo: *Me too.*

Me: *I've got to talk to Josh tomorrow after work, at Finnegan's ...stuff about Monica and whatever—want to meet me there around 7* *and we can decide what to do from there?*

Bo: *I've got a better idea. I'll text you in a little bit.*

I didn't text back; I just smiled at my phone.

"Ember," Monica said dreamily, "it's so nice to see you happy."

"I'm always happy, you know that. My happiness and men are mutually exclusive. Though, it *is* nice when they intersect," I winked.

"You know what I mean."

We sat for a couple of hours, and I was supportive as Monica yelled, cried, laughed, and cried some more about her breakup with Josh. When there were no more tears left I drove her home – she wasn't in any condition to drive on a number of levels. After she was safely in her apartment, I returned to mine. I ambled up the stairs, reached for my phone, and texted Bo.

Me: *I really do miss you*

I hit send and immediately jumped at a beeping noise at the top of the stairs. *What the hell?*

As I rounded the corner I gasped at Bo sitting on the top step, just outside my door, elbows planted firmly on his knees, hands clasped in front of him. *Sitting on that 'Welcome' mat under which my resolve hides, I see.*

"What are you doing here?" I could barely contain the ridiculous smile crossing my lips.

"I told you I wished I could see you." He shrugged, cocked his head to the side and drew a slow smile.

"Well, you made good time, weirdo stalker." I was quite aware of the roughly 2.5 hour drive time from Concord to Barnstable. I sat next to him on the stairs and leaned my shoulder on his. I was emotionally drained, in all ways good and bad. Bo curled his arm around my shoulders and kissed the top of my head as he drew me in.

"You smell good," I whispered as I turned my face toward his neck, kissing it softly.

"Mmm, you do too." He buried his nose in my hair. "Come take a walk with me?"

"A walk? It's nearly midnight."

"We'll drive down to the beach. The moon is huge. Please?" He stood and held his hand out to me.

Oh, what the hell.

I was thankful for the unseasonably warm weather as we strolled down the moonlit beach, hand in hand. Bo didn't speak during our five minute drive, and I didn't interrupt the silence. The past twenty-four hours were weighing heavy on me.

"Sorry, again, about today. It was all so much—Josh and Monica, my parents last night..." I shook my head and gazed at the heaving sea.

"November, stop apologizing. We've had a lot thrown at us from all different directions. How was the time with your parents?" His sincerity was palpable.

I wondered if I would smell the sorrow if I didn't know his parents were dead. I stopped where I was and folded down to the sand, begging my tears to stay at bay. I hadn't had a lot of time to process what my parents and I had spoken about the night before. *Reckless abandon.* Raven's words echoed through my body as I remembered that I need to commit with my heart or my mind.

"They were all raised eyebrows, mouths open; they saw the open guitar case and asked what was going on."

"What'd you tell them?" Bo sat next to me and gave me a little nudge.

Don't cry. Don't cry. Don't cry.

"Um..."

Don't cry!

"November," he lifted my chin with his index finger and turned my face toward his, "what is it?" The pure light from the moon flooded his eyes with concern.

Don't cry.

Too late.

As soon as I blinked, tears spilled messily down my face. I didn't try to wipe them away, and I didn't break my gaze from his. Bo's forehead creased momentarily as he watched the tears—filled with so many things I wanted to tell him—fall to the sand. He didn't look away as he brushed the salty confusion from one of my cheeks with his thumb.

"Ember..."

"Bo, it's just..." I wiped my eyes, finally, and turned my face back to the ocean. "I've never felt like this with anyone. Not just physically either. You've burrowed yourself deep in my soul. All the evidence my parents needed was the guitar I've never really played, just sitting causally in my living room. You've sparked something in me..." Out of the corner of my eye I saw him half-smile.

"You're crying because of how you feel about me?" He kept the grin as he tried to understand.

"It's not about you, it's about *me*. I am not the person that Fantasizes about running away with hot, guitar-playing man-gods." I was able to force a laugh through my tears, "There's this part of me that's longed for you for so long, and when you showed up it was like an ice-cold shower shocking me to life. I like structure, predictability, an unbroken heart..." I shot a glance in his direction and he seemed to cringe at 'an unbroken heart'.

Bo moved to a kneeling position in front of me, commanding my attention.

"November, if your heart was mine it would never break." His hands tightened around mine as he spoke the sweetest words my ears had ever hosted.

"Even in a thousand lifetimes?"

Shit! I dropped Bo's hands, flew to a standing position as he flinched, again, against my words, and I walked away. I was embarrassed that I let that slip out, and suddenly felt angry that he would tell Josh, and not me. When you feel that strongly about someone, you tell them.

"Josh..." he half whispered to the now vacant place I had previously occupied. He stood up and briskly followed my pace down the beach.

"Ember, I shouldn't have said anything to *anyone*." He wisely stayed slightly behind me, seemingly trying to judge my level of anger.

"*A thousand lifetimes,* Bo!? You feel like you've known me for a thousand *freaking lifetimes?* That's a bit intense, don't you think?" I didn't slow my pace.

"You just told me that I shocked your soul to life and you're accusing *me* of intensity of emotion?" His firmness road-blocked me.

"But I told *you*, Bowan. You told Josh, and he used it as an excuse to break up with my best friend!" Bo stared out at the ocean unapologetically.

"Ember, I'm really sorry about what happened with your friends. I'm sorry that Josh freaked after we talked. Look at me—that has *nothing* to do with us." He grabbed my shoulders, forcing my eyes on his. "I have never felt this way about anyone in my entire life. And the other night, at your place, when we—"

"Had sex?" I interrupted.

"That's not the phrase I would use, but, yea. That was the single-most mind, soul, and earth shattering experience of my life." His eyes searched mine in a panic.

"Bo, I haven't ever felt this way about anyone either, and it scares me." I looked just past him to avoid being consumed by the intensity of his now nearly black eyes.

"Even about Adrian?" He dropped his hands from my shoulders and backed up a step to gage my reaction.

"Excuse me?" My brow furrowed in sardonic consternation. "You're seriously bringing up Adrian *fucking* Turner? I told you it was ancient hist—wait... Did you see him today when you went back to Concord?"

The question suspended in the space between our bodies.

"He is a member of our legal team and was briefed on today's meeting." *Oh, that's it? You're going to leave it at that?*

"You couldn't have briefed him over the phone?"

It occurred to me that my reaction to Adrian's name during the meeting did not sit as well with Bo as he had led me to believe. It appeared Mr. Y-chromosome drove 2.5 hours to size up my ex-boyfriend with fresh eyes.

"Wait a minute, Bo, you didn't tell him..."

"I didn't tell Turner about us. I needed to sign some contracts for some other things, and I told him the meeting went well. I told him that you and Monica both spoke fondly of his abilities, and that the two of you would be arriving with your boss early next week." *Oh shit.*

"Hm." *Ember, get a damn grip. Hm?*

"He seemed quite pleased about you ladies coming to Concord." Bo's face fell, as if he was trying to work out the history between Adrian and me.

"Look," I took a deep breath at the realization that this night was not going as envisioned. "I know that you said I didn't owe you an explanation about Adrian—"

"You don't."

"Bo, just shut up and sit down for a minute," I instructed as delicately as possible.

I told Bo about my relationship with Adrian, and that we intended it to be mainly sexual; no strings attached. Bo looked up at me rather sympathetically when I shrugged and told him that when I thought I wanted more, and he wasn't ready for that, we called it a day—no hard feelings.

That was the Disney version of our break-up, it was all Bo needed. The only thing lacking resolution at this point, I told him, was me giving him a piece of my mind for this business deal.

"Ha, well, I'd like to be there for that, if you don't mind." Bo's ego seemed intact, and his disposition relaxed at the thought of me verbally assaulting Adrian. "He's a smug bastard, but he's damn good at what he does," Bo lauded.

"Yea, I was afraid of that." With an eye roll I checked my phone and saw it was approaching 1:00am. "Can we get going? It's late."

"Of course, let's go." He grabbed my hand as we headed back down the beach to his car.

When we reached the parking lot, a truck drove past, startling me away from the enchantment of the ocean with a jump. My hair stood on end and I reflexively tightened my grip on Bo's hand as a very familiar pickup truck drove into the distance.

"What?" Bo returned my tight grip.

"Nothing, can we go please?" My heart was in my throat. I knew there were a lot of trucks in the world, but not a lot of rusty blue ones that held Bill and Max over a week ago. *Shit, you didn't even forget their names.*

Bo's eyes darted around, and he ran his hands fiercely through his hair as he got in his car and shut the door. My heart raced the entire way back to the safety of my apartment. And, like the drive to the beach, on the way to my place we didn't say a word.

When we got to my door, I fumbled with my keys, dropping them on the floor. Bo swept them up gracefully and opened my door. He came in behind me and I took a concentrated breath before facing him.

"Thank you for driving me home." I smiled while grabbing his hand.

"You're shaking, Ember, are you really OK? What the hell happened?" He led me to the couch.

"Nothing. It's just... remember the night we first met, when Monica said I saw someone get beat up?" *I can't believe you're about to tell him this nothing of a story.*

"I remember." His eyes widened slightly as he furrowed his brow.

"Well, aside from the fight, I did see the truck that two of the guys were driving." I paused to study his reaction. He didn't seem to have one; he was waiting for more.

"It looked *exactly* like that truck that drove past us in the parking lot tonight, that's all. It startled me. I know, it's silly."

I bit my lower lip and shook my head.

"Ember, if you were scared you should have told me." He ran his thumb across my chin, but seemed anxious. "You said two of the guys. There were more?" he pressed.

"Yea, one more. He left after the rest of them..." I trailed off not wanting to recall the event.

Bo studied me carefully, as if I was a bomb ready to explode. He didn't look convinced by my story as his eyes flashed with what looked like fear.

"I've had a really friggen intense week, here." I held my hands up and darted my eyes around the room for affect.

"Hey, I get it. It's OK." He took a tense deep breath before continuing, "Let me help you take your mind off of it." His own words relaxed his face.

Yes, please.

Bo parted my knees with his, and leaned into me, relaxing me back on the couch. I clasped my hands tightly around his neck; forcing his tongue into my mouth as he moaned. I poured all of my frustrations, anxieties, and passion into that kiss. *I'll show you a thousand lifetimes.* I roughed his leather jacket over his shoulders, and he tossed it on the floor as I kicked off my shoes.

I could barely breathe in response to his touch. I didn't want to think about words.

He pulled away, searching through me with his eyes, as only he could do. He scooped me into his arms and carried me to my bedroom.

"This is a little dramatic, don't you think?" I rolled my eyes at this superfluous gesture, but secretly I loved feeling so feminine.

"Just let go a little Ember," he said in complete seriousness.

"Let go? Right, because it's so starch-collared to bust out my old guitar, sleep with a man two days after meeting him, and consider dropping everything to run away with him. I really *must* learn to let my hair down." I giggled as Bo laughed loudly, setting me on my bed.

"I just mean you've got to get out of here," he said as he tapped my temple.

"Just feel, for once. Don't think. Feel." He pressed against me.

"Like this?" I playfully grabbed him through his jeans.

"Ember," he stifled a laugh, "I'm serious, turn the rest of it off."

He moved my hand to his neck as he slid me up the bed. A quick moan escaped my throat before I thought about it.

"See? Feeling is good. Thinking... thinking is bad." The corner of his mouth twitched in to a wicked grin before he focused his lips elsewhere.

Bo's lips moved like they were sketching me into his long-term memory. Chills waltzed across my skin against his touch. *Just feel.* His words echoed through my body as I shifted underneath him, reaching for his shirt. Bo waited until both of his arms were out of his shirt—kissing me the whole time—before he paused to tug it over his head. I sat up to remove my tank and bra. When they were gone, he pressed back into me, the warmth of his hard, bare chest captured my innermost desires.

I reached for the button on his jeans, but once again his hand stopped me. He brought my hand above my head and planted urgent kisses down my arm and torso before stopping at my waistband. He popped the button on my jeans with his teeth, eliciting a gasp as my response. He removed his hand from mine and slid my jeans and panties down with care. As he stood on the floor at the foot of my bed, he dropped his jeans, sank to his hands and knees on my mattress, and crawled predator-like back between my legs.

His lips started at my belly button this time, and I sensed their final destination. Immediately, my hips started to shift, anticipating his arrival. As his mouth reached my inner thigh I grabbed his hair.

He continued his oral exploration as I eagerly felt all he had to offer.

"Bo..." I needed more. More *feeling.*

Sensing my impatience, he quirked the hottest grin I'd ever seen as he kissed his way back to my mouth. Inexplicably, his pace slowed and he rested his forehead on my naked chest.

"I love this," he sighed into my neck. "Just, this...you." *Did he just insinuate that he loves me?*

"Hey," I sighed in to the top of his head. When his Atlantic eyes met mine beneath his soft eyebrows, it was all I could do to keep myself from coming apart underneath him.

I pushed a little on his shoulders, forcing him to roll over. I parted his legs and sat between them on my knees. I sat back on my heels and stared for a minute at his flawlessly gorgeous body. It wasn't just gorgeous for what I could see on the outside; but gorgeous for what I knew burned beneath the surface.

"What?" He smiled as he crossed his hands behind his head, elbows out.

The minute his lips moved, my intentions shifted and my shoulders sank at the feelings I had for this man who lay before me. I loved him, and as my smile of seduction morphed to one of love, my soul nodded. *I told you so.*

"What?" He repeated, now sitting up on his elbows, his head cocked to the side.

"Nothing." I crawled overtop his body and placed my hands on either side of his shoulders.

Still, I stared. My mind just agreed with my heart for the first time in as long as I could remember, and I had no map for this course. *I love Bo Cavanaugh.* I didn't push the thought down; I just let the feeling run through me like the waterfall love is intended to be: loud, dangerous, and beautiful. Bo broke my soak in the pool of adoration with his deepest kiss yet. *They just keep getting better.*

After a few minutes of our lips dancing to longing, desire, and unspoken love, I rolled off of him and onto my bed. He placed his arm around me and I snuggled into his chest, breathing him in. His chin rested on top of my head as I listened to him fall asleep; the rise and fall of his chest deepening, slowing.

With sleep gaining its footing over my body and mind, I pressed my lips into his neck. As I pulled my lips away, I whispered softly to his sleeping body, "I love you."

CHAPTER ELEVEN

Waves danced gloriously over my feet as I strummed my guitar at sunrise. Seagulls echoed my fret squeaks as the ocean breeze carried the melody across its white caps. The song was as familiar to my fingers as it was my ears; it was one my parents played when I was a child, and it was the only song I knew by heart.

Throughout the night, Bo's hands slid up and down over the curves of my spine. I was momentarily jealous of his guitar as I pressed back into his tight hands. I woke early in his arms, both of us still naked from the night before. I slid out of bed and put on my cropped jeans and Princeton sweatshirt. I left a note on my pillow:

Heading to the beach to catch the sunrise.

You looked peaceful—didn't want to wake you. Be back soon.

If my mom could have seen me on that beach, I'm sure she'd call in a priestess of some sort to marry us on the spot. I'm not a 'guitar-playing on the beach at sunrise' kind of girl; not until Bo Cavanaugh waltzed in and made quick work of rearranging any notions I had about what I *thought* I wanted and needed out of this life.

When I finished the song for the third time, thoroughly satisfied that I had expressed all I needed to at that moment, I stood to head back home and get ready for work. I dusted myself off and turned around; my heart fluttered at the sight of him. Bo stood against the weathered split-rail fence that separated the beach from the parking lot, arms and ankles crossed. My pulse quickened as I neared him.

His face wore a sleepy grin.

"Good morning."

"How long have you been standing here?" I asked, my gut teetering on the razor's edge between desire and embarrassment.

He reached behind him and handed me my case.

"Long enough to realize you're a complete liar," he chuckled. "You can *really* play, November."

"Now you're the liar, *Bowan*. Besides, that's just a song I learned when I was basically an infant. It's the only thing I can play." *But it did sound really damn good.*

"I've got news for you, Beautiful. That might be the only thing you've memorized, but if your fingers can do that, you *know* how to play." He put his hands on my shoulders to emphasize the point.

"You walked here?" I nodded to the empty parking lot. "How did you know where I was?"

"Well, I didn't think you'd tell me you were at the beach and go to some random place where I couldn't find you. I just came to where we went last night." *Hmm, he's on to me.*

"Well played, Cavanaugh." I hoisted the case and headed across the parking lot.

"Please, Secret Goddess of the Guitar, let me," Bo murmured with a slightly less-than-teasing tone as he took the guitar from me.

Bo held my hand on the ten minute walk back to my apartment. We were quiet for most of it; a peaceful quiet that was a respite for the mind and soul. I received a text from Monica saying she was walking over to pick up her car from my place. I texted her back that I wasn't home, but told her to use her key to enter my apartment if I wasn't back by the time she arrived.

She waited on my steps, her wicked Cheshire grin partially hidden behind her coffee cup.

"Morning, Monica." Bo didn't miss a beat as we approached her.

"Bo," Monica chirped cordially.

"OK, ladies, I'll leave you to it. I'll call you later." Ignoring

Monica's watchful eye, Bo cradled my neck and planted a pillow-soft kiss on my expectant lips.

Neither Monica nor I moved a muscle as we watched him drive away. I slowly turned around, well aware that my facial expression was fair game for Monica's scrutiny.

"How ya feeling this morning, Mon?" A girl could try.

"Shut the hell up and get upstairs. *Nice guitar*." Monica shook her head and gave an exaggerated eye roll as we headed upstairs.

When we entered my apartment, I set the guitar by the couch and sat down. Monica stared at me expectantly, tapping her foot. I smiled a little before speaking.

"What?" I jested.

"Screw you. Where were you? It's not even seven-thirty!" She sat across from me on the couch, her eyes brimming with excitement.

"Playing my guitar... on the beach," I said with a shrug.

Monica shook her head in an apparent mix of wonder and disbelief.

"What!" My eyes bulged.

"Damn it, November, I have known you for eight years and I have never once heard you play that guitar. I didn't even know you still had it. Now, after another hot night with 'Cavanaugh the Casanova', you're all 'hot girl playing the guitar on the beach'?" Her glare begged me to retort.

"First of all, *Monica,* it wasn't that kind of 'hot night'." I cocked my eyebrow mockingly. "We slept together—as in sleep. Second of all," I exhaled dreamily, "yea, I'm all 'hot girl playing the guitar on the beach,' and I don't know what to do with that."

It was true; the first thought I had that morning had been to go play the guitar. A night sleeping in bed with Bo and I woke up with *that* on my mind.

"What else is going on up there?" Monica nodded to my head.

"I love him." Shock didn't overtake me as I thought it might.

"You love him." She nodded like we were talking about the

weather.

"Monica, I'm *in love* with this man and I have nothing snarky to cloak it in! Help!"

"Ha! Ember, that really *is* love!"

We burst into a fit of laughter, before I got dressed for work. As we walked down to our cars, Monica turned to me.

"You know what you have to do at work today, right?"

I don't have to tell my boss anything—yet.

"What?"

"You've got to call Adrian, before he calls us."

All blood and feeling left my face. "Nice buzz-kill, Mon."

"Well, he knows damn well that it's been about twenty four hours since you learned of his involvement. Wait. Did Bo see him yesterday in Concord?" *Man, she's good.*

"Yea, for some contract stuff. But he did tell Adrian about me and you learning about *him*. He said Adrian seemed 'pleased' to be talking about us, whatever that means.

"Hmmm." She seemed to be working something out in her head. "Let's call him. By let's, I mean you." She winked at me as she got in her car and drove away.

"Adrian Turner, please." I held my voice steady on the phone. Monica watched me. She looked like she was boiling with excitement.

"May I tell him who's calling?" the unsuspecting secretary responded.

"Of course, November Harris from The Hope Foundation."

"Seriously?" Monica whispered. "As opposed to the November Harris from the *'Girls You Sexed Up foundation'*?" I threw my pen at her.

"Just one moment, Ms. Harris." I was clicked to hold.

I mouthed to Monica that I was on hold but in an instant, I wasn't.

"Adrian Turner here." His voice hadn't changed at all. It purred through the phone and headed straight for the recesses of my brain. *No! You don't live there anymore, Turner*

"Adrian, hi!"

"November? How are you?" He did his best to sound surprised.

"Oh, listen to you, acting all surprised that it's me when your secretary took my name," I teased while Monica shot me a 'thumbs up'.

"Witty as ever, I see." Adrian's voice retained its purr.

"Listen, Adrian—" I was ready to attack, but he cut me off.

"I know, I know. I should have called you when I first started discussing you guys with DROP, but I knew you'd probably avoid me or tell me to screw off." His playful defensiveness brightened the conversation.

"Yes, Adrian, you *should* have called. We're adults. You made it weird by being all sneaky." My voice was intentionally flat.

"Anyway," I continued, "I just wanted to connect with you and clear that up before Monica and I meet with all of you."

"Actually Ember, I'm heading down to Barnstable today—didn't Spencer tell you?"

Suddenly I was on an out-of-control carousel. I needed air. I no longer had a few days to prepare to meet Adrian in Concord; I had mere hours. If he was coming all the way to Barnstable, he'd want to see me for sure. *Shit!* And, no, "Spencer" hadn't said anything to me about this. The look on my face drew question from Monica's eyes. I covered the phone and whispered that Adrian was coming *here* today. Her pace flushed the same color I suspected mine was.

Didn't Spencer tell you?

"No. I haven't seen Mr. Cavanaugh since our meeting yesterday, and I haven't checked my e-mail. You were my first order of business," I lied through the phone with confidence.

"First order of business, was I? Good to hear. I'll be in town this afternoon to meet with your lawyer and check out some office prospects. I'd love to get together and catch up; tell Monica I say hi."

"Sure, that sounds great. I will. Bye, Adrian." I stared at the phone for a few seconds after hanging up, collecting what little thoughts I had.

"So?!" Monica nearly screamed.

"Adrian says hi," I teased ; she threw my pen back at me.

"Apparently he's coming here to meet with our lawyer today and to look at some potential office spaces. He'd just fucking love to get together and 'catch up'. He asked if 'Spencer' told me he was coming."

The bottom of my stomach slipped away as I repeated the words. I began to question if this wasn't the real reason Bo drove back to Barnstable last night and met me at my apartment at nearly midnight; he wanted some alone time with me before Adrian got to town. Bo seemed so threatened by Adrian. I wondered why Bo wouldn't just tell me that Adrian was planning on coming.

"Maybe he didn't want Adrian in your head. He just wanted to enjoy time with *you*," Monica suggested after I shared my thoughts with her. It seemed reasonable.

"I guess. I wonder what shit Adrian is pulling."

"You should call Bo," Monica said.

"Call Bo about what?" Bo's voice rounded the corner before he did, and he leaned against my office door. His eyes fell on my still-flushed face and filled with apprehension.

"Uh, well, I just got off the phone with Adrian. He says he's coming to town *today* and wondered if you told me. I told him I hadn't seen you since our meeting here yesterday, and hadn't checked my email yet today." I focused my eyes on his.

"Why didn't you tell me he was coming, *Spencer*?" The cool accusation caused Monica to shift in her seat.

Bo lifted his chin and confidently retorted, "November, check your email. You will find one sent yesterday evening, informing you of Mr. Turner's intended travels. It was sent to you, Monica, Carrie, and your lawyer." His voice was stained with equal parts command and irritation.

"I see."

"I prefer to keep work at work, November."

He had a point; not once had we discussed work in our private time. Adrian, however, wasn't "work." I knew it, and so did Bo. Accusing him of withholding information clearly hurt him. Still, I was beginning to think I didn't care for Spencer, the alter ego to my beloved Bo.

"Well, I'm outta here." Monica gave no further explanation as she slid past Bo and down to her office.

I stared at her empty chair a moment before returning my stare to Bo, who remained standing with his hands in his pockets.

"You're awfully formal this morning," I accused as I leaned back in my chair, crossing my legs.

"I told you, November, I prefer to keep work at work."

"Well, in that case, won't you have a seat?" I threw a *screw you* eyebrow in his direction while I gestured with my hand to an empty seat across from my desk.

While I had been the one hell-bent on keeping my relationship with Bo professional as far as work was concerned, I was caught off guard by his distant language. The walls inside me began their ascent. Bo sat stone-still, never breaking our apparent staring contest. He opened his mouth to speak, but I was having *none* of that. I got up and shut the door to my office before I continued.

"I know, *Mr. Cavanaugh,* that you prefer to keep work at work, as do I. However, I take it rather personally when something like Adrian Turner coming to town warrants nothing from you other than a group email." I sat down, retained my crossed arms and legs position and continued.

"A group email covers things like meeting times, Spencer, not information like *Adrian.*"

"Please stop calling me Spencer, Ember," he charged through clenched teeth.

"That's your work alias, isn't it? And, are we *not* at work?" *Check your e-mail my ass.*

"It's your tone I don't particularly care for, *Ms. Harris*."

Now I didn't care for *his* tone, and I was about to go for the kill.

"Last night, after you spoke with Adrian and knew of his plans to travel here tomorrow, you came to my house. We went for a walk on the damn beach *at midnight*. On that beach I cried about my feelings for you. On that beach *you* asked me about Adrian, Bo— *you* brought it up. I told you all there was to tell about him, and still you weren't satisfied enough with my story to give me the decency of letting me know he was coming to town?" My interrogation rivaled anything I'd seen on Law & Order. *Push those tears back. Now is not the time.*

"You knew that Monica and I had no idea he was working for you. He is clearly up to something, and even you called him a smug bastard." My jaw was painfully tight.

Bo broke under my intense visual scrutiny. He threw an exaggerated breath to the floor as his hands held his head. When he sat up his face was different, it was Bo—not Spencer. I suppressed my petty guilt at my uncompromising tone because I hadn't yet heard what he had to say.

"November, I'm sorry," he acknowledged, "I drove all the way back here with the intention of telling you about Adrian in person. He asked how you were doing. It killed me to tell him that you seemed happy when I couldn't tell him that I felt I had a part in that. He smiled and wondered, out loud, if you were involved with anyone worthy of you. I just had to shrug."

His honestly paralyzed me. Adrian was fishing for information, the way many people do, but it was to the wrong person, and no one could say a word.

"He lit up about seeing you again and it gnawed at my insides. I drove all the way back here to—"

"Pee on my leg." I cut him off. While I knew he was working for an apology, the barbarism of this whole thing was suffocating.

"Jesus, Ember, give me a break!" He ran an exasperated hand through his hair. "It's not like that. Once you opened up to me about your parents, Adrian, and your feelings for me, I couldn't ruin a perfectly good night. I wanted to talk to you about it this morning, but when I saw you in the sand with that guitar... the rest of the world stopped. I knew in that moment that Adrian Turner, Josh and Monica, work; none of it mattered." He reached across the desk and put out his hand. I surrendered, setting my cold hand into his sweaty palm. *You make him sweat.*

"Ember, please, don't be upset with me. I'll fire Turner if it means we can forget about all of this," he pleaded. *Pleaded.*

I wanted to weep in response to his honesty. Instead, I took a deep breath.

"Bo, it does matter. All of it matters, that's the point. We just have to navigate it. We can't blow past the storm in favor of calmer waters. And, please don't fire Adrian. He's good at what he does; he'll figure out why you fired him and probably sue your ass off." I smirked and inhaled again, knowing I needed to respond to his bearing-of-the-soul here in my office.

"Look, I'm sorry for being so taciturn in regards to Adrian. We were young and it was painful when it ended. I wouldn't feel the same now, but my 21-year-old self still feels its rawness. So, yeah, it pissed me off that I wasn't given a heads up. I could have shared the full emotional bloodbath with you, but I didn't want that in your head. I don't want your ex-girlfriends in *my* head." *Ouch.* That was the first time I actually considered ex-girlfriends.

"November, any ex-girlfriend I have pales in comparison to you. They're irrelevant." He dismissed them figuratively with his hand. *Guess I'm his girlfriend.*

"Why does Adrian matter?" I relaxed back in my chair, pulling my hand from his.

Bo sighed, "Because he looked a little too satisfied to be talking about you, November. I think his twenty-one year old *and* his current self still remember you fondly. *That's* why it matters."

"I'll have no way of knowing if what you say is true until I see him tonight—he wants to 'catch up.' You can't be there. If you are, he'll know something's up."

Bo's face fell ten stories.

"Weren't you going to meet Josh tonight?" *Nice distraction.*

"Josh is an asshole. He can wait."

I stood up and crossed over to Bo; he stood to meet me in the center of the office. I reached for his hands—the only peace offering I had at the moment.

"I need to get some work done; I have to help Monica plan this trip to Concord. I'll call you tonight after I meet with Adrian."

"Are you upset with me?" Bo gave my hands a tender squeeze and just barely caught my eyes.

"I'm not, I promise. I just want to get through today and tonight. I'll call you after I deal with Adrian. To be honest, I don't want to catch up with him but I have no real reason to *not* want to besides you." I drew the corner of my mouth up sweetly to reinforce that I really wasn't mad.

"OK. Talk to you tonight. Please be careful." He knit his eyebrows together working out God-knows-what in his head.

"I always am."

Bo leaned in and gave a quick, sweet kiss to my neck before heading out as he shouted good-bye to Monica.

I turned my attention to my work and prepared for tonight's meeting with Adrian. My work email held the information about Adrian's travel plans, as Bo promised.

A new email came in just as I was heading out for lunch—it was from Adrian.

Hey Ember,

I'm looking forward to tonight. Let's meet around 7. Where should we meet?

111

Talk to you soon,
Adrian

I responded immediately.

Hi Adrian,
You caught me just as I was heading out for lunch.
Let's meet at Finnegan's—you'll find the address online.
See you at 7.
Ember

I was thoroughly satisfied with the brusqueness in my email, yet my insides started to twist with uncertainty. I wasn't worried that I would run full-speed in to Adrian's arms. I was worried that he might expect me to, being that he's a "smug bastard" and all. Bo's depiction of Adrian kept a smile fresh on my lips for the rest of the day.

CHAPTER TWELVE

"How am I even supposed to dress for something like this, Monica?" I spewed panic.

It was 6:30pm. I shuddered at the thought that Adrian was in Barnstable, looking forward to "catching up." Monica was lounging on my bed as I rifled through my closet. She hadn't spoken about Josh since last night; she was in her "not talking about it right now" phase.

"Hmmm, wear those dark skinny jeans there and that black fitted tee." Monica pointed and smiled. "Oh! Those impossible nude heels, too. There, that'll do the trick."

"What *trick*, Monica?" I bristled at my own irritation. "Sorry, what trick?"

"Oh, come on, Ember. You want to look sexy and confident, without being irreverent. You haven't seen the boy in four years; you're even hotter than you were then. Hey, maybe he got fat!" Monica bounced at the thought.

"I highly doubt Mr. Lacrosse got fat, Monica, but, thanks for trying. OK, I've got to get going if I'm going to show up first." I grabbed my clutch and headed for the door.

"OK," Monica said as she followed me down to the street, "give Josh the middle finger for me."

"Will do. You OK tonight?" I knew she was using humor to mask her still-fresh pain.

"Yea. Just call me when you get home, alright?" She gave me

an encouraging smile.

"Mon, I gotta tell you, I'm a little nervous about tonight. Adrian and I haven't seen each other face-to-face since graduation. I mean, it wasn't weird then, but I have this feeling that it will be now." I twisted my hands at the thought.

"Well, Ember, I guess it's a good thing you're going. You need to decide if you can emotionally leave Adrian in the past since he *and* Bo are in your present. Then, you can go about planning your future." She winked as she got in her car.

I climbed into my car and took a deep breath. The drive to Finnegan's was just long enough to recall the last night I spent with Adrian.

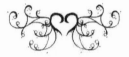

Neither one of us was having sex with other people, but we *had* agreed that we didn't want the stress that could come with being in an exclusive emotional relationship. We spent the summer before our senior year on the Princeton campus working separate camps and summer schools. It was really just the two of us, without all of our friends around, and it was so much fun.

At the end of the summer, it happened. We had just spent a fantastic night together and he was asleep on my bed. I sat in the chair on the other side of the small room, staring out the window and crying.

"Hey, Em, are you OK? What's wrong?" Adrian rolled over to find I wasn't there and caught my moon-lit tears. He rubbed his eyes and shifted to a seated position on the edge of the bed.

"Adrian," I slumped my shoulders and shuffled over to the bed, where he was waiting with open arms. "I'm so sorry."

"Babe, what's going on? What are you sorry for?" He wiped a tear away from my cheek. I'd never let him see me cry before, and I think he was scared.

"I'm sorry. I can't do this." I choked on the words swelling in my throat.

"Can't do what?" He couldn't imagine what was coming.

"I love you, Adrian, and I'm sorry. I thought it was just in my head; just a reaction to Monica's breakup with Grant..." My heaving sobs were met by Adrian's firm grip of my shoulders.

"Baby, I..." He didn't have to say anything. I willed him not to. "I love you, too."

"Adrian, stop! That's not what we're doing here; we agreed. Look what just the *thought* of losing something I don't have is doing to me. I'm not ready for this."

His hard kiss silenced me.

"I love you, Ember. It's OK."

"It's not OK, Adrian. We both know it. We can't keep doing this now. Not with all of *this*." I flapped my hands in a scattering motion between us to indicate what a mess it had instantly become. I didn't need, or want, a pity "I love you" from Adrian.

Adrian's eyes fell heavy between his lap and my face. After what seemed like several minutes he took a deep breath, exhaled for a year, and kissed me in a way that only he could kiss me.

We made love that night, for the first and last time. I cried, he cried, and we realized it was all too much. The fear of a deeper broken heartedness if we continued down the road that the L-word had dumped us on was stronger than the will we had to carry on. We ended things right then and there.

We saw each other in classes through junior year and remained cordial, but we ended the study groups. We saw even less of each other during senior year and, once we reached graduation, our paths never crossed again.

Until tonight. I parked at Finnegan's and took a cleansing breath, grumbling a little at the sight of Josh's car. I knew he'd think I was there for him. *No, I'm here for a different ass.*

With a second cleansing breath, I opened the door and headed straight to the bar to talk to Josh.

"Hey, sorry I didn't text you but we'll have to talk some other time. I've got to meet someone." I realized this was the first time I'd seen Josh since he broke up with Monica. He was pale and rather disheveled.

"Don't worry about it Em. He's over there—the guy you're meeting." Josh waved his hand to the back of the pub.

Still facing Josh, I straightened my posture and froze.

"How do you know..."

Josh chuckled, "I've seen his face many times in your old school photos. Plus, he asked if I would point you in his direction when you arrived."

"Well jeez, Josh. Thanks for the heads up. I was supposed to see him first." *Like he knows what that means.*

"Ha!" Josh let out a loud laugh. "Don't worry, I'd say whatever you're going for worked; his eyes haven't left you since you walked in." Josh gestured to my outfit.

"Damn straight they haven't. I'll talk to you later." I turned just slowly enough to be dramatic, but fast enough not to be obvious.

There he was. Adrian Turner. *Holy shit.*

He had, according to Josh, been watching me the whole time, but when our eyes met, his lit up. I walked toward him with the I-know-I-look-good saunter I had practiced in my apartment with Monica. He smiled and gave me a nod as he stood from the booth.

Take a breath, flash a smile.

Unfortunately, Adrian hadn't gotten fat at all. No, the past few years had done him nothing but unequivocal favors. He was still as broad and muscular as his Princeton lacrosse days, but a striking maturity graced his face that parted my lips. His flawless milk chocolate skin looked like it could melt under the heat of my gaze.

His hair was different; short dreads were replaced by a tight buzz cut, and an equally close-shaven goatee. He wore khaki shorts and an un-tucked cerulean button down shirt. He'd rolled the sleeves to his elbows, exposing boulder-like forearms, and the top three buttons were unbuttoned. *Water, please.* I wondered idly if Bo's reticence to my meeting with Adrian had to do with how incredibly beautiful he is—surely men notice if another man is attractive.

"November Harris," Adrian greeted with incredible congeniality. He stretched out his arms and I went in for the hug. *Damn.* It was easier to question his motives when I couldn't smell him. He smelled like Princeton, lacrosse, and my dorm pillow. He smelled like Adrian, *my* Adrian. He gave a whisper of a peck on one of my cheeks before holding me at arm's length.

"Adrian Turner, look at you. All grown up and a big-shot lawyer from Harvard Law. How are you?" *That's right, Adrian, keep looking.*

"I'm better now, girl. It's been a long time." His eyes blossomed with a sincerity that travelled to my gut, sprouting a pang of guilt for avoiding him for so long.

"It has. And, you only had to work-stalk me to make it happen." I winked as I took my seat.

"Ah, come on, that's not at all how it was. I happened to have a connection that DROP wanted me to explore." He gave a sly shrug. *Smug indeed.*

"You had no connection, you pompous ass," I laughed through the truth.

"Truth be told, I was only hoping that you still worked for The Hope Foundation when I presented the suggestion. You're the only girl I know who doesn't have Facebook, so internet stalking was out of the question. I couldn't ask Monica so I had to go the old fashion route." He winked, and the bottom of my stomach fell again.

Josh brought us some beer, on the house. He was still trying to smooth things over with me in regards to Monica, even though it had only been two days since he smeared her heart all over her apartment. I thanked him dismissively and turned back to Adrian.

"What's your problem with the bartender?" Adrian's delivery was innocent.

"Josh? He's one of the managers here. He was Monica's boyfriend, until Tuesday night; it's weird territory at the moment." I shrugged honestly.

"How is Monica? I half expected her to show up with you tonight."

"She didn't want to be around Josh, obviously. You'll probably see her at some point this weekend. We'll likely be here tomorrow and Saturday; there's live music here Saturday." I sensed I was beginning to ramble, so I took an indulgent sip of my beer.

"Yea, Cavanaugh's playing here Saturday, right?"

I spit some of my beer back in to my glass. "Uh, I guess so, he played here last weekend. He uses 'Bo' for music, though." I shrugged impassively. *Confident, nonchalant honesty, Ember. Don't show your whole hand just yet.*

"Yea, that's right. Is he any good?" His tone was unreadable; my palms began to sweat a little.

He's amazing, his soul is deeper than any ocean. I'm fairly certain angel's weep at the sound of his voice , and sing his songs to those who are in pain.

"He's really good. He knows his stuff, that's for sure." My palms broke into a full sweat. "Hey, let's go sit outside." *Fresh air.*

Adrian grabbed two more beers from Josh before holding the door for me, guiding me outside with his hand on my lower back. His touch didn't send electric shockwaves of passion through my body, but it didn't feel horrible either—which was a bit disconcerting. I'd hoped it would bother me, to have Adrian touch me. It didn't. It was grounding somehow—familiar.

"Um, let's walk a little." I was too unnerved to sit.

An air of familiarity walked us down the beach. I didn't feel like the emotionally wounded twenty-one year old who wouldn't allow him to love her because she was scared. I shared a couple of good years with Adrian, and it was actually refreshing to see him. My heart, however, sat with a man named Bo, who had decided that Adrian was a smug bastard. The thought made me chuckle out loud.

"What?" Adrian responded.

"Nothing. Just this." I motioned between the two of us. "Here we are, walking on the beach in Cape Cod, potential business associates. How are you Adrian? Are you happy?"

Adrian shrugged, "I'm happy. I have a great job, I get to work with a lot of great people and agencies, and I live mostly in Boston." *This is news.*

"Boston?"

"Yea, I travel a lot between the different agencies I help represent. Not a bad life having to travel all over New England, if you ask me." His tone sounded melancholy.

"What about your girlfriend? Does she mind all the travel?" I looked up at him expectantly. *Please tell me you have a girlfriend.*

"Nah, no girlfriend for me, Ember." He turned to the ocean and sat in the sand.

Crap.

"You OK?" I carefully positioned myself next to Adrian in the sand, intentionally avoiding physical contact.

"Ember..." His voice was tight.

Shit.

"Hey, what's wrong?" I immediately realized I was echoing his words from our last serious conversation. I couldn't be cold with Adrian. He'd given me no reason to.

"Ah, man." He was wringing his hands tightly. "I'm just, uh, I just want to say I'm sorry." He reached out and rubbed my knee for a second before clasping his hands back together.

He turned toward me with clouded eyes, biting his lower lip.

"Adrian, what could you possibly be sorry for?" I had an idea, but my pulse raced. My pulse had always raced around Adrian.

"I know it was a long time ago, but I shouldn't have done that to you—told you I loved you because I was scared to lose you. I lost you anyway, and we were both hurt. You told me to stop, you said I didn't love you, but it was all I had left to try to hold on to you."

"Adrian." I stopped him. I'd heard enough. "We were too young, that's all. I got scared. I knew how I felt for you and it was unfair; you weren't looking for a relationship." My memory winced against the pain.

"Ember, I loved you even before we had sex for the first time, but I was too chickenshit to admit it." *This is also news.*

"Adrian, it's in the past, OK? No need to drudge it up." I stood and brushed the sand from my body. The charge that I thought didn't exist between us threatened in the distance.

Adrian stood, and his soft fingertips grazed my hand without expectation as we turned to walk back down the beach. I considered grabbing his hand; it would be so easy, so us. Instead, I pretended not to notice and continued drinking my beer; his fingertips courting mine for the rest of the walk.

When we got back to the deck at Finnegan's I was relieved to see Monica sitting there, out of her house. *Sitting there with a suspicious look on her face, but sitting there nonetheless.*

"Monica, good to see you!" Adrian approached Monica and as she stood up to hug him, he lifted her and swung her around. She looked far less than impressed.

"Adrian. Boy, you know how to make an entrance," Monica said flatly.

"Well, ladies, I'm going to head inside for another beer." He squeezed my fingertips for a split second before ducking inside.

"What the hell was that all about?" Monica regained her seated position.

"Friggen Adrian." I gulped before telling her about our conversation on the beach.

Monica leaned forward, her eyes nearly bulging out of her head.

"He told you he *loved* you?!"

"Back then, not now, Monica—relax."

"No, Em, no man walks on the beach to tell a girl he was 'just having sex with' five years ago that he loved her *five years* ago." She had a point, and I swallowed it hard.

I wanted Bo to come to the bar; I reached for my cell phone which Monica quickly snatched away.

"Hey, Asshole, what are you doing?"

"You may *not* call Bo until we address Adrian, Ember," Monica's voice was clipped and serious.

"Monica, did I miss something? There's not anything to discuss." *Nothing I want to discuss.*

"Adrian 'I fool around but love no one' Turner admitted that he was in love with you. It may have been five years ago, but he's still got it for you. I saw the way you two were walking back here. It was like you were walking to class all over again."

I shrugged, but my shoulders suddenly felt heavier. "So what, Monica, I'm not in love with him anymore."

"How do you know?"

"What the hell are you saying? You know I'm in love with Bo. What's your deal?" My voice rose. I was pissed.

Monica's eyes filled with tears. "Look at what just happened with me and Josh. We fell hard and madly in love with each other two years ago and now—nothing. Josh says I might not be his core-shaker. Ember, I *know* that Bo told Josh that he feels like he's known you for a *thousand* lifetimes, and I know that right now you feel that way too—but is it the smart choice?"

Her words tripped me. Monica was telling me to think about love, to think about my feelings for Bo. I'd spent the last week riding the waves of feeling and emotion, playing my friggen guitar on the beach, and now my best friend was telling me to use my head. Hurt splashed across my face.

"Look, I'm sorry, but if you want to be sure about Bo, don't you think you ought to be sure about Adrian first?" The words seemed to pain her as she spoke them.

"What the hell? You said that you've never seen me happier.

I'm singing more, playing the *guitar*, I whispered to Bo that I loved him as he slept. I'm in *love* with him Monica and it supersedes any feelings of love I ever thought I had for Adrian. We made sense on paper five years ago, with our intellect and our ambitions. But that was it, just stats. I don't really see how that translates to right now." I stood up and huffed to the door.

"Em! Wait!" Monica followed me. "I'm sorry. I shouldn't be doling out relationship advice when I'm still hurting. You're right. I haven't ever seen you so happy. I just—"

"It's too late, Mon, you're already up here," I said as I tapped my head.

As I stormed through the door, my knees nearly gave out at the sight of Bo and Adrian at the bar, drinking and chatting with Josh. All three of them looked up at Monica and me at the same time, a mix of emotions splayed across their faces. I looked back at Monica, who's eyes amplified in a "what are we going to do?" sort of way. I grabbed her hand and headed for the far exit; quickly stomping out any residual anger I had toward her.

"We're going to Lost Dog and we're going to get drunk," I said, loud enough for at least Josh to hear.

She smiled like she'd just won the lottery. We breezed past the three men who sat there with dumbfounded looks on their faces, each for their own reason.

CHAPTER THIRTEEN

One finds themselves at Lost Dog in only the direst of situations. It's dark and more than a little dingy, but the liquor is cheap and flowing; exactly what Monica and I needed.

I was mad. Mad at Bo for our pseudo star-crossed situation, mad at Adrian for showing up; really I was mad at Adrian for being involved at all. I was mad at Josh for breaking Monica's heart, mad that Monica made me think about what feelings I might have for Adrian, and mad that I wanted to run away with Bo and play the guitar on every beach in America.

"Do you think they'll follow us?" Monica sounded breathless, as if we were in an action movie.

"Who the hell cares? We've had a century's worth of shitty days between the two of us this week." We took my car to get there faster and we were at LD, as we called it, in less than two minutes.

The pounding wails of Lil' Jon were the only rewards for muscling through the sweaty belligerence of the entryway. We tore up to the liquor buffet with purpose.

"Two shots please!" I shouted into the bartender's pierced ear.

"What do you want?" He leaned in to hear my answer.

"Does it look like it matters?" Monica shouted in to his other ear.

With a knowing grin, the bartender set up two shot glasses and urgently filled them.

"Here's to us. We love each other unconditionally and would

never screw each other over!" Monica shouted.

"Truth!" I tipped my head back, and let the burning liquid coat my throat with indifference.

Monica and I rarely went out with inebriation in our sights. That was a pastime typically left in college. However, the past week had beaten the hell out of me, and I'd had enough. I fully intended to take it out on whatever the bartender was pouring.

After our third shot Monica got a text message.

"What fresh hell is that?" I asked in a surly voice.

"Christ. It's Josh. His first text to me in two days and he tells me that he, Adrian, and Bo are on their way here. Evidently they're concerned." Monica put air-quotes around the last word and I hooted loudly.

"Concerned are they? Hey, Blake, another round please!" Blake the bartender poured us each another shot.

"Monica, this is bullshit. I'm in loooove with Bo." The fourth shot was finding its way in to my speech.

"Yea?"

"Bitch-of-it-is, I can't jump all over him when he gets in here because Adrian mother-fucking Turner is with him. And Josh is a dick, Monica—a total dickless dick," I garbled.

"Ha ha ha. Yea." Monica's eyes started to gloss over and she was swaying to the beat of a song in her head. "And, don't forget, Adrian still looooooves you!" She pointed at me and giggled before her eyes shot to the door.

"Super, the three musketeers are here!" I mocked. "Come on, screw them." I dragged Monica to Lost Dog's excuse of a dance floor.

I positioned myself so I could see Josh, Bo, and Adrian standing all cross-armed against the bar while Monica and I shook it like it was our last night to shake it. It took the last semi-sober look I had left in me to gauge their reactions.

Josh looked rather like a deer in the headlights. Monica hadn't so much as looked at him at Finnegan's, and I guessed that this was the first time they'd been in the same room since their break up. Adrian smiled in amusement at our display, but his face seemed to retain a bit of the emotion from our conversation on the beach. My observation pivoted to Bo, and our eyes locked as he stood uncomfortably to the side of Adrian. Despite the dim lighting and my profuse buzz, I could tell his clenched jaw held the worry his face couldn't—not in front of Adrian.

"Look at them. What are we, property? Poor Bo, look at his face." Monica made a puppy-dog face and I smacked her arm.

"Poor Bo? You were just telling me all about the paper-perfectness of me and Adrian!" I shouted through dance moves.

"Oh, Ember, what*ever*. You've got two men who love you; champagne problems, sister."

"Come, we need more drink." I walked us intentionally to the side of our self-appointed guardians.

"Gentlemen." I nodded with a mocking smile. I was starting to feel the extra-snarky confidence that comes from so much alcohol.

I slipped between Adrian and Bo and asked the bartender for two more shots.

"Wait!" Monica shouted over me. "Make it five!"

I handed shots to a relieved-looking Josh, and Adrian—the always willing participant in all things booze, before turning to Bo.

"No thanks, I'm set." Bo held up his hands.

I shrugged and swallowed his shot, followed immediately by mine, before slamming the glasses back on the bar. His hand gripped above my elbow as he breathed into my neck.

"Don't do this." His voice bristled with anger, making me a little uncomfortable and, therefore, angry.

"What the hell are you talking about?" I hissed in his ear, yanking my arm out of his grip.

"Turner clearly dumped something on you. I can see it on his face and yours. I'll step back while you deal with it." The matter-of-fact way the words rolled off his tongue threw my head back, and filled my eyes with tears.

"Just like that, huh?" Bo's willingness to stand down raised a red flag of betrayal in my drunken head. I realized in that moment that I was seeking for him to remind me why I loved him, and not Adrian. This wasn't helping.

Bo reached for my arm again, but I yanked it away—instantly hoping Adrian didn't notice the awkward exchange. I stumbled back to the dance floor with six shots in my system.

The heady combination of liquor and men blended my brain in to a vortex of bad decisions. I grinded with faceless strangers like I was back in the AXP house in college; it felt so good to scatter my sexuality on the dance floor and watch men clamor to scoop it up. Sooner than I'd hoped, my rapid alcohol consumption caught up with me and I stopped dancing. When the floor kept moving, I knew it was time to go.

"You OK?" Monica slurred in to my direction.

"No, and neither are you. Let's get out of here."

We stagger-danced our way to the door and poured ourselves out onto the sidewalk, bracing ourselves briefly against the brick exterior wall. My head was spinning wildly.

One...two...three... Adrian, Josh, and Bo followed behind us almost immediately, taking stock of the situation with their eyes.

"You ladies need to get home," Adrian asserted as he dug in his pocket for his keys.

"Come on, Mon," Josh encouraged as he reached for her, causing her to flinch backward.

"*Don't* you touch her," I snarled, slapping his hand away. "You lost your right to do that days ago *Josh*." Monica gave me an appreciative smile as Josh stood there looking helpless. He ran his hand through his hair.

"What the fuck, Ember? What do you want me to do, leave her here on the sidewalk?" His voice was slightly louder than I cared for.

"What I want *you* to do, *Josh,* is leave us alone and go work on finding *your* thousand lifetimes somewhere else. I promise you it's not on this sidewalk." My resentment bored through his eyes. Josh and Bo exchanged an uncomfortable glance that, thankfully, escaped Adrian.

Josh swallowed hard, turned on his heels, and walked away with his head down. For a split second I felt bad for him, until I saw the tears streaming down Monica's face.

"Thank you," she managed, "If you weren't here I probably would have let the asshole take me home and made a fool out of myself trying to get him in to bed."

As I made a move to walk toward her, dizziness overhauled my brain. I swayed too far to one side and fell toward the sidewalk.

"Shit, November!" Bo's voice cut through the haze just before his hand grabbed my forearm, yanking me upward and into his chest. "Dammit," he exhaled into my hair. "Are you OK?"

"Yea. Sorry." I left my forehead on his chest while I grappled for some sort of equilibrium.

"Nice save, man." Adrian's voice confused me at first, as if I was having a dream, forgetting he was in my real life again. "I'll get her home."

"It's OK, Adrian, Bo can drive me." Regret slapped my drunken mouth.

"Ember, don't be crazy, you know I'd never let you leave with a guy you barely know. I'll take you and Monica home. Catch up with you tomorrow, Cavanaugh." Adrian looked at me like I was crazy before wrapping his arm tightly around my waist, guiding my arm around his broad shoulders. Monica fell into his other arm.

Adrian's words twisted Bo's face in angst. What was he to do? He couldn't chase after me without revealing everything to Adrian, causing a host of problems for everyone involved. No, he had to stand on the sidewalk and watch as I stumbled to the parking lot in the arms of Adrian Turner.

I chanced a glance backward before getting into Adrian's car; Bo pressed his forehead on the brick building and thumped his hand listlessly against it once, before turning and walking back into the bar. If my ears weren't ringing I'm sure I would have heard a testosterone-filled growl.

I started pointing the way to my apartment when Monica insisted we drop her at her place. She said the heated exchange between Josh and I sobered her up quicker than she would have liked. I shrugged and guided Adrian. As Adrian walked Monica up her stairs, I pulled out my phone. My drunken ambivalence to Adrian's personal escort was boiling into anger as I thought about Bo walking back into the bar. Thumbing for his number, I wondered if he went back in to the bar to get drunk. *Maybe he went home with someone.* I hit send.

"November," Bo answered in a tone so clipped I couldn't tell yet if he was drunk. *Or with anyone.*

"Bowan." Brazen. That's what I was going for.

"November, where are you? Are you OK?" Anxiety and concern absorbed his voice.

"*You*, Spencer Bowan Cavanaugh, know *precisely* where I am. I am in the front seat of a *very* nice BMW that, incidentally, belongs to one Adrian Turner." I paused for a minute.

"*You*. You just stood there..." While I knew it wasn't fair to accuse him of abandoning me, I was livid at his assumption that I had *things* to work out with Adrian.

"Are you going back to your apartment?" He was nearly yelling out in frustration. Or concern. Or both.

"Adrian's going to take me wherever he's going to take me, Bo. *Thanks to you.*"

Wow, that was cold Ember. Even for you.

"I was trying to respect your privacy. I don't know what you and Adrian talked about, and I've already been accused once of peeing on your leg—as you put it. I couldn't do it Ember, I couldn't go face-to-face with Adrian about who was going to take you home in front of everyone on the sidewalk." I thought his voice cracked, but the liquor scrambled my signal.

"Oh really? Not even with the power of a *thousand lifetimes* behind you?" I turned off my phone and threw it into my clutch with renewed resolve.

Adrian climbed back in to his car, giving me a curious once over.

"Monica's fine. You look pissed, though. You OK?"

"Just drunk as hell, Adrian... take me home." *I don't care how that sounded.*

"As you wish." He smiled. *Oh, you think you know what I meant.*

Adrian pulled up to my building and opened the car door for me, since I evidently lacked the capacity to do so in my current state. It wasn't until I stood up that I felt the full effects of my foolishness, and stumbled for the second time. Adrian caught this pass.

"Whoa," he forced through gritted teeth as he righted me. "Let's take it slow on the stairs. Take off those ridiculous shoes and hand them to me." I did as he asked. *Damn, he's being rather thoughtful.*

Adrian led me up the stairs just as he had away from the bar, his solid arm secured around my waist. I took the opportunity to breathe in his scent once more.

"Mmm."

"What?" He looked at me from the corner of his espresso eyes.

Crap, I said that out loud? "Nothing." I let my head rest on his shoulder.

"Hold on as tight as you can." He said gently, as if he was talking to a child which, really, is how I was behaving.

When we reached my door, I pushed my clutch in to his stomach, *his rock hard stomach.* The door graciously supported me as Adrian unlocked it. He resumed his hold on me as he opened the door and flipped on the light.

"Thanks. You're sweet," I slurred into his ear as he set my heels by the door.

He walked me over to the couch and guided me down before heading to the kitchen. He returned with a large glass of water and sat down next to me.

"Drink this, ya drunk," Adrian teased as I took the water from him. I rolled my eyes and took a huge gulp.

"Why are you being so nice?" I demanded, setting the glass down.

"Why wouldn't I be?" He seemed shocked by my question.

"I don't know. I was just prepared for the smug bastard I worked you out to be in my head." What little conversational filter I carried was long gone.

Adrian laughed and shook his head, looking at the floor.

"Smug bastard, huh? Well, I guess I deserve that after tracking you down and assuming you'd want to meet me for a drink." He left his forearms on his knees and looked up at me, his face unreadable.

"That's right you deserve it. Especially when you tell me you really loved me five years ago. Why would you say that?" I guzzled more water but still felt incredibly drunk.

"Because it's true. And, I panicked. When I talked to Cavanaugh..." He stopped himself. *What is it with these two and using each other's' last names only?*

"When you talked to Bo, what?" *Bo. See, filter gone.*

"I think he likes you, Ember." His eyes squared in complete seriousness.

"Do you now? And what would make you say something like that?"

Besides the fact you've had song sex, real sex, and he feels like he's known you for...never mind.

"I could tell tonight. He had this look on his face when you and Monica tore out of Finnegan's, and again when he saw you at the other place." Adrian struggled to find the words.

"It's like he was protective of you, like he was seeing the stars for the first time, or something." His mouth took on a disappointed frown.

"When the hell did you become an expert face reader, and poet, Adrian 'all the ladies want me' Turner?" I was anxious for his answer.

"Because, November, it's the same look I saw when I looked in the mirror every single day that I was with you."

Oh.

"Adrian, I..."

"Come on, you need to get to bed." He stood quickly and held out his hand.

I held his hand all the way to my bedroom and, for a second, it felt like the old "us." Unexpectedly, he turned toward the window as I unabashedly took off my pants and

crawled into my bed.

"Nothing you haven't seen before, Turner," I deadpanned. He didn't respond. When I drew the covers up, he turned around with his hands in his pockets.

"You're so drunk. I don't feel comfortable leaving, Ember." The poor boy looked tortured.

"So don't," I yawned and rolled over.

I patted the side of the bed next to me, and he obliged. Adrian removed his shoes, and nothing more, before climbing in to my bed and folding his hands behind his head. Instinctively, I rolled over and nuzzled into his chest. He sighed a conflicted huff, reached down, and stroked my hair. I suddenly wished Bo was with me, and I was again mad at him for not being there.

I clumsily propped myself up on one elbow and looked into Adrian's eyes. The sexual tension between us was as palpable and undeniable as ever. The intensity of the moment overtook me; I leaned in, my lips reaching for his.

"Ember... Adrian pressed on my shoulder, stopping my down-ward motion.

"What?" I said rather petulantly.

"You're drunk. Drunker than I ever remember seeing you. I can't do that to you, and I can't let you do it to yourself."

His words were rather sobering, and my soul pulled itself out of the dark hole it had fallen into and mouthed *thank you*. Feeling only slightly defeated, I resumed my nuzzling of his chest; this I would not regret in the morning.

"Thank you." I smiled up at him.

"For what?"

"Taking care of me tonight." Sleep fell heavy on my eyes.

"Always." He kissed the top of my head as I drifted off to sleep.

CHAPTER FOURTEEN

"Ow. What the... ? Ow." I pulled the blanket down from my face, only to return it immediately at the brightness of the sun.

My memories of last night were thoroughly clouded. I recalled everything in precise detail up until the point Monica and I saw the guys walk into Lost Dog. From that point on it was just flashes of liquor and Lil' Jon.

"How are you feeling?" A deep voice whispered from above my head, scaring the hell out of me.

"Shit!" I flew to a seated position and looked to my right, regretting the sudden move immediately. I grabbed my head in a weak attempt to ease the throbbing pain.

"Whoa, take it easy Em. I'm sure you've got a killer headache after last night's performance." Adrian smiled.

"Adrian?" I was squinting, trying to keep as much sunlight out of my eyes as possible.

"Ha! Ya, it's me. Disappointed?" He coyly smiled as he accurately sensed my reaction. I took note that Adrian was fully dressed in the clothes he was wearing last night, save for his shoes, which were on the floor. I was wearing the same shirt, but my face flushed when I noticed my absence of pants from underneath my covers. I looked over at Adrian in horror.

"Where are my pants?" *Classy question, Ember.*

"You tossed them over there." Adrian motioned to the other side of the bed with his hand.

"Oh. So, we didn't…" *God, could this be any more humiliating?*

"No, Ember, we didn't." His voice was terse.

"Disappointed?" I shot his previous question back at him.

"I'm disappointed you'd think so little of me, frankly." He shook his head and swung his legs to the side of the bed. "We never even had drunk sex when we were together, Ember, What makes you think we'd start now?" He wasn't looking at me so I couldn't read his face.

"I'm sorry, last night is *very* fuzzy. Oh, damn, I was an awful bitch to Josh, wasn't I?" I covered my eyes with my forearm and laid back down on the bed.

"Seemed like he deserved it a little," Adrian chuckled. " I'll go make some coffee; come out when you're ready. Take it easy when you stand."

Suddenly, I remembered a lot about last night. I remembered yelling at Josh, Bo catching my concrete dive, leaving with Adrian, and then Adrian catching me. *I shouldn't wear those shoes anymore.* My stomach dropped as I remembered yelling at Bo on the phone, and then trying to kiss Adrian in my bed. *What a mess.* I walked wearily to the kitchen, where I saw Adrian pouring coffee and checking his Blackberry.

"Seems like our boy Bo really has it bad for you." Adrian smirked at his Blackberry.

This conversation feels familiar. Oh, yea, last night…

"What do you mean?" I wandered to the living room, recalling painfully that I had to be at work in an hour.

"He e-mailed your boss and told her that the four of us got together for a dinner meeting and we all got food poisoning. You're off the hook for work today." Adrian wore a wry smirk as he tucked his Blackberry back in to his khaki's.

"That was thoughtful." I tried passively.

"Yea, OK, we'll go with thoughtful." Adrian sat next to me on the couch.

"What's your problem with Bo?"

He didn't hesitate before he launched into his spiel. "First, you call him *Bo,* meaning you know him outside of work. Second, he likes you. Third, you like him. Those are my issues with Cavanaugh.

"Cutting right to the chase this morning, Council? First," I retorted, "Monica and I happened to see Bo play at Finnegan's last weekend. It wasn't until Monday that we learned we'd be working together. Second, maybe he does. And third, maybe I do." I shrugged, not breaking eye contact. *Conversational filter clearly hung over, as well.*

Adrian's forehead creased and he closed his eyes for a moment.

"Adrian, *please* don't say anything to anyone about Bo." I was walking the fine line between self-preservation and revealing too much.

"Is there anything to tell?" Adrian studied my face, imploring the truth from me.

His question sent chills through my body and froze my face. I opened my mouth to speak, but Adrian put up his hand.

"Never mind, I don't think I want to know. I'd never say anything, Ember. I respect you... and your decisions." He seemed sad. "Just be careful, OK?" His eyes darkened as he put a firm hand on my knee.

"Thanks, Adrian."

I felt a little weird talking about this with him, especially since we hadn't properly and soberly addressed what we'd talked about on the beach. My face paled at yet another piece of last night's puzzle. Adrian talked a lot about his feelings for me in the past, but hadn't suggested that they were any different in the present.

"You OK?" Adrian asked.

"I need to check on Monica," I lied. I didn't want to rehash his feelings for me or further discuss my budding romance with his coworker.

I quickly texted Monica:

Me: *Morning. You OK? Did you hear we got the day off due to "food poisoning" courtesy of Bo?*

Monica: *Hey, I probably feel better than you do, Hot-Mess-Express. So grateful for food poisoning right now. I'll come over later...when I decide to move.*

Me: *Adrian stayed here last night. NOTHING happened. Don't call, I'll call you. I just needed to get that out there.*

Monica: *You're lucky outside noises still hurt my head this morning or I'd ignore your request to not call. Literally dying waiting for your call.*

I put down my phone, took a huge breath, and returned my attention to Adrian.

"Ooooh," Adrian said in a revelatory tone, leaning back against the couch.

"What?" I narrowed my eyebrows.

"That's why you so easily suggested that Cavanaugh take you home last night. There's already something going on between the two of you, isn't there?" It was like he was working out a math problem in his head and didn't like the answer.

I chuckled for a split second, until I blanched under my own revelation.

"Nooo," I sounded like I was speaking to a toddler, "that's why you *insisted* on taking me home." My volume rose as I stood up in front of Adrian. "You already knew, didn't you, Adrian, because I called him Bo in front of you and you told me you noticed a certain "look" on his face when he talked about me." My eyes were wide with anger.

Adrian glanced to the floor before standing. His eyes finally met mine.

"I'm right, aren't I?" My voice burned with fury.

My heart raced as I realized how misplaced my anger at Bo was last night. Not only was he truly trying to respect me, but both of us were manipulated by Adrian. Smug was a kind adjective compared to the ones going through my head at that moment. Betrayal is not something I take lightly. I stormed by Adrian, crudely opened the door and stood next to it with my arms crossed and eyes narrowed.

I couldn't even begin to rationalize the reasons Adrian would splinter himself between me and Bo. Did he want me back? If so, why, and did I even care? Either way, I was so upset I couldn't talk to him about it, not yet.

"Ember, come on." That was all he could manage as he walked toward me.

"Don't say anything about me and Bo to anyone, OK?" My tone was only a hair below a yell.

"I won't. I'm sorry. Please be careful, Ember." His voice sounded sincere again.

"Well, *Bo* hasn't manipulated me lately, has he?" I arched one hell of an eyebrow.

"No, I guess you're right, he hasn't. But, you don't know him well."

"And you do?" I snipped.

Adrian shrugged unconvincingly, let out a sigh, and brushed my cheek softly before I turned away.

"Adrian—"

"Ember, look, I'm here until tomorrow. I want to try to get together again—just the two of us. There are still some things—"

"I'll see you later, Adrian. I'm too angry to talk about this right now, but we *will* be talking about it." I opened the door wider as I interrupted him, solidifying my stance in anger.

He turned and walked uneventfully out the door and down the stairs. When I heard his car drive away, I collapsed on the couch in tears. I had shared some sweet moments with Adrian last night only to find out he manipulated the whole situation, and for what? Adrian didn't even make a move last night—maybe he felt guilty; he damn well better.

I called Monica and told her everything. She wanted to come over, but I needed some time alone. When I heard a knock on my door, I hung up the phone and angrily walked to answer it, preparing for round two with Master Manipulator.

I threw the door open rather ungracefully, and found Bo standing there, hands in his pockets and his head hanging slightly; he looked thoroughly tortured. I burst into tears at the sight of him, threw my arms around his neck, and sobbed heavily into his shirt.

"Ember, what happened? Are you OK?" He took a slow step into the apartment; my arms still around his neck, his arms around my body.

He gently unwrapped my arms from his neck, took my hand, and led me to my couch. When we sat, I placed my head back on his shoulder and continued to sob irrepressibly. Bo rubbed my shoulders silently, before he sat me up.

"Did Adrian do something to you?" His chilling look ceased my tears.

"N-no, not like that," I managed to spit out, though my breathing was erratic from crying. Bo looked confused.

I told Bo about Adrian helping me up the stairs, rolling my eyes at the embarrassment all over again. I sheepishly admitted that I tried to kiss him in my drunken haze, but he rebuffed my offer and slept on top of the blankets *with his clothes on*. Finally, I took a deep breath before telling him about Adrian's motivations for taking me home last night; that I understood only seconds before I kicked him out of my apartment. When I finished I just stared at Bo, awaiting his reaction. After a thoughtful pause, Bo's forehead smoothed as he released a sly grin.

"Cunning son of a bitch, isn't he?" He let out a muffled laugh.

"What?"

"Not only did he manipulate the situation in his favor so he could take you home last night, but he didn't even try anything with you. Man, had you not figured out what his game was, he could have walked out of here looking like a knight." Bo lifted his eyebrows in mock-awe.

"Bo, I was mortified when I woke up next to Adrian this morning. I was so angry at you last night for just letting me go with him, even though I knew you really had no choice. But when I put his whole puzzle together, I felt awful. I wanted to wake up next to *you* this morning." I stared down at my hands, my eyes refilling with tears.

"Bo, I feel scuzzy and need to shower last night off of my body. Will you wait for me?"

"Of course." His gaze reignited me and I wanted him right there. I pressed my lips hard into his mouth before heading to the shower.

The shower is undoubtedly the best place to think; the hot running water drowns out all the background noise from the brain. The haze of my hangover was beginning to wash away and I could finally assess my feelings in private. While my stroll down memory lane with Adrian was nice, it was also clouded by misinformation and underhanded motives. Adrian admitted that he panicked when Bo mentioned me; it sure seemed his motivations last night were guided by someone trekking on what he'd assumed was still his territory. Meanwhile, this beautiful man was waiting for me in my apartment and I wanted to be his, all his.

Suddenly, it didn't feel like a choice *between* anything. No, it wasn't a choice between the logical and the romantic, and it wasn't a choice between my head and my heart. It was a choice *for* my spirit; for all the things that make me...me. I loved Bo Cavanaugh. I realized I needed to tell my boss about my relationship with Bo— before the Concord trip.

I was, therefore, choosing Bo. Choosing Bo and me. Choosing us. My soul smiled and hugged me. *Thank you.*

I turned off the shower, briskly dried my hair, and walked into my bedroom with a towel wrapped around me, startled to find Bo sitting on my bed still looking a bit conflicted.

"Better?" He asked.

"So much," I replied. "You OK?" I sat next to him, towel still wrapped around me.

"I have a confession to make." He grinded his palms on the tops of his thighs.

"OK?" My heart rate rose slightly as Adrian's words of caution bubbled to the surface of my brain.

"Wait. Can I ask you something first?" I continued, not waiting for a reply, "What did you do last night after Adrian took me and Monica home?"

"What do you mean?"

"Well, I saw you walk back in to the bar. And, now, you're wearing the same clothes," I said, passively grabbing his shirtsleeve.

"That's what I wanted to talk to you about." His tone was level, if not slightly calculating.

A million possibilities flew through my mind. Actually, only one did; maybe he went home with someone else. If he did, would I be mad? Would I have a right to be mad? We've never seriously discussed a relationship between the two of us, as such. *No, you've only talked about a thousand lifetimes and shocking me to life.*

"Last night, after you left, I did go back into the bar; but that was only to prevent myself from chasing after you like a fool." He smirked to himself.

"As soon as I saw Turner's car pull away, I drove to your place. I was going to wait for him to leave and then come see if you were OK. You must have called me when you were at Monica's place, because I was in front of your apartment and you weren't there."

I opened my mouth to respond, but he held up his hand. "I waited in the lot across the street to make sure he brought you home, as he said he would. Yea, I felt a bit like a stalker, but he's fast with women—that much I do know—and I was worried about you. When you got to your place and I saw you stumble again, I nearly jumped out of my car. But, I saw that he was being kind to you, and I just wanted him to get you inside and then leave. He didn't leave. I waited... and waited... and waited..." Bo drew this out for affect, his voice constricting around the words. He looked up at me, apparently awaiting a reaction. It finally dawned on me.

"You were out there all night..." I whispered.

"I knew how drunk you were. I didn't know if he'd..." Bo looked out the window, unable to verbalize his fears.

"That's how you arrived just after Adrian left, impeccable timing." I smiled.

"You're not mad?" His brow creased.

"Mad?! Bo, that's fucking romantic. How did Adrian look when he left this morning?" I wanted to know if my brutal rebuffing of him had any visual effect.

"Completely deflated." A boyish grin took over his face.

Jackpot.

I couldn't hold back any longer. I grabbed Bo's face and pulled him down for the most healing, soul reviving kiss I had in me. He responded by pinning me on the bed, one arm still hooked around my waist. I fisted his hair, eliciting a moan from his throat as he released his arm from under me and ran his hands roughly through my wet hair. I grabbed him through his jeans causing him to hiss in anticipation. I started undoing the buttons on his shirt one by one; Bo sat up and pulled the shirt off over his head. His eyes were smoldering.

Without saying a word, Bo opened my towel and pulled it out from under me, tossing it—and last night—to the floor. His hand sculpted over every curve of my body; I was his. I deftly undid his belt and pants with seduction playing across my lips, silently begging him for more. He kicked his jeans to the floor as my hips grinded against him.

"Mmm," he moaned in to my neck, assaulting it with delicious kisses.

I rolled over and sat astride him, planting my lips on his earlobe and tracing them down his body to his navel. In one quick movement, I was suddenly underneath him once more. I squealed like a child about to open birthday presents. I grabbed him and reached for a condom from my bedside stand.

"No," he flashed a wicked grin, "this one's on me." He pulled a condom from his pants pocket on the floor.

He slowly and deliberately rolled the condom on; an anticipatory moan escaped me as I watched him. Gently, he parted my knees and positioned himself between them. I was breathless as his hands stalked up the sides of my body on the mattress. It was all I could do not to beg him to enter me; thankfully I didn't have to wait. He sank slowly and beautifully into me as we let out simultaneous sighs of relief. I couldn't justify why we'd only done this once before.

Our rhythms quickly synched, and I was meeting him every step of the way. He slowed down for a moment, pulling back slightly to look at me. My forehead crinkled inquisitively.

"You are so damn beautiful." He shook his head as if he was trying to rationalize it.

"*You're* so beautiful," I replied, pushing my hips further into him, grabbing his head and leading him back to my mouth.

Being with Bo was like throwing myself into the ocean; invigorating and breathtaking. The swell of my orgasm built like a tidal wave, and I dug my fingers into his back; he quickened his pace in response. We climaxed nearly in unison, our bodies keeping the beat of our love song.

When our breathing returned to normal, Bo lifted my chin. " I wanted to tell you something the other night... but you fell asleep." He looked nervous.

"Anything." I shifted through my lashes to focus on his face.

Bo pressed his lips against my forehead.

"I love you too."

CHAPTER FIFTEEN

My face flushed and my eyes filled with fresh tears as Bo kissed my lips and spoke again.

"I love you, November Blue Harris," he breathed in to my ear.

"I love you, too, Bowan." A single tear glided down my cheek in blissful ecstasy.

"You mean you don't want to call me Spencer?" He teased.

"Not if I don't have to," I grumbled, thinking of work. *Call your boss.* "Hey, you said I fell asleep the other night when you wanted to tell me—but you were already asleep when—"

"When you told me?" Endearment eddied in his eyes.

"You heard me?"

Bo shrugged, "I wasn't asleep." He flashed the most all-American smile I'd ever seen. "I wanted to tell you the second I woke up, but you were gone. When I saw you on that beach playing the guitar, Ember, it was as if my world had stopped. I loved you more in that moment than I even had the night before. I was in awe. You rendered me speechless and I wondered all day if I could find a word better than love to express my feelings for you. I couldn't. The word is so simple, so beautiful, but so complex—so you."

Do people really say things like this? I need a fainting couch.

"You're unbelievable in the most brilliant way." I kissed the dimple left exposed by his lingering grin.

I sat in awe, once again, at his beauty. He was physically flaw-less—the kind of perfection you only find in books; but also kind, gentle, talented, sweet, caring, and protective. He survived his parents' death and took care of his sick sister as she battled drug addiction, ultimately leading him to my office door. The thought of how we met drained the color from my face and my mouth frowned in thought.

"What is it?" Bo sat up.

"I've got to call my boss. I don't feel right continuing this without letting her know. It's the right thing to do." I took a deep breath and got out of bed to put clothes on.

As I walked out to the living room to get my cell phone, Bo hollered down the hall, "Always in your head, Harris!"

"Ha! Not since I met you, *Cavanaugh.*"

A newfound feeling of freedom came from choosing happiness, wrapped in Bo Cavanaugh and his friggen guitar; a feeling I wanted to carry with me for a long time. I took a deep breath and dialed my boss's number.

"November? I'm surprised to hear from you, are you feeling OK?" Carrie's concern sounded genuine. *Thank you for food poisoning, Bo.*

"I'm feeling a little better, just really dehydrated at this point. Thank you for understanding. We all had the fish last night," I lied.

"Glad to hear it, we'll need you ladies healthy for Concord on Monday." *Right, that.*

"Carrie, that's sort of why I called..."

"What is it?" Carrie's tone was suddenly anxious.

"Bo—er—Spencer Cavanaugh and I actually met the Friday before he came in to our office for the meeting with all of us. Monica and I saw him performing at Finnegan's; he uses his middle name, Bowan, or Bo, except for business when he uses his birth name, Spencer." Words emptied from my mouth with barely enough grace to sound like an adult. Bo entered my living room and sat on the couch next to me.

"Well, that would certainly explain the awkward tension I felt between the three of you on Monday," Carrie laughed. "It's no big deal, kind of funny actually."

"Yeah," I drew out for effect, "see, we spent a lot of time together that weekend, because we really hit it off on Friday night. We were so involved with talking about music and our families, we never talked about work. I—"

"You like him?" Carrie cut off, her tone still light.

"Yes. Very much. I tried to keep everything separate and private this week. I was hoping to wait until we decided if we were going to partner with DROP. You know, why make an issue when there doesn't need to be?" My face was an inferno of embarrassment and nerves.

Bo laughed to himself as he patted my leg. *Glad you find this amusing.*

"November, it's fine," Carrie reassured, eliciting an exaggerated sigh on my part. "I appreciate your disclosure; it shows real maturity on your part. I suppose since Spencer, Bo, whoever," she chuckled before continuing, "runs DROP, *his* personnel staff doesn't have an issue with the relationship, and neither do I."

"Carrie, thank you so much for understanding." I gave Bo the thumbs-up.

"The only time we'd have to worry about it is if there is a dissolution of the relationship, and thereafter." The word "dissolution" pinched my heart, but she was right.

"Understood. Oh, and Carrie? I guess in the interest of complete disclosure, I should let you know that a member of DROP's legal team, Adrian Turner, and I dated in college. Before you say anything, I had *no* idea that he was involved with DROP and Bo had no idea Adrian had been involved with me. But, it was Adrian's idea for DROP to approach us, among other non-profits, because he knows me and Monica." I told Carrie all of that in one breath, as well, and saw Bo's eyes widen in response.

After a brief pause, Carrie broke in to laughter. "Ha! That's... well, good luck with... all of that, Ember. David Bryson and I have worked out the itinerary for the trip, I'll email it to you this afternoon. Take care, hun." And just like that, she hung up the phone.

Relief flooded through my body and oozed out of my pores. *You're free to be with him, nothing is holding you down.* I looked up at Bo and he smiled a knowing smile.

"She's fine with it," he said matter-of-factly.

"Yes. As long as your people are OK with it," I teased.

In a flash, Bo had me pinned beneath him on the couch, my head cradled in his hands.

"I think I can talk them into it," he said with sexy authority, burying his face in my neck.

"I really do love you, Bo." It felt so good to say it without the pang of guilt by way of ethics.

"You have no idea, November..." Was all he could breathe out before we lost ourselves in the riptide.

"Play that song again," Bo whispered into my ear as we lay together on my couch.

"Why?" I rolled my eyes at the thought. Singing in front of people was one thing; the fact that he accidentally heard me play the guitar was another.

"It was beautiful, and you were beautiful playing it. Do you have it written down anywhere?" *He's serious.*

"Uh, no. It's the first song I learned, and that was before I knew how to read music; I never thought to transcribe the notes." I sat up, put on my robe, and lazily reached for the guitar.

"Hand me your music comp. notebook and I'll transcribe it for you as you play." Genuine excitement laced his face as he pulled his shirt down over his head.

"Um, I don't have a comp. notebook. What part of *I don't play* missed your ears," I said with mocking eyes.

"You're killing me! Wait here, I'll get mine from my car." He grabbed my chin and gave me a butterfly-inducing kiss before he dashed to his car.

When he returned, he sat on the couch and handed me the guitar I'd left sitting in its case. My breath rattled through the room as I inhaled.

"Why are you so nervous?" Bo asked in complete seriousness.

"Well, this is a little intimate. I've seriously *never* played for anyone besides my family. You sneaking up on me at the beach doesn't count." My face heated beneath his smile.

"Babe, we've covered intimate quite well already. Play." He slapped the notebook off of my knee and sat back, pencil in hand.

Babe? I like it.

With one more cleansing breath, I shifted so I was sitting cross-legged, facing him. I threw the strap over my head and rolled my shoulders to help relax, which didn't really help. I closed my eyes and started strumming the lullaby my parents taught me when I was little. It is a slow, swelling song that hangs mainly in the lower register; it sounds like the guitar is putting itself to sleep. It flows wonderfully and could cause lovers to dance and cry at the same time.

Once I let go of apprehension enough to feel the song through my soul, I lifted my head to look at Bo. He was studying my fingers, scribbling notes and rhythms as fast as he could. When he caught my eye, he nodded in encouragement, and returned to work. His hands were beautiful. His long fingers sat artfully in his masculine hands; it looked like he could break the pencil any minute, but his hand glided gracefully across the page.

When I strummed the last cord, Bo asked me to play it again so he could fill in the parts he'd missed. I had no sarcastic comment for him—I wanted to do it. I could play this song for *this* man all day. When I finished the second time, he looked at his notebook and gave me an accomplished smile.

"Gorgeous. Hand me your guitar so I can see if I got it right." I surrendered it without hesitation.

He set the notebook on my coffee table and began to play. They were the same notes, and the same beat, but it sounded so much more beautiful coming from his fingers. He studied the notes closely the first time through. When he finished, he immediately started again. This time his eyes were closed, but his forehead disclosed his concentration. He was trying to feel the notes as they should come, and he didn't miss a single one. His body swayed slightly as he rode the wave of notes coming out of his guitar. I grabbed my cell phone and recorded him playing. He cracked a smile when he opened his eyes and saw the phone, but looked to the page and kept playing. When he finished, I pressed stop and impulsively sent the video to my mom.

Me: *This is Bo. He's using my guitar. He wrote the notes to that lullaby as I played them–this is him testing his transcription.*

Within two minutes my phone dinged a response.

Mom: *I see you chose reckless abandon. Excellent. Love you :)*

My heart swelled anew when I saw my mom's message.

"Who'd you send that to?" Bo asked.

"Raven—uh—my mom," I shrugged and smiled.

My phone dinged again, but this time all sensation left my face and my stomach threw itself out the window.

"What's wrong?" Bo set the guitar down.

"It's Monica. She says that Josh is there, and he's drunk—she's freaked. It's ten a.m.! Shit!" My heart raced into my throat.

"I'll drive." Bo shut the door behind him as I was already halfway down the stairs.

The two mile drive to Monica's house felt inordinately long; I counted the feet with each heartbeat. Bo reached across the car and put his hand on mine.

"Has this happened before?" he asked.

"Not that I'm aware of," I shrugged, "but they've never broken up before."

"So, we don't know if he's aggressive or anything?" Bo's dark tone refreshed my anxiety.

"I guess not, but Monica didn't indicate anything..." A sob choked my throat. If Josh was drunk now, he was still drunk from the night before—when I verbally assaulted him.

"Maybe I should go up first and check it out—make sure everyone's OK." Bo said as he pulled in front of Monica's building.

"Thanks, but screw that. She's my best friend and he's being an asshole. We'll go together."

I sent Monica a text to let her know we were downstairs, rather than ringing her bell, so she could buzz us in. As the buzzer rang and the door unlocked, I looked at Bo and grabbed his hand for a split second before sprinting up the stairs.

"Jesus, hold on!" He flew after me.

As I reached the top of the stairs I heard voices and paused a second to listen.

"Josh, just drink the water." Monica sounded annoyed, which was a good sign. On that note, I decided to knock and enter.

"Mon?" I entered cautiously and tried to keep the anxiety out of my voice.

"Hey Ember, Bo, come in." Monica held the door open and mouthed "Thank you." I squeezed her arm in response.

"What the *hell* are you two doing here?" Josh sputtered venomously through his teeth.

"Shut up, Josh. I couldn't get you to leave, so I *asked* them to come," Monica spat angrily. She stood cross-armed by her still-open door.

"I told you, I'm not leaving until you hear me out!" Josh yelled.

My wide eyes were still assessing the scene as Bo crossed in front of me and sat on the coffee table across from Josh.

"Have you been home at all since last night, man?" Bo reached for the glass of water.

"You mean since *that bitch* told me off?" Josh gestured in my direction. Bo's free hand clenched into a fist against the table. Fury and hurt punched my gut and pricked at my eyes.

"Fuck off Josh," I started. Bo tried to silence me by putting up his hand, but I didn't follow. "It's hardly my fault that you broke up with Monica. How *dare* you call me a bitch after you tried to take her home last night. Now you show up here like a drunken scumbag and demand that she *listen to you?* You're better than this. Get the hell out of here and come back when you sober up." My voice was angry and strained as I successfully fought off tears. Bo's eyebrows shot up at my retort.

Josh stood and walked over to me until we were almost toe-to-toe. The venom and pain in his eyes commanded the hairs on the back of my neck to attention, one-by-one. I could smell the booze on his breath. I met his stare dead-on with a racing heart. A vacuum of suspense sucked all the air from the room; no one spoke, and no one moved.

"Josh, come, take a seat." Bo slowly approached Josh, putting his hand on his shoulder.

Seeming to snap out of it, Josh looked at Bo and took the water, raking his hands through his hair. "Man, you have no idea how fucked up this is..."

I took Monica by the hand and walked with her to the bedroom while Josh rambled to Bo.

"Holy shit, what the fuck was that all about? Monica, what the hell happened?" I whispered.

Monica's anger boiled over; tears steamed off her hot cheeks. "He just showed up here, all wobbly and slurring, telling me how sorry he was, and maybe we were at the beginning of our thousand lifetimes of knowing each other." Tears turned into sobs as I pulled her in to a hug.

"God. What did you say to him?"

"Nothing, I don't want to have this conversation with him drunk. I texted you and tried to get him to drink some water. I don't want him to leave right now because he's too drunk to drive—which is how he got here."

A soft knock on the door sent my pulse racing again.

"It's Bo, can we use your shower?"

Monica and I stared at each other quizzically and shrugged.

"Uh, yeah, go ahead," Monica said suspiciously; a fresh grin toweled her tear-stained face.

We heard the shower start, followed by garbled noises of protest coming from Josh. Monica and I peered down the hallway just in time to see Bo toss a fully clothed Josh into the shower.

"Shit that's freezing!" Josh exclaimed as he sat slumped on the shower floor.

"Don't come out until you get your act together." Bo walked toward us. "Are you OK Monica?" He asked empathetically as he put his arm around her.

"Much better now, thank you. I've got some of his clothes here. He can change into them." She turned back to her room.

"Are *you* OK?" Bo turned his question to me.

"Yea, why? Oh, the bitch thing?" I shrugged impassively. It really didn't bother me.

"I almost decked him. Are you always that confrontational?" Bo asked, annoyance punctuated his question.

"Only when people are being asshats. Please don't waste a punch on Josh, I like your hands." I took them into mine, kissing the anger out of his knuckles.

Monica returned with dry clothes for Josh and we all looked at each other, silently discussing who would deliver them. Bo grabbed the clothes, opened the bathroom door, turned off the water, and tossed the clothes on the floor.

"Dry off and put these on." He slammed the door shut, his remaining anger streaked through the door frame.

The three of us waited in the living room for Josh. I wondered how Bo knew a cold shower would help sober Josh up, but I pictured his sister and thought better of the question. Within a few minutes, Josh was back in the living room. He sank into the recliner on my side of the couch and reached for his glass of water, which inadvertently caused me to flinch.

"Ember—" he started, but I raised my hand to stop him.

"I just want you to drink that damn water so we can get you home." I couldn't make eye contact with him.

I wasn't mad about him calling me a bitch; I was still mad at him for breaking up with Monica in the first place and then showing up at Monica's like a total degenerate. He'd honestly panicked when Bo told him that he felt like he's known me for a thousand lifetimes. Who does that?

"You don't have to take me home, I've got my car," Josh said seriously.

"Dude, I didn't cave your face in when you called Ember a bitch, but I *will* if you try to get into your car. Let's go. Em, I'll come back for you OK?" Bo said as he headed toward the door, one arm behind Josh.

As soon as the door closed, Monica collapsed on the couch in tears.

"Monica, I'm really sorry about yelling at Josh last night, and about him coming here." I sat next to her and put my arm around her.

"Em, it's not that. I am *so* sorry for trying to get in your head about Adrian." She wiped her eyes.

"Mon, it's fine. You're hurt, and you apologized last night."

"No, it was a *really* shitty thing to say. Maybe I'm jealous of what you seem to have found with Bo and that was my way of acting out. What the hell happened with Bo last night by the way?"

Her mouth hung freely open when I explained how Bo sat in his car and watched outside my building all night. She chuckled when I told her Bo saw Adrian's downtrodden exit from my apartment.

"Wow, that's intense. Hey, what do you think Adrian's real issue with Bo is? His reaction seems a bit overblown for it to be just about jealousy." Monica's words echoed my exact thoughts.

"I don't know, but I plan on dragging it out of one of them."

Bo returned after a few minutes and assured us Josh was safely at home in bed.

"K, Mon, I've gotta go home and catch up on some sleep. Carrie said she'll email us the Concord itinerary today. Oh, and Carrie now knows about me and Bo and she's fine with it," I said nonchalantly.

"Yes!" Monica nearly knocked me over with a hug. "Are you guys going out tonight?" *Shoot, I forgot, we're supposed to have plans.*

"Yeah, actually, it's kind of a surprise." Bo said shyly. "But, we'll likely end up at Finnegan's later; it's open mic night after all." Once again his face lit up with a playful grin.

"Great, see you guys then!" Monica half-cheered. "Bo, thank you."

"No problem, Monica." He gave her a tight hug.

"Call me if you need anything at all today, OK Mon?"

"Have so much fun tonight." She whispered while she ushered me out.

The drive back to my place seemed much faster now that Josh was safely in bed and Monica was relatively OK. When Bo pulled up in front of my building, his phone rang.

"Hey, while you take that I'll run up and get your comp. notebook." He nodded as he answered.

I bounded down the stairs happily, excited for whatever tonight would hold. Bo's angry voice bellowing from his car stopped me.

"Don't *fucking* start with me. I'll be back tomorrow night," he growled. When he saw me, his face changed. "Look, I'll call you later. Bye." He took a long breath as I opened up the passenger door.

"You OK?" I asked cautiously.

"Yeah, asshole friends." He shook his head reflexively and stretched out his hand, "Thanks Ember, I'll pick you up around seven, OK?" He smiled with a glint of deception. "I've got a surprise to work on before then."

"Sure, see you then." I smiled as I shut the door.

"Oh, and Ember?" He put the car in to drive, keeping his foot on the brake, "I love you."

"I love you too." I winked back.

As he pulled away from the curb, I heard his phone ring again.

"What!" he snapped as he drove away.

CHAPTER SIXTEEN

As 7:00 approached, anxiety crashed against the jetty's of my insides. I was excited to see what Bo had planned, but I had some lingering suspicions. Why did Adrian seem guarded about Bo? What was Bo yelling about on the phone earlier? As I pulled my hair loosely back at the nape of my neck, I resolved that I would ask one or both of them to spill it—there was something going on and I fully intended to find out what it was.

I decided a glass of wine was in order. As I leaned against my counter, welcoming the red relaxation through my system, I thought back on my crazy-beautiful week. This gorgeous man fell into my life, and disarmed me with a single kiss. The irony that I initiated said kiss was not lost on me. Exultant chills sauntered down my spine. The very first kiss we had in the parking lot told me nearly everything I needed to know; it was alive, passionate, longing.

It really *did* feel like we'd known each other for a thousand lifetimes in that first kiss, I just didn't have those words at the time. Now, I stood in my kitchen, ready to spend more time with him, anticipating the next time I could kiss him. I loved him. Butterflies fluttered drunkenly through my system when I heard a knock on the door. They dropped dead when I opened it.

"Adrian, what the hell are you doing here?" I let out an exaggerated sigh.

"Can I come in?" His voice was eerily urgent.

"No, you may not. I've got plans." I stood in the doorway with no intention of letting him in.

"Ember, let me in, I just want to talk to you." Urgency turned to agitation.

"Adrian, I've had a long fucking day. Josh showed up at Monica's this morning, drunk out of his mind, begging for forgiveness or whatever, and I just want to go out. So, if you would..." I slid past him and shut the door, putting both of us in the stairwell.

I jogged past him, down the stairs, deciding to meet Bo outside as a way to get Adrian out of my apartment.

"Wait!" Adrian yelled as he grabbed my arm tightly and yanked me back.

"Ow! *Don't,* Adrian!" I huffed, my cheeks fighting the heat. He released my arm immediately.

"Shit, I'm Sorry. Is Monica OK? He put his hands in his pockets as he tried to change the subject. *Good place for your hands—keep them there.*

"Yeah. Hey, I know you have some stuff you want to talk to me about, or whatever, but can it wait until we're in Concord? I've got plans with Bo tonight, and then Monica and I are going to watch him sing tomorrow. I just can't fit you in my head right now." My frankness never sat well with Adrian, and this time was no different.

"That's nice, Ember. So, that's all I am to you? Someone who takes up space in your head?" He stayed one stair behind me, but that didn't soften his antagonizing tone.

When I reached the bottom stair, I turned around and looked him square in the eyes.

"Look, Adrian, I've had enough surprises from you this week, wouldn't you say? Just, please, leave it alone for now." I opened the door and jumped at the sight of Bo, leaning against his car, arms crossed in front of him. I couldn't tell if it was in relaxation or defense.

Oh, hell.

Bo nodded his chin up at me and opened the passenger door of his car, but his eyes never left Adrian. I looked back as I climbed in, and noted that Adrian's eyes bored through Bo, as well. I had nothing to go on; no idea why they were like this with each other. It wasn't because of me and, if it was, Adrian needed to screw off because *we* were not an option. Not one single word passed between Bo and Adrian before Bo got into his car, and Adrian into his. When Adrian pulled away, Bo gripped his steering wheel in apparent frustration.

"What was that about?" Bo asked, looking at me out of the corner of his eyes as he pulled away from the curb.

"No. What was *that* about? That was like a friggen showdown." I pointed my thumb to the sidewalk, wide eyed.

"He just seems to be at your place a lot," he said with a hint of accusation.

"Yes, he does, and I'd like for *you* to explain why."

"I told you, the man's jealous. But, I also saw the look on your face when you walked out the door—you looked upset." Bo's eyes remained on the road.

"I was upset that he showed up unannounced when I told him we could talk later."

I reached for Bo's hand, and ran my thumb along his knuckles until his shoulders relaxed. I intentionally left out the bit about Adrian grabbing my arm and pulling me backward on the stairs.

"Sorry," he relented.

"Me too. Come on, let's just go and have some fun. I can't tell you how tired I am of discussing Adrian Turner." I glanced out the window to clear my thoughts.

"Hey, I wanted to run something by you..." Bo broke our few minutes of silence as we seemed to drive aimlessly around town.

"Yea?"

"Turns out I have to head back to Concord tomorrow morning. I was wondering if maybe you'd want to come with me? Monica could meet you there Monday for the meeting and you could ride home with her afterward." Bo sounded hopeful.

"Absolutely," I said without hesitation.

"That was quick." Bo chuckled as he pulled into Finnegan's parking lot. *Freakin' Finnegan's? Really?*

"Bo, I love you. What, exactly, is there to think about? I'll tell Carrie I'm going to extend my room stay by two days."

"Or... you could just stay with me, at my place," he suggested bashfully.

Two nights with Bo, alone, at his place? Mother, may I?

"Sounds perfect." I smiled, "What are we doing here? I thought you had a surprise; Finnegan's is no surprise to me." I cocked an eyebrow and he chuckled.

"First surprise is I'm going to play a set here tonight, since I won't be around tomorrow. The second surprise is... still a surprise." He winked as he got out of the car.

As we walked in, I was instantly annoyed at the sight of Josh behind the bar. I chose to ignore him and asked Bo to grab me a beer while I found a table. I watched Bo and Josh talk for a minute; Josh even cracked a smile. Bo nodded back in my direction and then stayed at the bar while Josh headed toward me. *What the hell?* As Josh got closer I straightened in my chair and could feel my nerves tense. I was not in the mood for another round of name-calling. He took a seat next to me and I raised my eyebrows, signaling him to get on with it.

"You're looking better," I said snidely. He didn't acknowledge my sarcasm before he began to apologize.

"I'm so sorry for how I treated you last night, *and* this morning. After you yelled at me, it hit me—I can't live without Monica. Look what happened to me after 48 hours away from her." Josh shook his head and looked to the floor. "She hasn't talked to me since I left her apartment this morning, but I think she's coming here tonight and I *really* need to talk to her Ember; I need to get her back—I'm such an ass." His jaw tightened as he cursed himself.

"Yes, Josh, you are. I'm sorry for yelling at you. You were drunk and hurting, but I went into defense mode for Monica. I'll text her, but if she's not ready that's not my fault—are we clear?" Josh nodded and I sighed as I texted Monica.

Me: *Hey. At Finnegan's—Josh is working. He's on bended knee telling me how badly he needs to talk to you. Judging by the look on his face I'd say you should give him a few minutes.*

Monica: *Boys are dumb—be there in a while.*

"She'll be here in a bit," I said flatly.

"Thank you." Josh gave my forearm a squeeze before heading to the stage to introduce Bo.

Bo sat down on the center stool. I noticed the second stool to his left and concluded I'd be singing with him again at some point. He spoke his thanks in to the microphone.

Swiftly, a low-toned melody drowned out any lingering applause garnished by the patrons of Finnegan's. My senses labored in slow motion as I lifted my eyes to the stage. Bo was looking down at his hands as they floated across the guitar that was producing a lullaby—my lullaby. *Holy...* I could almost see the red in my own cheeks as I watched him, up on stage, playing the song he had transcribed only this morning.

When he finished one line of the wordless melody, everyone clapped politely as my cheeks stung with what I was sure was crimson.

"Thank you, I just started working on that this morning. A beautiful woman played it for me." He smiled while looking at me across the bar and my breathing increased. "Ember, will you come up?"

I felt faint when he said my name, knowing that all of Finnegan's now knew *I* was the 'beautiful woman' who played that song.

"That was lovely," I said as I reached the stage and kissed him on the cheek, ignoring the crowd. They responded with requisite "oohs" and "ahs" as I settled down on the stool. "What are we going to sing?"

Bo leaned his head away from me slightly as that sexy smile of his graced his face. He ignored me and started strumming the lullaby again. I stared, confused, until I felt a tap on my shoulder. I turned around and all the air left my body. Monica stood there with an impish grin on her face—holding my guitar.

"What the hell?" My response produced a rumble of laughter from the crowd, and from Bo.

"I picked it up on my way here—I was on my way when you texted," Monica whispered, unable to contain her smile.

Shaking the daze from my head, I absentmindedly reached for the guitar and slung it over my shoulder.

"Come on," Bo urged, and the crowd clapped.

I took a deep breath, the desert in my throat was thankful that I wouldn't be singing, and closed my eyes. I kept them closed long enough to regulate my breathing. Fleeing from their hiding place, my eyes opened to see Bo staring at me, perhaps questioning his move to surprise me with the guitar. I wasn't upset; this was the most romantic thing that I'd ever witnessed and it was happening to me. I gave him a reassuring smile and joined in seamlessly. It was the first time I'd *ever* performed with the guitar, but I relaxed after just one line; beacons of light and exuberance shone from my core, highlighting the awestruck crowd.

"Keep playing that—don't stop," Bo said, as I focused on the task quite literally at hand.

In a second I heard a higher melody that harmonized perfectly with what I was playing. I looked over at Bo and he cautioned a proud grin as he played this beautiful compliment.

"I wrote this part today, for you," he said into the microphone.

I stopped hearing the applause long before it ceased. My eyes blurred with tears; I begged my fingers to hold on to the notes they knew. Bo wrote music for *me*. Music is the original love letter, and Bo Cavanaugh was reciting his to me for all of Finnegan's to witness. It is as public a proclamation of love as one can receive and each chord he played had a direct line to one of my heart strings.

There weren't any lyrics, but Bo intermittently hummed a husky-sweet melody in to the microphone, as if he were trying to work out lyrics in his head. This was surely more beautiful than words could ever be. I saw my parents do this regularly when I was a child; at night after I went to bed they would stay up and just play music with each other. My dad would strum something and my mom would respond with her voice, the piano, or her own stringed instrument. I would peek at them out on the porch from my bedroom window but they never noticed; they were lost in each other the entire time. It filled my heart with such joy then, and now I could feel it first handed as it sent me through the stratosphere.

Any love I thought I had for Bo Cavanaugh before this very moment paled in comparison to what exploded through me on stage. Reckless Abandon was left in the dust, her chest heaving in the after-effects of this gesture. I thought that if that was as good as it would get, I wanted to stay forever; if it was going to get even better—Heaven help me.

With one blink, tears trundled down my face; luckily we were nearing the end of the song. When I reached the last bar and stopped, Bo continued for another couple of lines. The higher melody was perfect, and he wrote it *for me*. When Bo finished and the crowd clapped, I could no longer hold back. I set my guitar down, grabbed his face, and sank my thanks into his lips right there on stage while the crowd yelped and whistled.

"Did you like it?" Bo whispered, grazing a tear off my cheek as I pulled myself away from the kiss.

"Bo," I faltered through a thesaurus of gratitude, "it was absolutely perfect."

I dabbed under my eyes and looked out to the crowd, where I saw Adrian was standing cross-armed near the door. His eyes connected briefly with mine before they fell to the floor.

"I'm going to take a little break, but I'll be back," Bo said before he silenced his mic and led me off stage.

Monica accosted me before we hit the bar.

"November, Jesus! That was the sexiest, sweetest, most romantic thing I've ever seen!" She squeezed me with all her might and I reciprocated. She was right.

"Ember," Josh approached us cautiously with wide, round eyes. "I had no idea you could..." he trailed off, looking at me for approval to continue.

"Thanks." I smiled and he relaxed.

Bo grabbed my shoulders from behind me and kissed my neck. Elation ebbed when I heard Adrian's voice.

"That was good, *really* good." Adrian's compliment sounded forced; he could barely make eye contact with me as he leaned in. "I get it," he whispered; his lips an inch from my ear.

"Yo, Spence, can I talk to you outside for a minute?" Adrian turned to Bo. *'Spence' is it?*

"Sure, be right back babe." Bo kissed my other ear before he headed out the door.

Once Bo was out of sight, I told Monica that he'd asked me to go to Concord with him the next morning.

"You're going to go, right?" Expectation poured through her words.

"Of course I am, as long as you don't mind travelling there alone. We'll ride back together." I tried to control my beaming excitement.

"You go. Have yourself a fantastic weekend of love, and music, and whatever the hell else it is you two perfect creatures do."

Josh came up behind me and handed me a beer. He was standing next to Monica, but her eyes remained focused on my face.

"Uh, Mon?" Josh cleared his throat as he tried to capture her attention.

Monica's stance collapsed, and her shoulders slumped as she turned toward Josh. Her head dropped, but Josh lifted her chin with his index finger, bringing her eyes to his. They stared at each other, saying nothing with words, but their eyes spoke volumes. *There's a thousand lifetimes right there.*

I don't know if it was the complexity of the situation between Josh and Monica, my own feelings for Bo, or the raging war between where I was and where I wanted to be, but when I watched Josh and Monica stare at each other, fresh tears begged for release.

"Guys, I love you both. Josh, I hate how shitty I've been to you, but Monica's my soul-mate best friend. I'll get out of your hair so you guys can talk." I hugged them and headed to the back door before either of them could respond. I gave a quick glance over my shoulder and saw Josh tenderly place his arm around Monica's shoulders as they walked to a table in the back.

I started to open the door to the deck, but stopped briefly when I noticed a heated exchange between Bo and Adrian. I could see the sides of each of their bodies; both of them retained clenched jaws, spoke through gritted teeth, and motioned wildly with their hands.

"This is going too far..." was all I heard from Adrian's mouth before I started yelling.

"What the hell is going on?" I fumed as I walked boldly up to them.

They stood motionless, their eyes dueling. I slid between what little space they had between their bodies, causing them to each take a step back.

"I've had enough of this awkwardness between the two of you, and I *know* it's not because of me." I hung on the word 'me' as I arched my eyebrow at Adrian. "Now, one of you better tell me what this is all about or I'll leave and not speak to either one of you again." *Poker face activated.*

Long seconds passed as Adrian and Bo held a soundless conversation. I took one step forward, *enough of this*, and made my way to the door before Adrian grabbed my arm. *Again, really?*

"Ember, *wait,*" he said, clearly conflicted.

"Let go of her, Turner," Bo said harshly, without reaching for my other arm. "I'll tell her."

My pulse quickened, and the heat of anticipation scorched my ears.

"Tell me what?" I shook free from Adrian's lingering hold.

I turned my back to Adrian and faced Bo. His face looked like it was about to shatter under the punch of pain.

"Bo, tell me what?" I said with more assertion, my hand on his arm.

He stepped back, which threw me off balance emotionally, and my hand remained suspended in air for a split second before I let it fall haphazardly to my side. I turned around and looked at Adrian, who just nodded in Bo's direction with a look of concession. I slowly turned back around to see Bo seated with his elbows on his knees, his hands clenched around his hair.

"Ember," he lifted his head and shot me an exhausted gaze. "I'm being blackmailed."

CHAPTER SEVENTEEN

"Blackmailed? By who? For what?" Thoughts flew out of my mouth before I could filter them.

Bo's elbows remained on his knees as he searched my face. His eyes ran red with pain, and I had to look down. He swallowed hard and looked past my shoulder, to Adrian. I turned on my heels and met Adrian's eyes.

"Wait, *you*?" I said to Adrian.

"No, Ember, I'm not," Adrian said unflappably, as if he was prepared for my reaction. "I'm on his legal team—remember?"

"Are *you* being blackmailed or is DROP being blackmailed." I had three trillion questions, but I stuck to the most basic as my head wrapped around the world 'blackmail.'

Bo looked up at Adrian, who gave him a nod.

"It's just me. The only connection this has to DROP, of course, is my money. Otherwise, this is one hundred percent personal." A grim line set across his brow.

"How long has this been going on?" I asked.

"About six weeks," Bo whispered, still seated.

"OK. So you," I pointed to Bo, "knew you were being black-mailed when you came to town. And you," I pointed to Adrian, "knew he was being blackmailed when you recommended our agency to him?" the basement of my voice flooded with anger.

Adrian took a step toward me, but I stepped back, stopping him.

"No. I've only been consulting with DROP's legal team for a

few weeks. I was consulted specifically for the purpose of finding a collaborating agency. It wasn't until after the initial contacts with Hope were made that I was informed of the blackmail." He gave me a minute to process, before continuing.

"Once it looked like the collaboration was going to go forward, and I could tell you two were developing... feelings for each other, it became a problem for me on an ethical level. I didn't want to involve you with something like this. But, my hands were tied as far as what I could tell you." Adrian shrugged and took a seat next to Bo.

"But Bo, you had no problem involving me?" No thought was sacred.

"Ember, you're not involved, nor did I plan on you ever finding out. This is a personal attack by some assholes. Adrian was convinced you'd find out anyway, especially when he couldn't get you to stay away from me." Bo's mouth hooked into a seductive, wicked grin.

"Adrian, why do you feel it's so important for me to know? You and I are in agreement that I'd probably find out anyway; wouldn't that have boded better for you, in the end?"

"What are you talking about?" Adrian looked at me curiously.

"You could have told me right away, right? You've been cryptic all week, telling me to be careful around Bo, and I still can't tell if that has to do with me and Bo or just me. Was this for his protection, mine, or yours?" I spoke frankly and laid it all out for Adrian.

"Ember," Adrian sighed, "I don't understand why you think I'm such an asshole. Aside from really wanting to keep you safe, it kills me to see you with someone else. I miss you, Blue."

Blue. A lacy black corset tightened itself neatly around my throat with a wide satin bow. My eyes tripled in size, as if they were trying to hear what he'd said.

Adrian, and Adrian alone, had called me "Blue" when we were an "us." His honesty held my heart captive and misted my eyes. Never, in the history of ever, had Adrian Turner been that vulnerable. He seemed to sense his slip; he bowed his head and jammed his hands into his pockets. The ocean quieted its white caps, and the stars hushed as the world awaited my response.

"Adrian, I've missed you too. I honestly didn't know how much I'd missed you until I saw you. I'm glad we reconnected, but you have to admit this is fucked up—even for us. You should have told me about what was going on, or at the very least encouraged Bo to tell me sooner than this. I know you're bound by laws and oaths, and all of that, but you know *me* and I respect confidences."

Blue? I'm expected to speak after that, and you can't even look at me?

"I guess you're right..." he trailed off, meeting my stare with his espresso eyes.

Bo sat back during my exchange with Adrian. There were years of history pulsing rapidly between Adrian and me. Bo seemed to be chewing the scene against the inside of his cheek. I was still feeling off-balance when I realized some of my earlier questions had gone unanswered. I buried "Blue" in the sand for the moment.

"What's the blackmail about, Bo?" I asked bluntly.

"The past. It doesn't even really have to do with me. It's nothing I've done or said or anything like that; I'm just the one with the money." He shrugged, trying for passive, settling for anxious.

"Do you know *who* is blackmailing you?"

"Yes." Black passion leaked from his voice and beckoned a chill through my core.

"Who?"

"He can't tell you that right now," Adrian cut in quickly, before Bo had even opened his mouth to answer.

"OK. Well, are you in any physical danger?" I stood up and walked toward Bo, who seemed worn out by this confession.

"He's not," Adrian cut in again, but I noted that Bo hadn't made any motion to answer 'yes' or 'no.' "If he were," Adrian continued, "this would be a *much* different situation and we wouldn't be having this conversation at all." As Adrian finished, Bo looked up at me hopelessly.

This was a lot. We both came to the table with various pieces of emotional baggage, for sure. But, the fact that Bo's involved black-mail, and Adrian, was a little too much for me to handle. I had to sort this out to the best of my ability. I was still madly in love with Bo, that much was certain, but there was still something lingering on his face that heightened my senses; never mind "Blue," who was still buried in the sand.

Of course, neither one of them could be completely honest with me regarding this situation because of ethics and laws. Irony raised its mocking eyebrow at my previous anxiety regarding telling my boss about my relationship with Bo. Those ethics paled in comparison to this freak-show.

I needed to take a walk and consider if I could go forth with the business end of the trip to Concord knowing what I knew. Could I tell Monica? I couldn't think about all of this with these two men sitting in front of me, watching me for a reaction. I stood up.

"I've got to take a walk. I'll be back in a few."

"I'll come with you." Bo stood and reached for my hand.

"Dude, let her go. She needs a minute," Adrian replied self-righteously.

Bo turned to Adrian, "I think I've got this Turner, *thanks.*"

"No. Bo, Adrian's right, I need a minute." I gave his hand a reassuring squeeze, wincing at the fact that 'Adrian's right' even came out of my mouth. But, he *was* right.

Bo squeezed my hand back before dropping it.

"It's OK, Bo, really. I just... need a minute." I kissed him softly on the cheek.

As I headed off, Josh poked his head outside and said, "Bo, you're up." I looked back, gave him an encouraging wave, and watched him head inside before I turned back around.

A half hour later I was left with more questions than answers as I made my way back to Finnegan's. I was madly in love with Bo Cavanaugh and, for the first time in my life, love was enough— more than enough—to carry me through whatever questions remained.

I spotted Bo leaning against the exterior wall of the bar as I got closer; his eyes broke into relief when he gauged my face. I returned a smile of reassurance, as he started walking toward me at a more-than-cautious pace.

"You came back," he said.

"I told you, I just needed a minute." I forced an over-hopeful tone to calm his apparent nerves.

"Or thirty," he teased as he caught up to me in the sand, just outside the back deck.

He wrapped his arms around my waist, securing me to him.

"Where did you think I was going to go?" I asked as I pulled way. Bo held me at arm's length.

"Well, that was a lot of information." Bo released one hand from me and ran it through his distressed hair.

"Actually, it really wasn't and I'm fine with that. I need to tell you, I ran through a lot of scenarios in my head, and they all led me back here, to you. You're you, Bo, and I'm me; there's going to be stuff that we have to work through as we get to know each other's nuts and bolts. No one ever just spills it all out on day one." I poured all the passion I could through my eyes as I looked at him.

"I've said it before, and I'll say it again—you're perfect, November. I was so distracted during the last set I played; those seven songs took an eternity to get through. I didn't know if I'd find you out here when I was done. As soon as I saw the look on your face I knew that no matter what your mouth said, your heart was still mine." He held my face the entire time he spoke, and punctuated it with a longing kiss.

I wrapped my arms around his neck and held on for dear life—

my new life. A life that would forever, hopefully, include Bo Cavanaugh. I certainly wasn't going to throw all of that at him, but I knew my decisions from there on out would be based with this fact in mind; Bo is mine. Our lips touched, and our tongues intertwined for what felt like the first time in days. I ran my hands roughly through his hair as he grasped the back of my neck. I grazed my hands over his shoulders and down his tight arms, resting them on his hips. He pulled me in tighter.

"Uh, mhmm?" A throat-cleansing cough pulled us apart.

I pulled away from my favorite reality to see Josh standing awkwardly in the doorway.

"Joshua," I said teasingly, "what can we do for you?"

Bo laughed as he placed one last kiss on my neck and turned around.

"I was, uh, can I talk to you?" He shrugged as he walked toward me.

"Oh, sure, of course. Bo, could you give us a few?" Bo looked at me with a sarcastic smile. "I really do mean just a few."

"Ha!" He brushed my hair over my shoulder. "Sure, I'll go inside and play a few more songs."

"Great!" Josh entered. "They'll love it. Everyone's bummed you're leaving town."

Just like that the wind left my sails. I was heading to Concord with Bo, and would be there until at least Monday afternoon, but what would happen after that? I really hadn't given much thought to "then what" until Josh spoke. Once again I was left with more questions than answers, but reminded myself that love was the answer I'd settled on during my walk.

"You OK Ember? You look pale," Josh asked.

"Yeah, it's just been a crazy couple of days." I nudged Bo inside. He didn't seem convinced by my answer, but his hand gave mine a quick hug before he headed inside.

Josh sat at one of the tables just off the deck, and I sat down next to him. He fidgeted with his hands. Although he'd asked me to talk, I gathered I was going to have to be the first one to speak.

"Where's Monica?" I cracked the silence.

"She was still tired from last night. She headed home when she realized you were still walking, or thinking, or whatever. She said it was OK if I talked to you." Josh's nerves were audible above the surf.

"Josh, it's OK, we're friends. How'd your talk with Monica go?"

"Good. I was *such* an ass to back away from her because I was scared. Truth is, I didn't back away from her because I thought she *wasn't* my 'thousand lifetimes'; I backed away because she is." For the first time since he stepped outside, Josh's eyes met mine. *Holy shit, he's serious.*

"Well why did you—I'm sorry, what?" I looked at him as if he had just spoken in a foreign tongue.

"Yea, I know, total guy move, right? I was just so blown away by what Bo said he felt for you. He was, at least in part, describing how I felt for Monica and it freaked me out. I've never had any commitment issues, but I panicked." Josh shook his head in disbelief as he heard his own words.

"I wish you would have at least said something to me before you turned her into a crying mess. I can't begin to tell you how little I thought of you in that moment. Ha, well, it looks like I'm telling you how little I thought of you. I knew something was off with how quick and random it was; you didn't even look her in the eyes Josh. Christ! Really, you should have talked to me first." I narrowed my eyes, condemning the past he was trying to forget.

"No," he shook his head, "I couldn't. I would have had to tell you what Bo said, and that's his business, not mine."

"Ha. Now *that* is a total guy move," I laughed as I stood and walked over to him. "So, I'm guessing you guys are OK?"

Josh stood and welcomed my hug. I loved Josh dearly, and the fact that he was my best friend's boyfriend made the reunion that much sweeter.

"Yea, but she said if I pulled a stunt like that again she'd make out with Adrian Turner in front of me."

I broke out in full-bellied laughter at the thought of Adrian, who makes every guy instantly insecure, kissing Monica to spite Josh.

"She's not kidding, and he'd totally do it, too. Hey, where is Adrian anyway?" I was silently thrilled that I didn't think of him from the time I left the deck until this very moment.

"He took off after he came inside. He told Mon he'd see you guys in Concord on Monday." Josh shrugged.

Instantly I was irritated. He couldn't even say goodbye to me after all the mess that took place outside? Noting the look on my face, Josh offered more.

"He didn't want to watch you and Cavanaugh, so he bolted."

Despite my annoyance, I was grateful for his departure. I would tell Monica about the blackmail issue after the meeting on Monday; I didn't need her all freaked out during our meeting with Tristan MacMillian and William Holder. I was more determined than before to make this collaboration between our organizations work; a thousand lifetimes upped the ante, after all.

We walked inside to catch the end of Bo's set. He was singing something that must have been his, because I didn't recognize it from anywhere. We only caught the last line that he husked in a sultry voice to the microphone,

"...*green eyes to blue*
and an I love you..."

Josh threw his arm around me in a playful squeeze.

"That boy has it bad, Em." Relaxed and fun Josh was back.

"What are you talking about, that's not about me—is it?" I asked, though I already knew the answer. "When did he have time to write that?"

"Musicians, write all the time in their head. Everything you've ever said or done in front of him is catalogued for future use." Josh was serious; he knew music and their musicians.

Bo thanked the crowd and left the stage with his guitar still slung over his shoulder. *Seriously, could he get any hotter?* As he got closer, his post-set grin turned to a passionate stare. The urgency in his unexpected kiss took the strength out my legs. As much as I wanted to leave for Concord with him tomorrow, I knew that would mean that the last week was coming to an end.

"Bo," I gasped as I pulled his waist closer to mine, tilting my head back, "take me home." Now was not the time for questioning.

CHAPTER EIGHTEEN

Darkness enveloped me as hollow footsteps threatened from behind. I ran faster. Even though I knew I was dreaming, it felt so real. Sounds of muted pain echoed in my ears as I screamed for help. In the distance I heard him call, "Are you OK?"

"Ember? Hey, Ember, wake up!" Bo's voice rang with panic.

I sat up in a flash, breathing heavily, looking around. *It was just a dream.* Embarrassed, my cheeks flushed. "Sorry," I tried to regulate my breath, "bad dream." Bo pulled me into his chest and kissed the top of my head as I struggled to pull myself back to reality.

"Hey, don't be sorry. I had vivid night terrors the year after my parents died." He squeezed me tighter, "What was it about?"

"Just... being chased." I shrugged as the nightmare slipped away.

"Well, good thing you run." He playfully rolled me over and swatted my butt, eliciting a horrifically girlish giggle from my throat.

"Can we go to Concord yet? Do you have to check out of your hotel?" I smirked as I stepped out of bed.

"We can leave whenever, I checked out last night." He winked as he rose to meet me at my bedroom door.

"Overconfident much?" I playfully punched him in the stomach as he slid past me and headed for the bathroom

I stared at the closed bathroom door, remembering our night. All the anxiety and stress from our morning dealing with Josh, to the revelation of Bo's blackmailing, slipped away as soon as we left Finnegan's.

When we returned to my apartment, I got in the shower. Having heard a small knock on the door, I poked my head out from behind the curtain; Bo stood before me in naked splendor. Wordlessly, I let him in. We spent several minutes soaping each other, washing the heavy off our shoulders and down our backs. He lifted me against the shower wall and kissed me without mercy or pause. He carried me to the bedroom before we collapsed breathlessly in each other's arms. Passion toweled us dry against my sheets until dawn. Yes, last night was a home run.

"Yo, Dream Girl, you OK?" Bo was suddenly in front of me, snapping me out of my memory.

"Are you picking on me for having a nightmare?" My brow furrowed.

"Jesus, no, sorry," he chuckled, "you're just...never mind." He smiled as he lifted me and spun me around. "Let's get the hell out of here," he breathed into my ear.

I called Monica before Bo and I left. I told her I talked to Josh last night, and encouraged her to spend the weekend really talking with him and working it out—they were so good together I couldn't bear the disaster that would follow a full break up.

As we headed off the Cape, I thumbed through Bo's CDs and his iPod.

"Indigo Girls, Alanis, *The Wailin' Jenny's*... are you sure there's not a vagina hiding in this car somewhere?" I teased as I looked back and mockingly searched.

Bo chuckled, "I like good music, and that is good music; there are some balls in there—keep looking." He grinned as he grabbed my hand and brought it to his lips.

After a few minutes of Mumford and Sons, I took a breath and forged ahead with the question I rehearsed in my head all night and this morning.

"What's the blackmail about?" I turned to face him.

Bo swallowed hard and released my hand, placing his back on the steering wheel. "I'm not really supposed to—"

"Fuck Adrian Turner." I cut him off.

"It's not just that, Ember..."

"Well either it's such a big deal that you should drop me off on the side of the road right now so I can run scared back to Barnstable, or it's handled enough that you can tell me. I don't get naked and tell just anyone that I love them, Bowan, you have to trust me. Trust is really important, you know." I realized with building irritation, that I hated not being trusted.

"November, you can trust me, too. I just don't want anyone to get hurt." His tone told me I'd pushed far enough.

"Sorry," I said as I turned my shoulders back to the windshield and let out a long breath. I reached for the "play" button again, but he stopped me.

"No, it's OK. Look, you're right; I owe you *something* after all we've gone through this last week."

"I'm sorry for pushing you, it's your business..." I conceded, though I really wanted to know.

"It's about Rachel."

"Your sister?" My pulse quickened as my voice rose.

"Yea."

"Does she know?"

"No." His face paled.

"What the hell?"

"They knew if they went to her for the money she'd probably tell me and I'd kick their asses. They were smart; they went directly to me, threatening to expose some nude and other graphic pictures of her from her drug using days. If she even remembers taking them, she certainly doesn't know they're still around. She's my Achilles's—I'd do absolutely anything to protect her, Ember. Those pictures, and that part of her life, need to burn with the assholes that have held onto them." He clenched his fist against the steering wheel before continuing, "No one else at DROP knows about it, not even David Bryson—just our legal team." He glanced at me out of the corner of his eye.

"Wow. You said you knew who was blackmailing you, though, so why wouldn't you just go to the police?"

"We have to build the case, and it's a small town. When you're as wealthy as my family is... I couldn't risk anything getting out before we were ready. I involved the legal team because they are from all over and didn't grow up with me, my friends, or my parents. When dealing with blackmail, you've got to push it to the breaking point to mount as many charges as possible," he replied unapologetically.

When we pulled in to Concord, I was momentarily disoriented by the lack of ocean. It reminded me that I needed to get off the Cape a little more. Bo drove me through town, giving me a drive-through tour of his birthplace. He pointed out his favorite restaurants, his high school, and we passed DROP's main office.

"Nice spot," I commented, "You can really do a lot with that location. What are some of your long-term hopes for the community centers?" We were in Concord for business, after all.

"Ideally I'd like to equip any and all centers we operate with a studio and, of course, instruments to use in those studios." A hopeful smile spread across his lips.

"That's an amazing idea! Music therapy is *huge*. I've never even been to a recording studio before, but imagine being a kid from desperate circumstances and being able to hear your instrument and your voice played back in your ear? Great idea, Bo! Technically, it would be Monica's department to help you on the ground level with that project—but, quite frankly, I call dibs." I nearly leapt out of my seat.

"You'd be awesome at it. But, wait a minute—*you've* never been inside a recording studio before?" His jaw unlocked for the first time since I brought up the blackmail.

"No. Why is that weird? Have you? Well, duh, obviously you have." I blushed at my idiocy.

"Ha. Yes, you're right and, I liked the experience so much that I built one inside my house." He straightened his posture, illustrating his pride.

"You have a recording studio in your *house?* Figures. Now your new name will have to be Lord Hotness of the Guitar and All Things Awesome." I laughed then stared out the window.

Several minutes after driving through the center of Concord, we turned onto what appeared to be a private road. We drove along its smooth surface for several more minutes, and I only saw two houses before we came upon an overbearing wrought iron gate at the end of the road. Without missing a beat, Bo threw his Audi into park, slid out of the car, and walked over to the gate. He pressed a few numbers on a keypad, and the gate slowly opened as he got back in.

"A gate? Really?" I wasn't dancing with the hippies anymore.

"What?" He shrugged passively, "It's not *my* gate—well I guess it is now but—it was my parents' house, Ember. I can't let it go." He drove through the gate and proceeded slowly down the driveway.

"I've never known a real-live person who had a gated driveway, you'll have to excuse me," I laughed, "I spent most of my time on farms, communes, a yurt..." The look on his face caused me to break in to laughter, "What?!"

"A yurt?" He howled.

"You heard it here first, Baby." I winked, "That was the last straw before I told my parents to cut the shit and let me be normal for high school. We lived in an apartment and everything—it was fucking glorious."

"That's awesome your parents would do that for you, pause their lifestyle for four years so you could settle."

"Yeah, they're swell—shit! They were going to be coming back through Barnstable this weekend and I totally forgot to tell them I'd be here; I've got to text my mom." I frantically dug for my cell phone.

Me: *Hey—I'm in Concord for the weekend with Bo—sorry for the short notice.*

Mom: *:)*

Me: *That's not a response*

Mom: *OK... yay! How's that ;)*

Me: *Be normal for once, would you?*

Mom: *We'll call when we're driving back up the coast to see where you're at. If you're still in NH maybe we'll swing by.*

Me: *You're impossible. Love you.*

Mom: *Have fun, Baby Girl.*

A wistful grin crept across my face as I put my phone back in my bag. Suddenly, my cheeks felt the heat of Bo's stare. I chanced a glance to my left and saw an unreadable expression on his face.

"What's wrong?" I asked

"You really love them, huh?"

Oh, the look was melancholy.

"I do. Being their daughter has been an eye-rolling experience, for sure, but they're great." I didn't want to elaborate too much in fear of opening barely healed wounds for him, or myself.

"Hey, do you have siblings? I never asked." Bo got out of the car.

"Nope, just me, and whatever children were living in whichever agricultural community we lived in." I smiled as I got out.

"Why don't you ever let me open the door for you?" He asked, creasing his eyebrows.

"Ha, are you serious? Um, well, for starters, my arms aren't broken." I couldn't have kept the sarcasm out of my voice if I tried.

"What am I going to do with you?" Bo huffed as he put his arms around my waist.

"Anything you want." I smiled, "But, could we get our stuff in your house first?"

We carried our bags to the grand front door; the house was absolutely gorgeous. To anyone outside of New England, the house might look ominous; it was clearly at least one hundred years old. It was white with black shutters—standard New England fare. A spacious widow's watch with a stained glass window on one side, and a regular window on the other, topped the house. I made a mental note to check the view from up there later. Bo produced a key from his pocket and opened the door.

The inside of the house was anything but antique; there had clearly been a massive remodel at some point. A large granite-floored foyer greeted us, with a grand, double-banister staircase just to the right. The foyer's ceiling was two-stories, and a window at the top poured delicious light.

"Impressive." My eyes took in the scale of the foyer and what appeared to be a dining area to the left.

Bo flashed a quick smile, "Yea, not bad for a lonely bachelor." He winked and led me up the stairs.

"How many bedrooms do you have?" I asked, noting several doorways down the straight hallway.

"Six. And three bathrooms upstairs," he said over his shoulder.

"Does Rachel stay here when she's on break from school?" I asked.

"Actually, she lives here most of the time, Durham's only about an hour away. She's staying on campus this weekend with some friends, though. She might be by sometime tonight to pick up some stuff."

"Will I get to meet her?" It was clear how much Bo loved his sister; I was jealous I didn't have a sibling with whom to share such a bond.

"Of course. And, if we miss her tonight, she'll be at the DROP meeting Monday. That's why she's staying on campus this week-end—trying to get ahead since she'll miss classes for our meeting." Bo stopped in front of a door half-way down the hall on the left, and cracked it open.

"This is my room. Well, *our* room for the weekend." He beamed.

I entered the room and felt instantly at home, it screamed Bo. A large well-made bed with dark navy bedding was positioned in the center of the wall opposite the door. The walls were sparsely adorned with family photos and a couple of autographed and framed posters of musicians.

My eyes found a family portrait on the wall adjacent to the bed and I approached it slowly. All four Cavanaugh's were smiling the trademark mega-watt smile. His parents were young, and Bo was the spitting image of his father. Rachel was pale with dark hair, just like Bo, but her eyes were darker. Vivian, their mother, was breathtakingly beautiful. While Bo looked slightly younger, maybe more carefree, this looked to be only a few years old.

"This is the last portrait of my family before my parents died." Bo startled me away from my thoughts.

"Oh, when was it taken?" I didn't break my gaze from the picture that held the gorgeous family.

"A month before they died. The pictures came in the mail a couple of weeks after their funeral." I could feel him staring at me.

"Holy shit, are you serious?" I turned and looked at him wide-eyed.

"Yeah, they saw the proofs, but never these. This was the best one; Rae and I each have one in our rooms."

"Rae?"

"Yea, Rachel's nickname."

"Cute." I smiled.

"Want a tour of the rest of the place?"

"You bet your ass I do." I slapped his butt and headed for the door. He tugged my arm and pulled me in for a deep, soft kiss.

"Well, up here is just bedrooms; Rae's is across the hall and all the way at the end is my parents' room. It just stays... well..."

"I get it." I squeezed his hand in reassurance as he led me back down the grand staircase.

Bo took me through the foyer and showed me the living room, expansive gourmet kitchen, office, and den before opening a door leading downstairs.

"Want to see the studio?" He asked with an impish grin.

"Yes!" I squealed like a little girl before I pushed past him and flew down the stairs to the full-height basement.

Bo opened the door at the bottom of the stairs and flicked on the light. Just like in the movies, there was a window looking into the expansive room. I could see the studio space itself and to the back was the control room, also with a large window. This was no DIY project; this was some state-of-the-art recording shit. I reminded myself to close my mouth as I walked in, lest I look the fool.

"Rae and Ash would *love* this." I stated out loud.

"What?" Bo asked, thoroughly confused.

"Ha. Sorry. My mom's nickname is also Rae, it's short for Raven. My dad's name is Ashby, but I call him Ash most of the time. 'Mom' and 'Dad' were out of the question for them when I was growing up." I shrugged as I entered the control room, grazing my fingers across all of the slides and dials.

"Wait a minute," Bo said, entering the control room behind me.

"I know, I know, it's weird to call your parents by their first names—it's just what it is." I smiled.

"No, *that* I get." He chuckled, "Your parents are Raven and Ashby Harris?" He placed his hands on my shoulders and looked me square in the face.

"Yes, my name is November, their names are Ashby and Raven, and we all share the same last name." I swallowed hard, thinking it was impossible that he was going where I hoped he wasn't.

"Cute, Ember. Let's try it this way; are your parents *the* Raven and Ashby Harris?"

I stood in shocked silence as he reached to a shelf of albums above my head, thumbing through them. When I realized what he was doing, I finally spoke.

"*Shit.* Are you fucking kidding me?" I whispered. My eyes

widened as blood raced to my face.

Bo pulled out a straight-up old school vinyl record. The cover read, "Earth Mama by The San Diego Six" and graced the pictures of my parents and four of their closest friends. I made no facial expression as he held the record up next to his face and smiled.

"How the fuck... you know what? Never mind. I can't believe this," I said all at once as I plunked in the chair behind me, burying my face in my hands.

"How could you not tell me that your parents are, or were, in one of the most popular indie folk bands from San Diego in the eighties and early nineties?" He grabbed my shoulders again and shook them playfully, like he was breaking the news to me.

"Um, how about because my parents were in one of the most popular indie folk bands from San Diego in the eighties and early nineties, and exactly *no one* our age knows about that? This is un-fucking-believable!" I broke into hysterical laughter, "Where did you even get that?"

"My parents had it in a huge collection of albums. I was sorting through their stuff after they died and found this gem. So, November Blue Harris, how is it that *you've* never been inside a recording studio?" He suggested I was lying.

"Well, Officer, maybe I did go in one when I was younger, but they were mainly touring. I think they only recorded one new album after I was born and I don't really remember that. So, it's possible that I crawled around a studio once or twice. I swear to you right now, do *not* say anything to Monica, Josh, or Adrian—none of them know." I snapped the record from his hand and looked at it, feeling a knot tighten in my stomach.

"What's the deal? They're awesome," he said a little less playfully.

I feigned indifference, "It's just..." I rolled my eyes and huffed, "It's just kind of a long story. It's not important." My eyes shot to the floor.

"Hey," he lifted my chin as he sat in the chair across from me, "what is it?" He spoke softly.

I looked to the left and the right, trying to find a topic of discussion to get us out of this Ashby and Raven vortex, but I couldn't; we *were* in a recording studio after all. I yielded a sigh and slowly brought my eyes to his.

"Fine. Look. Remember the first night we met and I told you about how my parents are hippies, and later I told you how I finally got them to agree to settle in one place long enough for me to attend high school?"

"Yeah."

"That's the sugared-up Cliff's Notes version. The truth is I was part of their little traveling show with Six—that's what I called them. They were recording the album in your hands while my mom was pregnant with me—which is why she's pregnant on the cover. It's actually kind of funny that you have the vinyl, they didn't make many. You may want to hang on to that." I laughed dismissively.

"Anyway, I grew up being home-schooled as they travelled up and down the West Coast. By the time I was fourteen, I wanted to go to a real high school so I begged, *begged* to be in one place for it. They smiled, said 'sure', and let me pick the place which is how we ended up on the East Coast. I wanted to be as far away from San Diego as possible." Tears betrayed my eyes.

Bo looked a little confused; I stopped him when he opened his mouth.

"You know, when we moved to Connecticut, it was the first time I had my own room for more than a few days. It was the first time we lived somewhere rather than *stayed* somewhere. I felt so proud of myself for convincing them to move, let alone three thousand miles away. It was empowering. I learned if I asked, I could get, hence my stellar grant writing," I laughed, "But as I went through high school I just got fucking pissed. I was a *kid* and they dragged me along in their life without giving me one of my own. They were so selfish while they touted free love, peace, and harmony; I thought they were such hypocrites."

"Well, it sure explains a lot about you." Bo wiped the tear from my cheek

"Sorry, I don't mean to be bitching about my parents. But that night on the beach, when we first met, you said 'You take what you get and you use it for what you want.' That's what I did with my parents. I got exactly what I didn't want, so I modeled my life the opposite way." I shrugged.

"Real mature," he huffed.

"Excuse me?" My face heated, drying my tears.

"You're so damn talented with your voice, and a clear natural on the guitar, and yet you won't do anything with it because of some life your parents chose for themselves? Sounds to me like they're still doing the choosing," his voice wavered between sarcasm and anger.

I opened my mouth to answer, stunned with shock, but I jumped up when I heard a door slam upstairs.

"Bowan? Bo?! Are you here?" A female voice tore through the house.

"Who the hell is that?" My scant jealousy irritated me.

"That," he smiled, "is Rachel. Prepare to meet my sister."

CHAPTER NINETEEN

"Down here Rae!" Bo hollered up the stairs.

I quickly composed myself from his 'mature' comment in order not to seem like a total snob in front of his sister, but I was still pissed.

Light footsteps bounded down the stairs. When Rachel entered, the whole vibe of the room changed. She was smaller than I thought she'd be, probably 5'4", and she was quite thin, but wore that huge smile I'd become accustomed to from Bo. He opened his arms for a hug, and his size swallowed her.

"You're early," Bo said.

"Yeah, need to get back to the campus library to get some work done before they close for the night." She beamed and turned to me.

"You must be November. It's great to meet you!" She squealed. I stuck out my hand but she wrapped her arms around me instead. *She's cute as a friggin button.*

"That's me. I gather Bo's mentioned me?" I smiled as I backed away.

"Are you kidding? You're all I've heard about for the last week." She shot a teasing glance at her brother.

"OK, Rae, that's enough." For the first time, I saw Bo blush, eliciting a giggle.

"Whatever, Bo, you have it bad for her—let's just get it out there. OK, so, do you guys want to get lunch?" Rae smiled at me.

"I'm starving, that sounds great."

As we headed up the stairs I realized I could be good friends with Rachel Cavanaugh; she had spunk.

When we returned from lunch, Rachel headed upstairs to pack her things for the weekend. I had pushed the blackmail to the back of my mind, which was good since Rachel didn't know, and I certainly didn't want to be the one to tell her. During lunch I got a glimpse of a young Bo Cavanaugh and it was quite a trip. It turned out that Bo played the piano until he started getting picked on by some of his friends, and then he begged his parents to let him play the 'much cooler' guitar. Luckily it worked out for him, though Rachel let it spill that Bo still plays the piano—which would explain its presence in the recording studio.

"You're sister's great," I said as I followed Bo into the kitchen.

"I love her so much. When our parents died we grew even closer; we're all each other have left. My parents have family on the West Coast, but we're not close with them." While his voice was sweet when discussing Rachel, there was a tense undercurrent of worry.

Bo's phone rang. His face darkened when he looked at the caller ID.

"Um, I'll leave you alone; I'm going to wander up to the widow's watch." I gave him a quick peck on the cheek, turned on my heels and didn't look back—having an idea what that call was about.

The winding stairway to the upper most point in the house was brightly lit from the sun. When I reached the top and opened the door, Rachel and I both jumped.

"Sorry, Bo got a call so I'm wandering." I stood outside of the room.

"Come in, silly. It's not like I'm naked in here," Rachel laughed.

When I entered, I gasped at the view. I didn't know the city limits of Concord, but was pretty sure I could see them from where I stood. The stained glass window cast rainbow shadows throughout the room, but enough natural light peered in to keep out the church feel. The windows went all the way to the floor, where Rachel sat cross-legged.

"Sit." She patted the dark wooden floor next to her. I sat, mimicking her position, and admired the view.

"It's so peaceful," I whispered.

"Isn't it great? I feel like I've spent half my life up here," she said wistfully. "So, you've had some meetings with Bo at your organization, right?" She turned to me.

"Yeah, we had a couple last week, including one with David Bryson," I said, looking back at her.

"So, then, you know 'my story.'" She put in air-quotes.

"Oh. Yeah, I do." I shrugged, trying to keep emotion out of my voice.

"I just don't want you to feel uncomfortable around me. I'm working on myself all the time. Everyone knows, most people aren't assholes about it."

"Most people?"

"Well, you know, when you're in your early twenties, your friends tell you they just want you to come out with them 'to dance' or just 'hang out.' Sometimes I can do that, no problem, but it's the days that I'm feeling sad, depressed, angry, or otherwise weak that I don't want to be around all of that. So, I don't go out, and they don't always get it." I was impressed by her maturity and confidence.

We sat in silence for a few more seconds, before Bo's footsteps drummed up the stairs.

"There you guys are," he said as he entered the room. "Rae, I thought for sure you sent Ember running for the hills." He sat between us.

"Ha. Hardly, Bo. You have no idea how happy it makes me to

finally see you happy," Rachel cooed as she rested her head on Bo's shoulder.

Watching them, it was the first time I realized that I couldn't comprehend the weight that had been on Bo's shoulders for the past few years. The thought sent fresh tears to my eyes; I excused myself and made a bee-line to Bo's bedroom.

When I got to his room I called Monica.

"Hey Em! How's the trip?" She sounded cheerful, which was a good sign as far as she and Josh were concerned.

"It's great so far. You should see his place—it's a fucking palace. He has a recording studio in his basement." I stopped there to avoid revealing my parents album that she had no idea about.

"You sound weird, is everything OK?" *How does she do that?*

"Yea. I met his sister, she's great Mon. She loves Bo so much, it's lovely to see but heartbreaking at the same time, knowing what they've been through." I felt better getting it out there, and the tears stayed at bay.

"Well, he's amazing, we all knew that. Have a great rest of the weekend and call or text me with the inappropriate details."

"Hey, wait, how are things with Josh?"

"All good." I could tell by the smile in her voice that he was standing next to her.

"Get a room. Bye."

Suddenly, exhaustion bested me. Bo and Rachel were still up in the watch talking, so I crossed over to the bed. As I lay back, on top of the blankets, the emotional ups and downs of the week caught up with me and I gave in to the warm embrace of sleep.

"Ember. Hey," soft whispers pulled me from a deep sleep. "Babe, wake up." Bo kissed from my forehead to my collarbone.

I peeled my eyes open. According to the alarm clock it was 6:00pm; I'd been asleep for a few hours.

"Shit, sorry, I was exhausted." I sat up slowly and tilted my head side to side. "Did I miss Rachel leaving? Did she go back to school yet?" I yawned.

"No, actually she likes you so much she wanted to stay and have dinner with us. She's meeting some friends right now and we'll catch up with her at the pub in an hour. Wanna shower?" Bo grinned ear to ear.

"Mmm. You bet I do."

I sat up on my knees and rapped my arms around his neck; pressing my mouth to his. He responded by forcing my hips back down to the bed. Without wasting time, I pulled his shirt up and tossed it on the floor. He did the same with mine, before reaching for my pants.

"I love you, November." He kept his hands on my face as he pulled away. Every single time he'd said that, he'd looked right in my eyes. This time was no different.

"I love you," I replied, gripping the back of his neck.

Whatever spell he had me under, I didn't want the cure. I could live the rest of my life bewitched by the likes of Bo Cavanaugh.

We showered and got ready to go meet his sister for dinner. I was glad that we didn't have sex before we left the house, neither of us would have been able to remove the grin from our faces.

"Hey, by the way, if you ever need to get into the gate at the end of the driveway, 7325 is the code," he said nonchalantly as we pulled off his property on to the road.

"How mighty trusting of you." I winked.

"Come on, Ember, you have my heart and soul, what's a gate code?"

"Are you serious? How do you come up with that stuff?! I mean, it makes me swoon, *seriously* swoon. But, come on." I stared at him with an open mouth.

"What? It's true. Look, I learned the hard way the lesson of telling people exactly how you feel because you don't know if it could be your last moment together." He stared straight ahead, driving down the road.

"Oh, true... Sorry." I turned back to the road.

When we arrived at the restaurant, Rachel was outside talking with some friends who were smoking. She beamed when she saw us.

"Guys! Over here!" She waved frantically.

"Hey Rae, do we have a table?" Bo asked.

"Yeah. Guys," she gestured to her friends, "this is Bo's girlfriend November. Hot name, right?" She bragged while I shook hands with her friends outside.

Girlfriend. The word made me blush as soon as it left her lips and it didn't go unnoticed that Bo reddened, too.

When we were seated inside, Bo asked if I wanted a drink. I shot a cautionary glance toward Rachel.

"Oh, please, go ahead. I'm fine. You're sweet." She touched my hand and narrowed her eyes playfully at Bo. "Don't fuck it up with her please, she's awesome."

Bo shook his head and wandered up to the bar.

"You're great, Rachel," I turned toward her while Bo got my drink.

"Please, call me Rae. And, *you're* great. Bo's been infinitely happier since he started spending time with you."

"What, is he typically depressed or something?" It dawned on me I had no idea how Bo was day-to-day.

"No, it's not really anything like that. It's just... since he started getting DROP off the ground again, he's been all business. He doesn't spend a ton of time with his friends—which is OK, because most of them are staunch dickwads anyway—but I sometimes feel he's missing out." She shrugged as she played with her straw.

A rather excessive giggle caught my attention across the restaurant.

"Who's that?" I nodded toward a slender strawberry-blonde woman talking to Bo. Her head was cocked to the side like a puppy.

"God, that's Bowan's ex-girlfriend. Can we say 'Stepford Wife'? This is a pub, lady, ditch the pearls already." Rachel barely looked in her direction, which I took to be a good sign.

"Hm. She's pretty, what's her name?" I asked, trying to be indifferent.

"Ainsley Worthington."

"Of course it is." It slid out before I could stop it.

"Ha!" Rachel spit some of her water back in her glass.

"What?" I cracked a smile.

"What do you mean, of course it is?"

"Seriously? Worthington? Could there be a wealthier name in all of New Hampshire?" I raised my eyebrows.

"Yep, Cavanaugh, which is why Ainsley's panties are all in a bunch over there," Rachel panned. "She and Bo were already broken up, but after our parents died she tried using his grief to get back in his pants because she's a complete tramp. Bo hasn't given her the time of day in four years, but bless her heart she keeps trying. It only got worse after he started playing here. You should see the spectacle she makes of herself." Rachel rolled her eyes.

"Rae, I think I'm in love with you," I laughed.

"Well, seriously, her family has plenty of money," she giggled, "Can't she stay away from ours?"

Bo nodded in our direction, and Ainsley looked at us, causing Rachel to smile and wave excitedly. I guessed that Rachel had words with her at one time or another by the way Ainsley forced a smile and a barely polite wave back. Ainsley gave Bo a quick hug before he turned and walked back to the table.

"Sorry guys," Bo said as he sat down.

"Yeah, we saw," Rachel said cynically.

"What? Rae, cut me a break! Ember, are you pissed?" Bo's voice rose to an unnatural octave.

"What? Me? Noooo," I exaggerated. "I don't know her, so it was less her personality that bothered me and more her hands' proximity to the rest of you."

"Ha, ha," Rachel hooted, "Bo, marry Ember today, right now. What the hell is Ainsley doing here anyway? Are there no other restaurants in Concord?" Rachel paused for a moment before her face lit up in a wicked grin.

"Oh the poor dear, she thought you were going to play tonight, didn't she? She didn't count on Ember—oh my God what did you tell her about Ember?" Rachel was nearly bouncing in her seat.

"She didn't ask. She probably thinks that Ember's one of your friends, and I'd like to keep it that way for now."

"Um, what?" I couldn't keep the irritation out of my voice.

"Smart, bro. You see Ember, as I said before, Ainsley is a tramp."

"Rae!" Bo said tersely.

"Prove me wrong Bo, prove me wrong. Anyway, she's a tramp, so if she knew Bowan was with a *girlfriend,* it would only make the situation worse. But, since she's left the restaurant with her tail between her trampy legs, feel free to engage in all the PDA you want."

"Classy Rae," Bo said as the waiter came to our table. We broke in to laughter and placed our order.

While we ate our dinner, I was overcome with the heartening feeling that Rachel was the sister I never had.

CHAPTER TWENTY

"Bye Ember, it was great to meet you," Rachel said as she climbed into her Lexus.

"You too. See you Monday. Rachel." I smiled and waved as she drove away.

"I had a great time tonight," I said to Bo as we headed back to his house. "Rachel's a trip, I like her a lot."

"She really likes you, too." Bo grabbed my hand.

"I love seeing you two together; makes me kind of bummed that I'm an only child."

"She's my world. Rather, was. Now you're in it too." He kissed a smile against my knuckles.

"I love you," I sighed as his kisses sent chills throughout my body.

When we got to the house, Bo led me wordlessly up to his bedroom. He kicked off his shoes and lifted my dress over my head before carrying me to his bed. He set me down and backed up to unbutton his shirt. He slid into bed next to me, pulling me close.

"I meant what I said before, you know; 'love' just doesn't cover what I feel for you, Ember." He kissed me from my neck to my ear.

Taking his time with sweet movements, Bo kissed my entire body. Our bodies moved together as they had since we met. I gripped his back with all my might, approving the pull from within. Bo kept his forehead on mine, our lips never parting as our bodies formed one picture of pure emotion.

Neither one of us made a single sound aside from our heavy breathing. My throat was choked with feelings I never knew I held inside; we made love—true love. The word 'love' seemed so bland in comparison to what happened between our bodies. I could barely wrap my head around what we expressed; there truly were no words. Our bodies spoke our souls' language.

As one motion flowed seamlessly to the next, I realized I could do this forever. Forever is not a word that'd ever been a part of my vocabulary; but as I drifted to sleep in Bo's solid arms, it was the only word on my mind.

The deepness of my sleep did not keep the dreams away.

"Hey, hey! Are you OK?" the distant voice echoed.

"Yes," I whispered, looking around for the source of the voice.

"Get out of here," the voice demanded.

"But—"

"Out!"

I woke breathless and in a panic, disoriented by my surroundings. I steadied my breathing when I remembered I was in Bo's bedroom but when I looked to my left, he wasn't there. The clock read 2:51 AM.

"Bo?" I climbed out of bed and threw on his t-shirt and my panties.

I paused in the doorway leading to the hall and listened, but couldn't hear anything.

"Bo?" I said again, heading down the stairs.

The cold granite floor of the foyer was unforgiving against my bare feet. A soft melody drifting through the air broke through the massive scale of the dark house. I made my way through the living room and kitchen and stopped at the top of the stairs leading to the basement. I could hear the music louder now; it was a single guitar playing in the studio.

What the hell is he doing down here at this hour?

I tip-toed down the stairs. The studio door was open, allowing the sweet melody to meet my ears. Bo's back was to me and he was hunched over his guitar; the only light came from a single lamp on the piano. He was shirtless, and sat only in his black boxer briefs. Goosebumps formed on my arms and I wondered how he could be comfortable in the cold room.

My eyes sketched along the strong lines and deep contours of his body. Each time he slid his left hand up and down the neck of the guitar, the muscles of his back flexed in response—a visual metronome. The large black cross on his back stood in stark contrast to the sparseness of the room and caused me to catch my breath. My soul begged on bended knees for me to run to him; to give in to the physical craving that burned at full heat between us.

"Hey." I rapped lightly on the door, to avoid scaring the hell out of him.

Bo turned around quickly and his eyes brightened, "Hey, did I wake you?"

"Hardly, you're all the way down here. I woke up and you weren't next to me so I came looking."

Don't tell him you had another nightmare.

"Well, here I am." He put his guitar down and opened his arms.

"Couldn't sleep?" I asked as I sat on his lap and wrapped my arm around his neck.

"I don't typically sleep well, not in the last few years anyway." His previously light tone was now raked with sadness.

"Oh..."

"I like having you here, November; it's nice to have someone else in this big, old house. Rae's here, but she stays with friends a lot to avoid driving back and forth to school every day." A blanket of loneliness swathed his eyes.

"I like it here; the house has a real family feel to it." I grimaced

TEN DAYS OF PERFECT

at my lifelong desire to live in a single-family house.

"Hey, about earlier, when I pushed you about your parents and how you grew up—I'm sorry. It wasn't my place. I can't imagine what my life would be like right now if I'd never had a place to call home." He grabbed my hips and turned me so that I was straddling him.

"Don't worry about it. I've never really thought about it that way before—my parents still calling the shots." I shrugged, "But, ever since I met you, I've considered another lifestyle entirely—you know, running away and all—so it's nearly a moot point."

I kissed him teasingly, but he grabbed my chin and pulled me in for the real deal; I could feel his grin on my lips.

"Rachel said you can still play the piano. Play something for me. I'll sit in the recording room; I've always wanted to hear how things sounded in there."

"What do you want me to play?" His reticence was poorly concealed.

"Whatever is on the stand," I said, walking into the control room.

Bo's brow crinkled a bit, then relaxed as he took a breath and headed to the piano. I looked around for the speaker switch in the control room and, when I flicked it on, I heard another deep breath come from Bo as he sat on the bench.

"Let's see what you got, rock star." I winked into the mic.

Bo didn't look at me, and I noticed his mouth formed into a slight frown. He tilted his head to one side, then the other, before stretching out his fingers and hitting the keys. He didn't warm up, he just took off. I was wrapped in the blanket of the dark, bittersweet song that came from the piano. Bo's shoulders moved in time with his hands; he was a sight to behold.

The droning repetitive tones from his left hand and the sparse, chilling high tones from his right collided in my throat, forcing me to suppress a sob. I didn't recognize the melody, but my body felt it anyway; anticipating each note. The single lamp remained on in the recording room, but I couldn't see Bo's face. His dark, arresting figure over the piano was unsettling. I needed to see him.

My palms broke into a sweat as I stood and crossed slowly to the piano. I was mesmerized at the intensity with which he played. I stood motionless behind him. This was different than his passion with the guitar, it was a different level of deep—it was haunting. Unable to resist, I carefully placed one hand on each of his shoulders. Bo slowly relaxed back into my body, but continued to play.

His skin was pulsing, burning with whatever emotion was coursing through his veins. I chanced a glance at the sheet music; my mouth ran dry as all the moisture from my body huddled in my eyes. It was hand-written on staff paper and titled, 'Goodbye', with the initials 'B.C' barely visible underneath it. I muted the sharp gasp that escaped my mouth with my hand; he'd written the song for his parents.

When Bo finished the song he sat motionless facing the piano. Without turning around, he placed his left hand on mine. Expelling a labored sigh, he blindly reached his right hand behind him and pulled mine away from my mouth; bringing it back down to his shoulder. He kept his hands firmly atop mine, never turning around. I swallowed hard, begging ineffectually for moisture to return to my mouth. Soon, the last lingering chord of the piano drifted away and silenced the room. Seconds felt like minutes as we stayed frozen, unmoving, letting the funeral hymn hang in suffocating silence around us.

I leaned forward and kissed the top of his head and he kissed each one of my hands. When he turned around, I nearly buckled at the sight before me; his eyes were black holes of sorrow and grief, yet still held unmistakable beauty. The space between his eyebrows sank into a deep crevasse of hollow pain. A tear threw itself down my face at the sight of his brokenness and I wanted to look away, but couldn't bring myself to emotionally abandon him.

He placed his forehead on my stomach for a second, taking a deep breath and pulling me to his lap. I kissed his temple and his nose before he grabbed each side of my face and drew me into his mouth. This kiss was different. It was pleading; begging me to understand, begging me to pull him up from the hole that opened as soon as he started playing that song. His grip moved to my waist and a restrained moan sprang from his throat.

I pulled my face away and stared at him. Tears flowed freely, now, down his cheeks; my thumbs couldn't wipe them all away before they splashed on my thighs. With one bottomless, primal sounding wail, his forehead pressed into my shoulder as he gave in to the music, his body quaking beneath my arms. Grief encased me; I buried my head in his neck and met him sob for sob, my legs wrapped tightly around his waist.

After what felt like several minutes, our mouths found and comforted each other between silent cries of love and loss.

"Ember," he forced apologetically between kisses and tears.

"Don't. I love you. This is what it means."

I didn't elaborate, and he didn't respond as we continued making love with our clothes on and our souls bared.

CHAPTER TWENTY-ONE

Sunlight speared through a tiny part in Bo's heavy curtains as I awoke in his arms. By the time we made our way back to his bed from the studio, we both buckled under emotional enervation and fell asleep immediately.

I peered up at a still-sleeping Bo. *How do guys look so young when they're sleeping?* Tilting my head, I kissed under his chin before nuzzling back into his neck. *Forever.* The thought rang loudly in my ears; my heart raced at the want of forever, and the realization that tomorrow morning would be the last time I woke in Bo's bed for who knows how long.

"Mmmm, I could get used to waking up like this." Bo just barely opened his mouth and eyes, as he tightened his arms around me.

His swollen, red eyes were the only reminder of being in the studio last night; I realized mine must look the same. Without question, he had played his song for me. I saw and tasted the suffering, but he never stopped. He didn't question when I absentmindedly asked him to play the music on the piano; he trusted me with his soul completely. He told me he loved me by baring the very essence of his soul, *without hesitation.*

"Good morning." I shifted upward and stretched my arms overhead. I combed my fingers through his hair.

He planted a kiss on each hipbone before sitting next to me, knees bent. He draped his arm around my shoulders and pulled me back in to him; there was no awkwardness in our silence—it was perfect comfort.

I reached for my cell phone to check any missed messages, and noticed an email I'd missed from last night. It was from William Holder, DROP's grant writer, telling me he was looking forward to meet me and wondered if he and I could schedule a time to go over our contacts.

"Do you have anything planned for today?" I turned to Bo, who sat staring at me with something playful in his eyes.

"Not really, we'll go out for drinks tonight since tomorrow will be a long day but that's about it, why?"

"I got an email yesterday from your grant writer asking to get together sometime so we could go over our contacts, and all that other boring grant writer nonsense. I figured since I was here, I could see if we could get the meeting out of the way before the *big* meeting tomorrow." I thumbed through the rest of my emails and texts.

Bo was silent for an inordinate amount of time. When I turned to see if he'd fallen back asleep, his face was twisted in deliberation.

"Something wrong?" I elbowed him.

"Huh? Oh, no, sorry, just spaced there for a minute. Does Bill know you're in town already?"

"No, I haven't emailed him back yet. Do I call him Bill, or is that just because you two are friends?"

"Bill's fine. Just email him and let him know you're in town, and that we'll be at McCarthy's tonight if he wants to stop in to introduce himself—we don't need to worry about other business stuff today," he dismissed, though I could tell he was pulling from reserves of lightheartedness.

Bo jumped out of bed and pulled on his blue plaid pajama pants that hung dangerously low off his hips.

"You're right. Today can be spent in frivolity. I'll email him," I giggled as I sat on my knees, heading toward him.

Bo stiffened. "I gotta head downstairs to the office for a quick sec; towels are all set in the bathroom if you want to shower." He placed a tight kiss on the top of my head before heading downstairs.

What the hell was that all about? Was he expecting me to talk about what happened last night? Shit, did I offend him by not mentioning it?

When I stepped out of the shower, I could hear Bo shuffling through his dresser.

"Hey, better?" I said into my towel as I dried my hair upside down.

"What do you mean?" He walked over and impishly messed the towel through my hair.

"You got all weird earlier, just checking." I shrugged, righting myself and wrapping the towel around my head.

"No, sorry, it's fine. I'm just tired." He slipped on his dark jeans, and pulled a snug emerald green shirt across his chest.

Shit, if that's not his color, I don't know what is.

He caught my lingering stare and straightened his shoulders proudly.

"Color of your eyes; looks good on me, I'd say." He smirked sophomorically.

"I'll say. What are we doing today? I need to dress accordingly, lest we run into the likes of Ms. Ainsley Worthington again," I quipped as I reached for my suitcase.

"*You* don't need to be worried about Ainsley, November." He was annoyed.

"Oh, I know," I added teasingly, "but I just want to make sure *she* knows." I winked.

"What am I going to do with you?" he laughed, as he lifted me in the air.

"As I said, anything you want." I pressed into his mouth desperately.

Our morning was spent ambling through town; it quickly became clear I was with New England royalty. Every shop owner engaged Bo in honest conversation, congratulating him on everything with DROP, and wishing him well with a pat on the back as he left. As we drove back to his house in the afternoon, my phone beeped with a text.

Adrian: *You're in town?*

Me: *What town? Don't you live in Boston?*

Adrian: *Concord, smartass... meeting tomorrow, remember?*

Me: *How'd you know I was here, Stalker?*

Adrian: *You caught me. I saw you and Cavanaugh walking through town today.*

"I didn't realize Adrian would be at the meeting tomorrow." I looked from my phone to Bo.

Bo shrugged. "Legal team. Does it matter? I can ask him not to come." Half his mouth turned up.

"I'm sure you could." I looked back to my phone.

Me: *yea, I'm staying with Bo... you really are a hopeless stalker Adrian*

Adrian: *Want to get together before tomorrow? I'm staying at The Centennial*

Me: *Nice try*

Adrian: *What? :)*

I leaned forward and thumped my head on the dashboard.

"What?" Bo chuckled.

"Fucking Adrian... he wants to get together before tomorrow. I told him the other day we could have some time to talk before the meeting Monday. Should I invite him to the apparent party we're hosting at McCarthy's tonight?" I asked, reminding him Bill Holder was planning on showing up.

"I suppose. Maybe I could tell Ainsley and we could make a real night of it."

I flashed him the middle finger before returning to my text.

Me: *Bo and I will be at McCarthy's tonight—9:00. Some of his friends will be there, too.*

Adrian: *see you then.*

"Well, if nothing else, tonight's going to be interesting. Hey, do you think we should hook Adrian and Ainsley up?" I jested as I pressed my head against the window. "Rachel sure has some choice words for Ainsley, what's that about?"

"Do you really want to know or are you going to get 'all girl' about it and use it to form some jealous rage?"

"Excuse me? What part of the last week and a half leads you to believe I'll act 'all girl' about *anything?*" My mouth dropped open in mock-horror.

"Ha! True. Ainsley and I dated a bit off-and-on in high school; you know-the whole cheerleader and football player deal?"

"Um, you played football? Oh, please tell me you were the quarterback." He tried, and failed, to suppress a grin as I spoke. "You were the fucking quarterback? Let me out now so I can go puke in the bushes."

"Hypocrite. Like Adrian Turner was some wallflower book-worm." Bo turned up his sarcasm.

"Fair enough. So you and the trampy cheerleader dated, trampy being Rae's word not mine." I cocked my head to the side, mimicking Ainsley's move from the night before, "Why'd you break up?"

"We went to different colleges; I went to UNH and she was down at Northeastern, it was kind of an easy out for me—the whole distance thing, since I didn't want to be with her anyway."

"You pig—love it. Rachel said she tried to get back together with you after your parents died? Better words than trampy are typically used to describe *that* kind of move." I rolled my eyes out the window.

"Yeah, it started innocently enough; I mean, we've been friends since we were little. After a few months she tried to move in on me physically and I called her on using my grief for her gain. She was pissed, but that's only because I was right."

"Well played." I nodded.

"That's really it. She still flirts with me constantly; it bugs the hell out of Rae and she's told Ainsley off a few times." A proud big-brother grin stretched across his face. "So, what about you and Turner?"

"Well, you know about all there is to know."

"Yea, Blue, I guess I do."

Ouch. Bo saw the tense look on my face.

"I'm sorry, that was out of line. Why'd you break up?"

"Well, like I told you, I told him I loved him. He said he loved me back, but I thought it was panic on his part. Wouldn't have mattered, we were too young."

"What was it, if it wasn't panic?"

"Well, the other night he told me he wasn't kidding, that it was love—that he really did love me then," I spoke in a near-whisper.

"What? What do you mean the other night?" *That was not a whisper.*

Oops.

"Oh calm down. He just thought the reason why I've basically avoided him since graduation was because I thought he was a jackass—"

"He *is* a jackass," Bo interrupted through gritted teeth.

"Easy! I know Adrian well enough to know that he wasn't telling me that to get back in my pants. *Believe me*, a guy like Adrian Turner does *not* have to use 'the L word' to get what he wants."

"What's that supposed to mean?"

"Well, haven't you seen him with women around here? Don't they just throw themselves at him? You said you knew he was 'fast' with women."

"I haven't spent much time with him apart from being with you; I just know guys like him."

"Oh, well, you'll see tonight—he doesn't have to do anything but walk in a room, kind of like you." I smirked.

"Oh for Christ's sake, *do not* compare me to Adrian." Bo rolled his eyes, exasperated, as he turned down his driveway.

"What the hell is your issue with him? As far as I can tell, he did you a huge favor by not telling me about the blackmail even though he had *ample* opportunity to. But, he let, or made, you do it. Did he make you do it?"

"No, he didn't make me do it Ember, Jesus. We covered this already; for a split fucking second Adrian knew you better than I did, and pointed out that you would likely figure the whole thing out eventually." The leather of the steering wheel groaned under his tightening grip.

"Right, and that split second is over, I'm all yours. I was all yours before Adrian ever showed up, and I'll be all yours long after he moves on." I pried his right hand off the wheel and smoothed my fingers across his.

Bo maintained the strained silence as he drove down his driveway and I shook my head thinking about going out later. *Perhaps I'll text Adrian and tell him not to come.*

"Is it going to be all weird tonight having Adrian there—if he decides to show up?" I asked as Bo exited the car.

"Oh, he'll show up. And, no, it's fine." Bo slammed the door. "Hey, why are you just sitting there—are you pissed?" He crossed over to my door.

"Just waiting for you to open the door." I shrugged and his face cracked as he let out a raucous laughter.

"Come on, let's get ready so we can go have a quiet dinner before we introduce Ainsley and Adrian—if Ainsley shows up, that is." Bo winked as he opened the door and swooped me into his arms.

"Oh, she'll show up." I mocked his previous tone, as he carried me up the front steps to his house.

CHAPTER TWENTY-TWO

"Oh, come on, are you really wearing that?!" Bo rolled over and buried his face in his pillow as I strutted across the room.

"You bet your sweet ass I'm wearing this," I purred in to the mirror, brushing off the bright red, backless halter dress as I steadied myself in my nude patent heels.

"OK, *why* are you wearing it? Are you trying to incite a riot?" His voice rang with lively wickedness as he lifted his head from his pillow.

"Ha, quite the opposite actually. I'm wearing this for several reasons. One, I look hot in it, two, you know I look hot in it, and three, there's no other way to prove to you that Adrian's not trying to get in my panties unless I wear this very dress. He'll look, don't be fooled, but if he has any residual feelings for me, they'll throw themselves on the floor in front of me." I turned to see him sitting slack-jawed.

Adrian totally has feelings for you, Blue. Let's hope he doesn't act on them.

"Alright, you cock-tease, what if he *does* throw himself in front of you?" Bo's laugh echoed in the room.

"Permission granted to kick his ass... if I don't do it first. And, I *never* tease—you know that. Now, get yourself all prettied up; you can't be seen with me looking like that."

"Alright, alright, I'll change. But first... I want to give you this." From under his bed, Bo produced a wrapped package with a card taped on the front.

"What's this?" I charmed, slinking toward him.

"A little something from the real me to the real you, November."

Ignoring the card, like an excited child, I tore the wrapping open. Inside was a hard cover music composition notebook; it was all black with no wording on the front. I cracked open the front cover and my eyes welled with tears. There, on the first page, was the lullaby, my lullaby, with Bo's original accompaniment, scribed in his hand.

Seeming to sense my lack of words, Bo grabbed my knee, "It was incomprehensible to me that someone with your talent didn't own one of these." He cocked his head, "I wanted to be the one to lead the way. You *need* to take yourself seriously here, November. I've been playing for years, and your raw talent supersedes most that have spent years in a studio," he encouraged through pleading eyes.

"Bo," I choked at the sight of my past and anticipative future together in one gorgeous visual harmony, sitting between us in the present, "this is..."

"Forever, Ember. Something brought me in to Finnegan's that night. Something sparked in me when we shook hands before you sang—"

"You felt that?" The memory of my first physical interaction with Bo warmed my senses.

"Hell yes, I felt it—it's what made me join in that damn *Wailin' Jennys* song with you. I couldn't deny the pull I felt to you and I had to test it out on stage. The crowd noticed too, Ember—it was like they were watching James Taylor and Carly Simon or something!"

Forever..." I dropped the book and sank into his body.

On the drive to McCarthy's, Bo stole several glances at me as I touched up my deep red lipstick. I was looking forward to having some uninhibited fun with him tonight, as tomorrow could change everything in terms of our flagrance around each other. If our organizations ended up collaborating—which I, hoped they did—we'd likely have to lay low while all the nuts and bolts screwed into place.

"Come back," he whispered, grabbing my hand.

"Sorry, just thinking about the meeting tomorrow." I returned my glance to the street.

"What's the matter?"

"I want the collaboration to work; it would be so great for both of our organizations and communities. Mostly, we'd have excuses to travel between our two homes, Bo. But, if it works we have to be careful, and discreet; if it doesn't, we're left as two people living nearly three hours apart..."

"It doesn't have to be three hours apart, Ember."

"Ha. What are you suggesting? That one of us moves?" I raised my eyebrows as high as they'd go and sat in shocked silence.

"What? Nothing sarcastic to tag onto that one?"

"Give me a minute..." I didn't need a minute; there was nothing sarcastic, rude, or dismissive to say to this.

"Well?"

"Well, what? Who gives up their job? I love my job, Bo—holy shit I can't believe I'm engaging in this conversation." My sweaty palms sought relief, but I couldn't mess up my dress. I shook them in the air.

"Are you freaking out? We're just talking, Ember." Bo's grip on my knee sent a calming current through my veins.

"Sorry, it's just, tonight, last night, the day before, and the eight before that I've thought of forever when I've thought of you Bo. Fucking *forever*."

He grinned, "And that's a bad thing?"

"It's a crazy person thing," I scoffed.

"Guess I'm crazy, too." His smile reached his eyes as he kissed my hand. "Let's just have some irresponsible fun tonight, and worry about all of this heady stuff tomorrow."

"Bowan Cavanaugh, are you going to try to get me drunk?" I batted my eyelashes dramatically.

"Nope, I happen to know you can do a fine job of that all on your own, Ms. Harris." He winked as we parked in front of McCarthy's Pub.

Despite the name, McCarthy's was more of a night club than a pub. Private tables surrounded the black dance floor. We were escorted promptly to one in the corner and given complimentary champagne; just another reminder of the weight the Cavanaugh name carried in Concord

"You sure know how to show a girl a good time," I toasted him and sucked down half the champagne.

Bo just shook his head as the waitress approached. He ordered for us and her smile lingered as she backed away from our table.

"Has it always been like this for you? The fawning and all?" My hands motioned back and forth in front of his body.

Even in the dim light of McCarthy's I could see Bo's cheeks redden, "Kinda, but it's hard to tell if it's because of me, my money, my parents..." He shook his head in thoughtful disbelief.

"Oh, it's you, for sure." My smoky stare did it's best to undo him.

"I'm thinking tonight that it's you; no one's eyes have left you since we walked in here Ember." His proud peacock look returned.

Looking around, I noticed he was right; we seemed to be the talk of McCarthy's. No doubt, all minds were wondering who the woman was with Concord's heir apparent; it didn't make me nervous. I felt proud and beamed the biggest smile I had.

As we ate our dinner, McCarthy's got busier, and I noticed a DJ setting up near the dance floor. I sat facing the door, which I always preferred, and that gave me the advantage of seeing Ainsley walk in before Bo did. I swallowed my second glass of champagne in one gulp.

"What was that about?" Bo stared at my empty flute.

"Told you she'd show up." I nodded in Ainsley's direction just as she caught my eye and the back of Bo's head. "Oh, would you look at how she just lights up like a Christmas tree? It's sweet, really." Sarcasm flooded our booth.

"Play nice." Bo playfully kicked me under the table.

Ainsley Worthington, all five-foot-four, strawberry blonde, and ice-blue eyes of her, walked toward us with what I now knew to be a cheerleader smile.

"Hey Bowan! I didn't know you'd be out tonight!" Ainsley cheered... *cheered.*

Is that octave truly necessary? Force a smile, Ember—smother her later.

"Yeah, I know it's a 'school night', but Ember and I have a pretty big meeting tomorrow so we're trying to loosen up beforehand." Bo reached across the table and grabbed my hand.

Activate launch sequence.

Ainsley's eyes immediately shot to our hands, then my eyes, then his eyes, and back to our hands. She took a deep breath and swallowed hard.

"Ahem," she cleared her throat and tried to pry her eyes from our hands to my eyes, "Ember, is it?"

Here we go.

"Yes, it is. November Harris, actually, pleased to meet you Ainsley." I broke my grip from Bo and stuck my hand out.

"That's an... interesting name." Her dead-fish grip held mine for a split second before she clasped her hands in front of her.

"Thank you!" *Two can cheer.*

Ainsley speared her eyes in to mine before looking slowly to Bo, who nodded almost imperceptibly to her.

"Well, I've got to get back to my girls, see ya later." She walked quickly back to her gaggle of friends.

"Jesus, I've never seen her back down like that before. Well done Ms. Harris." Admiration oozed from Bo's pores.

"It's the dress. Told you it's a good one."

As the second glass of champagne numbed my mouth, I noticed a large man across the dance floor. He seemed to be making his way toward us with a cocky smile on his face.

"Is that a friend of yours?" I shouted over the now blaring thumps of Ludacris.

When Bo glanced over his shoulder he released my hand and his shoulders sank for a minute. "That's Bill Holder."

"He's an enormous son of a bitch; did he play football with you?" The hair on the back of my neck stood higher the closer Bill came.

"He played, but not with me, he's Rachel's age. Let me warn you, he's great at what he does for DROP, but he's a massive asshole—real cocky."

While Bo's tone tried to be playful, it made me edgy. I suddenly wished for a shawl to cover myself with, especially when Bill's eyes settled on me. His imposing shadow strapped my shoulders against the booth and my pulse raced. I let out a long-held breath as he smiled—rather arrogantly—and gripped Bo's shoulders.

"Hey brother, what's goin' on?" Bill sat, uninvited, next to Bo, who rolled his eyes.

Seeming to ignore his inquisition, Bo nodded in my direction, "Bill, this is November Harris from The Hope Foundation. She's their grant writer."

Bill extended his massive hand across the table and, quickly, I put on my best business smile and returned the greeting, "Nice to meet you. Can I call you Bill?"

"Absolutely," he said unctuously.

The vibration from my phone made me jump half way out of the seat; it was a text from Monica.

Monica: *Hey Em! See you tomorrow, how's your weekend been?*

I smiled politely at Bill and Bo before I padded my text back.

Me: *Weekend's been great. Wait till you meet Rachel, Bo's sister—she's a riot. I actually just met Bill (William) Holder, their grant writer... he kind of gives me the creeps—huge guy. How are things with Josh?*

Monica: *Things are good, almost back to where they were :) Kick that Bill guy in the nuts if he acts like an asshole!*

Me: *Will do :-**

"So, Bill, Bo tells me you played football?" *Maybe if I get him talking more he won't creep me out so much.*

"Fuckin' right I did, State Champs, baby!" While his smile was genuine, his voice didn't settle right in my gut. *Something is off.*

"If you gentlemen will excuse me, I have to use the restroom." I forced a smile and slid carefully out of the booth; fighting the growing urge to run. *From what?*

Bo's eyes followed me all the way out of the booth and, I assumed, down to the bathroom. When I entered the bathroom I cursed my makeup for preventing me from splashing water on my face, like I so desperately wanted to. Instead, I took a few cleansing breaths against the cold tile of the bathroom wall, thankful for my backless dress. I picked up my phone and dialed Adrian's number; he answered on the first ring.

"Hey Em, did you get my text? I'm running late."

"No I didn't. *Shit.*" The gong of my heartbeat started to reach my ears.

"Everything OK?"

"Um, I just met Bill Holder. He's talking to Bo and I'm in the bathroom. He kind of gives me the creeps, Adrian..."

"Did he say or do anything to you?" Panic shot through the phone and closed my throat.

"No...why? Adrian, what's going on, does this have anything to do with—"

"Ember, I'll be there as soon as I can, just relax and hang with Bo, OK?"

"Where the hell are you anyway?" I couldn't calm myself down.

"On my way back from Portsmouth."

"Jesus, Adrian, that's like an hour away!"

"Relax, I'm more than half way there. Met up with some friends at Smuttynose and the afternoon got away from us." He sounded far more relaxed than I needed him to be. "Everything's fine, Blue. Be there soon." *Blue. He keeps doing that.*

He hung up without a goodbye and I was left, still near-panting, in the bathroom. *Blackmail, I meant to say blackmail to Adrian before he cut me off. Did he know that? Does he know something? Shit. Game face on, Ember.*

As I swung open the door with renewed confidence, Bo's figure in the doorway startled me.

"Shit!" I screamed.

"You OK? You're acting anxious." He placed his hand on my shoulder, his sweaty palm did not go unnoticed—nor did it help calm me down.

"Get in here." I yanked the buttons on Bo's shirt.

"Ember, what the hell, this is the woman's bathroom—"

"Bill Holder has something to do with your sister's blackmail, doesn't he?" I hissed, pressing my hand against the bathroom door.

Sweat beaded on Bo's forehead and the color drained from his face "Ember..."

"*Doesn't it?* That dude gives me the serious fucking creeps, Bo, *and* you called him a massive asshole. I had to ask myself, why would Bo have someone working for *his* organization who is a massive asshole?"

"It's not... holy shit..." Bo paced over to the sink and splashed water on his face. *Must be nice.*

"Look, I'm not going to say anything and I won't act any different to him out there, but I can tighten my guard around him for sure. Adrian didn't sound too pleased—"

"You called Adrian?" He growled through clenched teeth.

"Yes, psychopath. I called Adrian because Bill scared me and I wanted to know how soon Adrian was getting here."

"Why couldn't you tell me instead, Ember? Why did you have to run to Turner?" He stared into the empty sink, gripping it.

"No, this isn't going to turn into an Adrian vs. Bo thing. Does Bill have something to do with the blackmail? Just give me an answer and I'll drop it till later when we can talk about it at your house." I placed my hand on his steaming hot back.

"Yes. He does. And, it'll be all over soon, so don't worry about anything, OK?" With his head still hanging, he turned to look at me. His eyes were shrouded in exhaustion.

"OK, I trust you. Can we please go drink heavily now? That's the only way I can be around Bill Holder."

Bo's face warmed again against my words of reassurance.

"OK Rock Star, just don't tumble in those nosebleed heels like you did the last time you wore them," he chuckled as he led me to the dance floor.

"Deal, as long as you don't let me go home with anyone else like the last time I wore them." I shot my eyebrow sky high.

"Cold, Ember. Real Cold," he feigned hurt while theatrically grabbing his stomach.

On the way to the dance floor, we stopped by the bar and I opted for a cosmopolitan. One glance at the crowded bump-and-grind told me my drink wouldn't last two seconds out there before ending up down the front of my dress. With a smirk I poured the ice cold drink down my throat in one gulp, grateful for the instant calming effects of vodka.

"What, you want a repeat performance of that dog place?" Bo asked, referring to Lost Dog—the night Adrian took me home.

"I don't want those assholes spilling my drink." I nodded to the dancing fools. "Get me one more and I'll be set to go out and tear it up."

One more gulp of a cosmopolitan restored my equilibrium-and buried my inhibitions. Bo and I swung freely across the dance floor, though I couldn't seem to shake Bill's eye as he leaned back with his elbows up on the bar.

"I meant it, you know," Bo's lips on my ear caught my attention over Bill.

"Meant what?" I stopped dancing and grabbed his hips.

"Forever."

I staggered back, feeling the equal effects of the uneasy feeling in my stomach and the vodka.

"I meant it too, Bo... we'll just have to navigate it—"A tiny hand wrapping over Bo's shoulder stopped me.

Ainsley.

"Bo, can I steal you away for a minute?" Seduction was her game.

"Go ahead Babe, I need another drink anyway," I said, my eyes unmoving from Ainsley as I asserted my position.

Bo shot me a look of sardonic thanks as he moved across the dance floor with Ainsley. I turned back to the bar and ordered another cosmopolitan while I avoided the sight of them. I knew who he'd be going home with tonight; poor Ainsley.

"So, November, are you and Bo, like, a thing?" Bill Holder shouldered next to me and I could feel the steel of his arm muscles pulse in to me.

That was exactly the kind of question I was hoping to avoid until after the meeting tomorrow. So, I shook my head dismissively.

"Not really." I opted to look him straight in the eye.

"Oh, well, in that case, can I have this dance?" He placed his arm loosely around my middle.

Shit.

"I'd like to finish my drink first if you don't mind." I twirled out of his hold as fluidly as I could and leaned my front against the bar.

"Sweet moves, November." Bill wasn't going to go down easy. He stood next to me but put one hand on the bar across my back.

Perfect, now you're trapped against the bar. With one more turn I faced Bill, and looked over to Bo and Ainsley, who had no idea what was happening between me and Bill.

"I'm set, Bill, but thanks." I chanced rolling my eyes, not

knowing if it would set him off.

"Hey Bill, what's up?" A young man with a much calmer voice and sunnier disposition bounded beside Bill, slapping him on the back.

He was significantly shorter than Bill, and far less threatening looking. He had short bouncy blonde curls that gave me some sort of comfort.

"This gorgeous lady, here, is the grant writer for The Hope Foundation, and came here on Bo's arm tonight," Bill sneered. *Sneered.*

Chills exploded up my spine and bile bubbled in my throat as I forced myself to believe I was hallucinating the reason *why* Bill gave me such bad feeling.

"If she came with Bo, Bro, you better keep your hands off," his friend said in an eerily calming tone that inexplicably also gave me a bad feeling.

"Don't be such a pussy, dude, like I'd piss Bo off in here." Bill gestured with his hands.

An auditory memory pulsed through my ears; *Max, just get in the truck if you're going to be a useless pussy.*

No, it couldn't be.

I turned one more time so my back was to Bo, but I was no longer pinned against the bar.

"Take it easy, Bill, just trying to save your hide." His friend elbowed him playfully in the ribs.

He'll be here Bill, just take it easy.

Impossible.

Flashes of the night at the garage almost two weeks ago whipped wildly through my head; changing frames with each thump of the bass from the speakers. Bill sounded identical to the violent Bill from behind the garage—all that was missing was his calmer sidekick, Max.

Clearly I'd had too much to drink and my mind was playing tricks on me. Bill's imposing stature and snarling voice set off warning bells in my head, but he was a creepy looking guy anyway. I shook my head in an attempt to think rationally.

"Um, sorry, we haven't been introduced." I pointed my eyes to Bill's friend.

"This guy," Bill interjected, "works with us at DROP, too. He's the community educator."

"Oh, so you must be Tristan MacMillian?" I stuck out my hand as the bass from the stereo volleyed for position in my head over my heartbeat.

"Tristan's my dad's name," he smiled as he stuck out his hand, "my friends call me Max."

Run.

CHAPTER TWENTY-THREE

Are you crazy? Run!

My brain shouted to my frozen body as terror took over. It tasted like cayenne infused wine; it was disorienting and pulled beads of sweat to the surface of my forehead. I took one prey-like step back as my senses scrambled. In the last twenty minutes my brain received two very important pieces of information; one, Bill Holder is blackmailing Bo, two, the two men in front of me were most definitely the "Bill and Max" duo from the garage nearly two weeks ago.

"Hey, you OK?" Max reached out for my arm and I reflexively flinched back.

"I, uh, just need to get some air. I've had a lot to drink." My eyes moved from Max's to Bill's, and back again.

Turning my head to the dance floor, I finally caught Bo's sight. He put his hand on Ainsley's shoulder, mumbled something, and tore through the crowd toward me.

"Ember?" Bo gripped his hand on my sweat-soaked back.

"Get me out of here, now!" I raced toward the exit, not looking back.

Bo was just a second behind me as I sucked the cool, calming air in to my lungs outside McCarthy's.

"What the hell happened? Ainsley just—"

"This isn't about Ainsley, Bo. Those—those guys, Bill... and Max..." My erratic breathing was doing nothing to help my voice.

Bo grasped my shoulders and squared me to him, "They what, Ember? Did they say anything to you?" His fingers pressed in deep urgency against my skin.

"No. Those fucking guys were the ones, the ones behind the garage that I dropped my car off at two weeks ago. Why the *fuck* were they in Barnstable? Are they blackmailing other people?" I spewed all at once.

I became more aware of the sound of my breathing in the silent night. My eyes darted around, noting the desertion around Bo and me.

"I don't think so, Ember." Bo looked toward the door in growing fear.

"Well I've got news for you, they beat the hell out of some guy named Spike, and I—"

"What the fuck did you do, Cavanaugh?" the all-too familiar sneer followed us out to the sidewalk.

"Bill, *not now.*" Bo stood in front of me so I wasn't in the line of verbal fire.

"She knows *something*, Golden Boy, or she wouldn't have called you by your high school football name—no one calls you that anymore."

Bo's back stiffened as Bill's words hammered incoherently in to my head.

"Wait..." I stepped back slowly, dragging my toes with each step.

Bo turned to me and his pain-seared face nearly knocked me over.

"S-spike, is your nickname?" My head swirled as blackness overtook my peripheral vision.

In a flash, Bill was lunging past Bo and toward me. Bo threw up his forearm like a steel beam and stopped Bill from colliding with me; but he still managed to grab at my shoulder, knocking me off balance. Bo turned to steady me, giving Bill another swipe at me. He wrapped his hand around my arm.

"What'd he tell you, huh? Did he tell you about his slutty sister? Tell you how much money she owes me, that I took the job with DROP to get it back, but it wasn't coming fast enough?" He spoke through adrenaline, as Bo was lunging toward him.

I tried to pull my arm away but he only tightened his grip. Tears threatened, but for some reason I couldn't scream. I ducked in time for Bo's fist to connect with Bill's face, causing him to release my arm.

"Run, Ember! Go!" Bo hollered right through me. Thankfully, my fight-or-flight response chose flight in agreement with Bo, and I turned and ran. I heard nothing other than my heart beat and my heels on the sidewalk. My shoes did nothing to steady my frantic gait as I realized I had no idea where I was going.

Away.

My sight cleared as I focused on someone walking—no, running —down the sidewalk in my direction.

Adrian.

"Adrian! Adrian, help!" I managed a scream that tore through the quaint street.

I paid less attention to the scene behind me, and more attention to his face as we got closer. In one step, the pavement was no longer under my feet—it was under my face.

"Ember! What the hell is going on?" Adrian knelt beside me and grabbed my shoulders.

Stallion-like foot beats approached behind me as I pushed myself from the sidewalk. *Ouch.* For the first time since I ran, I looked back. Bo, Bill, and Max were a block behind me and Bo was holding them both back; but just barely.

"Those guys, Bill... and Max... they're involved..."

"*Jesus Christ*," Adrian fished through is pocket and produced a plastic credit-card looking thing, "here's my key for The Centennial, room 323, go!" He pointed in the direction he came from as he helped me to my feet before running toward Bo.

I kicked off my shoes and kept running, leaving them where I fell.

Taupe. That's the color I named the walls of Adrian's room at The Centennial. There was only a digital clock in the room, but I could hear the ticking of impossible time. I was growing anxious at the unknown fates of the men I'd left behind on the sidewalk

I must have been a real sight showing up to the classy hotel bloody and shoeless. I kept my head down as I ran to the elevator, praying not to run into anyone as I opened his door.

My muscles started to ring from the fall I took in those *damn* shoes. I rose and limped to the bathroom to survey the damage; my skinned elbows and knees were crusted in dried blood. My eyes lifted to meet themselves in the wall-length mirror; a fairly deep looking gash oozed blood from my right eyebrow—I turned aimlessly back to the room and sat carefully on the bed.

Taupe. Tick. Tock.

A soft knock on the door didn't startle me as it would have even two hours ago; I rose indolently and moved toward the door. There was another knock.

"It's Adrian, Ember."

I turned and walked back to the bed as I opened the door so he wouldn't see my face immediately. Adrian closed the door softly; more to appease me than the other guests, I assumed. I heard a clunk on the dresser and turned to see him set my shoes down; I cracked a half-smile but winced against the pain.

"Fuck, Blue, hang on," he said as he went to the bathroom and turned on the water. He returned with a wet washcloth and sat next to me on the bed, "I'm just going to clean off your face, OK?" I nodded, my eyes never leaving the infinite spot on the wall they'd chosen. When the warm washcloth connected with my wound, I leaned in to Adrian's hand and was able to finally start processing the events of the last couple of hours.

"Does anything else hurt?" he continued. I just shook my head.

"Where's Bo? Did he get hurt?" I asked, not moving my head from his hand.

"No, Cavanaugh's fine, don't know why those pricks messed with him in the first place—he's much stronger. They're at the police station; Bill and Max will be staying the night. Bo hung around a while to make sure you didn't have to come down and give a statement."

"What? Of course I do, right?"

"You didn't really have anything to do with the fight those three got into on the sidewalk; you ran away. Bo wants you as far away from this as possible." Adrian draped his arm around my shoulder.

"But, in Barnstable the three of them—"

"The three of them were in Barnstable? When?" Adrian leaned back, forcing me to hold my own weight. I noticed Adrian was wearing a tight red t-shirt, and wanted to smile at our wardrobe telepathy. I chose, however, to remain on the task at hand.

I told Adrian the story of the night when I dropped my car off at the garage, and the events that transpired thereafter. He listened intently, like the lawyer he'd become; furrowing his brow, nodding, and rubbing his chin.

"So you didn't *see* any of them." Adrian asserted.

"No, just heard their names and they were talking about Rae... but I thought it was 'Ray'. They called the other guy 'Spike,' which I now know to be some high school nickname given to Bo..." My thoughts drifted to Rachel who was still, hopefully, unaware of the situation.

As Adrian opened his mouth to speak, there was a frantic knock on the door.

"Adrian? November? It's Bo—let me in."

I rose, but Adrian's hand forced me back to the bed.

"Just sit, you're a mess," he said as he headed toward the door.

Inexplicably, Adrian opened the door just a crack.

"What the hell Turner, let me in! I need to see her, is she OK?" Bo was frantic.

"Just, OK, stay calm dude, she hasn't cleaned up yet," Adrian said as he backed away from the door.

"What the hell? Oh my God, Ember!" Bo fell to his knees in front of me, wrapping his arms around my waist and burying his face in my lap.

The dam broke, and in the span of time it took for him to utter the word 'God', I went from near-catatonic to a heaving, shuddering mess. He rose and met me on the bed, using tender strength as he pulled me toward him. When I finally pulled away, I saw my blood-stained tears resting on his shirt, and Adrian standing uncomfortably by the bathroom door.

"Bo, what the *fuck* was all of that?" I finally managed as I stood and crossed toward the bathroom to clean myself off. Adrian walked to the other side of the room as Bo remained seated.

I walked out after my face, elbows and knees were sufficiently cleaned, and found the guys in the exact same positions.

"Ember," Adrian started, "you were telling me that you saw, or heard, something with Bill and Max a couple weeks ago in Barnstable?" His tone was prompting.

"Yea, and apparently Bo—but they called him Spike..."

"That was my nickname in high school-long story," he chuckled.

"Why didn't I know about this, Bo?"

Bo stood and faced Adrian, "Those assholes knew I'd be in Southern New England for a couple weeks on business and they were getting impatient. I knew if I just got it out of the way at the beginning of the trip it would buy me a couple of weeks..."

"Damn it, Cavanaugh!" Adrian yelled. "A fight? Behind a garage!"

"Calm down, Turner." Bo held up his hands and dropped his voice.

"But you didn't *see* anyone?" Adrian continued, shifting his glance back to me.

"No, I told you that," I said as I crossed passed Bo, toward Adrian. I was their geographic center for the moment; I'd seen enough fights for one night, "It was dark, I was hiding behind a *fucking tree*, and I—" I stopped myself mid-sentence, dropping my jaw, and widening my eyes in horror at Adrian.

"What?" Adrian reached for me, but I turned to my right.

"What?" Bo asked.

I turned slower than I'd ever turned in my life and addressed Bo.

"When did you know it was me?" I choked, shaken by my own words.

One...

Two...

Three...

"*When* did you know it was *me, Bowan?*" I took one purposeful step forward and heard Adrian shift behind me.

"Ember," Adrian touched my shoulder, turning me back around, "what the hell are you talking about?"

"I saw *him* that night." The weight of the revelation did its best to crush me.

Bo touched my back, "Nov—"

"Shh!" I replied, not turning around, "I saw 'Spike' that night. It was nearly dark, he was shadowed under a street light more than fifty feet away. I heard the fight, one car pull away, I checked to see... "

I turned back to Bo.

"November..."

"When... the *fuck*... did you know it was me?" I recoiled as he reached for me.

Anxious sweat highlighted his forehead, "We were fifty feet away, I had no idea—"

"Bullshit! You realize there was a potential witness to whatever the hell happened and you don't use every *single* second to memorize every detail of what I look, sound, act like? Tell me, Bo..."

His shoulders sank and my rage ignited unlike anything I'd ever felt before. I lunged toward him with feral strength, and was as surprised as he when my palms connected with his chest, and he staggered backwards.

"*You knew it was me?*" How long did it take? Was it the second you saw me at Finnegan's, when I sang with you on stage?" I kept pushing and pushing him until he was against the wall. When there was nowhere left to push, I clenched my fists and pounded them in to his chest and shoulders.

"Ember, fuck, stop!" Bo tried to grab for my arms, but I was thrashing so erratically, he couldn't catch up.

"Was it after we kissed, after we had *sex?!*" Heavy sobs replaced desperate anger. "When was it, Bo, when did you realize that I was the scared shitless girl? Was it right away? Were you thrilled by the coincidence that I walked in to Finnegan's so you could hold onto me as an insurance policy; that I wouldn't say anything if I remembered who you were?" My fists pounded harder in to him and my voice was lost in my tears. Bo did nothing to stop the blows.

Suddenly, two hands gripped my shoulders from behind and yanked me away, "Ember! Get off him!" Adrian yelled as he moved one hand around my waist.

Adrian forced me down on to the bed and held his hands on my shoulders as Bo slid down the wall and buried his face in his hands.

"Will *someone, calmly* tell me what is going on?"

"When the fight behind the garage was done, I walked over to see if the guy who came by himself was OK. I couldn't see him because of the darkness, the distance, and the fact that I was scared as *hell*," I'd never attacked anyone before, and it left me quite breathless, "I'm now finding it quite convenient that it was *him* and he made himself so available to me."

"November, it's not like that, I had *no* idea it was you until—"

"Until when? Are you honestly telling me that you didn't know I was the girl at the garage *before* tonight?" I stayed seated and took a deep breath, which caused Adrian to relax his defensive stance in front of my body.

"When you walked on stage at Finnegan's you looked familiar, but I couldn't place from where." I started to respond but both Adrian and Bo held up their hands. "Then Monica mentioned that you saw some sort of altercation near your house, I thought it was a coincidence..."

I remembered Bo's over-concerned reaction that night, and more pieces fell into place.

"You brushed it off so effortlessly that I had no reason to believe it was you," he continued.

"When, did you know it was me?" Fresh tears formed and tumbled down my cheeks.

Bo sighed heavily as he stood and walked cautiously toward me, "Ember, that night when I came back early from my meeting here, and we walked on the beach..." He reached toward me but leaning back was my only response as he planted his knees in front of my feet.

"When we walked on the beach what?" I said blankly.

"We got to the parking lot, and there was a truck... "

"It *was* their truck."

"Yes." His head was hanging so low I could see the very top of the tattoo on his back where his collar opened.

"And *they* were in it."

"Yes," he mumbled, still looking at the floor.

I stood slowly, brushing off Adrian's hand, "It's fine, Adrian." I paced toward Bo.

My knees were level with the top of Bo's head as I continued, "I told you that the truck looked exactly like the one that night behind the garage—*exactly*. So that night you had all the confirmation you needed, and you still didn't say anything to me?"

Bo lifted his head and his face was twisted in regret. "What would have been the point?"

"The point," I snarled, "is that you *chose* not to tell me that it was you the entire time. The *point* is that the next day, and the day after that, we said we *loved* each other."

Adrian wiped his palms on the front of his pants and headed back to the window; this conversation was sucking the life out of the room.

"Ember, I had my suspicions, sure. But, what was I supposed to do? Tell a girl I just met that I was beaten up behind some garage? At that point I couldn't have told you about the blackmail without scaring you away or risking Rae's safety—I didn't know you. By the time I knew it was you, it was too late; I was in love with you." His shaky hand trembled against my arm, but I didn't move.

"That's the reason you *should* have told me!" I roared as I took one step back, causing him to drop his grip.

"Ember!" Bo raked his hands furiously through his hair as he stood, "I was backed into a corner! You were never supposed to find out about the blackmail, but it was all spiraling out of control so fast!"

"Holy—that's the reason my dreams of that night didn't start until *after* we met... it was your voice..." My eyelashes touched my eyebrows at the thought. "And even after I told you about the nightmares, nothing? Shit, that bruise you had on your stomach, that wasn't from helping your friend - that was from that night!"

"Ember, it shouldn't have ever happened like this! It was too late, I was so *fucking* in love with you I couldn't think straight..." I answered his step forward with one back of my own.

"You were *never* planning on telling me, were you? We were talking about *forever* and you were going to leave that out— forever."

"November—"

"Don't! It's too late." I raised my hands in defense as more tears plummeted down my face.

"No!" Panic rang through the room with a deafening howl.

I turned toward Adrian to avoid Bo's face.

"Get out," I said as emotionless as possible.

"Come on, Ember, it was just—"

I felt a breeze behind me and turned to see him on his knees again, hands clenched in his hair. I looked back at Adrian, who had to turn away.

"November, please, *please* try to understand," he pleaded painfully as he reached for my calves.

When his hands wrapped around my calves they slid a little under the sweatiness of his palms. He tried to stop their shaking by tightening his grip around me as he buried his face in my bloodied knees.

"Bowan when I met you..." *My soul shifted; my heart pulsed with fresh blood.* "Never mind, it was all a lie; I was just a pawn in some high-society bullshit blackmail."

"No! November, no!" His fingers dug deeper in to my legs.

I bent at the knees slightly, forcing him to look at me through tears and blood. When our eyes locked I took a deep breath, aiming for clarity.

"Trust, Bo. All that keeps two people together is trust. Love isn't enough. I don't trust you. I don't want to see you ever again. Get out." My throat locked and threw away its own key against the words.

Bo reached up and pulled me to my knees by the wrist, causing Adrian to rush to my side.

"Ember, please. Calm down. We can work this out, come on!" His plea wretched through my soul, and for a split-second I wanted to concede, but couldn't. I had been purposefully put in danger, lied to, and deceived.

I couldn't meet his eyes. I remained on my knees, begging the floor to swallow me.

Adrian lifted me from the other side, "Everyone needs to sleep on this, I think," he said with remarkable poise. After I was on my feet, Bo tried one more time to convince me to talk.

"Ember, can we just take a walk, or something?"

Adrian put his hand up, "Dude, tomorrow, OK? Everyone needs to sleep off tonight."

Crestfallen, Bo followed Adrian out of the room, looking at me one more time over his shoulder before the door closed.

CHAPTER TWENTY-FOUR

The water in the shower at The Centennial burned my skin. It was liquid therapy. I let the water boil over the raw skin on my face, elbows, and knees; inviting it to boil through my soul to no avail. I heard the door to the room click open and closed.

"Ember, it's Adrian—you OK in there?" The sincerity of his voice produced fresh tears that washed away with the shower.

"Yea, I'll be out in a minute. Thank you."

Turning off the shower produced an eerie silence; a foggy, suffocating silence. Not even the TV could be heard in the other room; Adrian was observing the silence as well. As I dried, I groaned at the fact that all of my belongings were still at the Cavanaugh house. Without pretense, I walked in to the room in just my towel and stared at my red dress, crumpled on the floor.

"Hey," Adrian called gently.

When I looked up, I saw him lift my suitcase and a bag onto the bed.

"How did you..." I paced toward my things.

"When I brought Bo back to his house he had me wait so he could get your things..." Adrian shrugged uncomfortably.

"Adrian, I'm so sorry for dragging you into this. I need to call Monica to come pick me up. I need to call my boss to tell her about everything..." *Dissolution of the relationship...*

Adrian sat next to me and put his arm around my bare, wet shoulder, "I'll call Monica. I'll just give her the basics and tell her that you'll fill her in in the morning. I'll take you home, but you need to get some sleep first. About your boss, Bo said he was heading inside to call David Bryson to tell him about the blackmail. David and Monica will fill your boss in. Don't worry about it tonight.

"Just like that..." I whispered.

"What?" Adrian lifted my chin.

"Nothing... I'll get dressed. Sleep sounds divine, I'm sore as hell."

"Here's some ibuprofen, take it." Adrian handed me the pills and a glass of water. "You're a tough shit, November Harris, I've never seen anyone so..."

"Pissed?" I laughed as I swallowed the pills.

"Yeah, pissed. Look, I'm sorry about what happened with Bo, I can tell how much you mean to each other." He pulled me in for a hug.

"*Meant.* And, I'm sorry you had to witness all of that." I spoke weakly into his chest.

"It was intense, that's for sure. But, I'm glad to know you can hold your own, Blue, that was something."

I stood to bring my clothes to the bathroom, but Adrian excused himself to the hallway so I'd have privacy and he could make phone calls. As I gave in to sleep, I could hear Adrian's muffled voice in the hallway, "Hey Monica, it's Adrian... yes, Adrian Turner. Look, something happened tonight. No don't freak out, everyone's OK for the most part..."

I woke early, thankful for a dreamless sleep. Stretching out in bed I could feel the pain of last night in every muscle of my body and soul. When I sat up on my elbows I smiled at the sight of Adrian

Turner sleeping in the desk chair. His head rested at an awkward angle against the wall, and his arms folded in front of him. The crinkle of the comforter as I swung my legs over the bed startled him awake.

"Sorry," I whispered.

"How'd you sleep?" He rubbed his neck.

"Great, actually. Turns out being chased, and trying to kick someone's ass really takes something out of you. Why didn't you sleep in the bed?"

"OK, Ember, you break up with your boyfriend and I slide in to bed with you that night? I'll pass on going *straight* to Hell, thanks," he laughed as he stood.

"Can we get the hell out of here?" I pulled my Princeton hoodie over my head, "or do you have all kinds of DROP shit to attend to today?"

"I'm taking a personal day. So, yes, let's go... Do you want to talk about last night?"

"Adrian, have I *ever* wanted to talk about *any* last night?" I smirked.

He stifled a chuckle, "I'm serious. That was some heavy..."

"I know... and I'm not ready to think about it again, yet. Can we get the *hell* out of here?"

The truth is, all I'd done since I woke up was think about it. I thought about love, loss, betrayal and pain. Bo trampled my trust, and I still couldn't piece it all together in my brain. I couldn't look at him anymore; not the same way I did that first night at Finnegan's. It was all different now. None of it could be taken back. Adrian caught my pensive stare at the wall and proceeded to load our things in to his car.

I thumbed through my phone as Adrian started his car and pulled down Main Street. I had a text from Monica that she sent last night:

Monica: *Ember, I talked to Adrian. Get sleep, I'll be at your apartment waiting for you tomorrow.*

I had an email from my boss:

November,
I received a call and email from David Bryson very early this morning. I also spoke with Bo. Take the week off and call me when you can. I'm sorry all of this happened. – Carrie.

Finally, there was a text from Bo:
Bowan: *I know you'll ignore me if I call, and I don't dare try to see you in person right now. I love you, November. When I said forever, I meant it. I'll never stop loving you. Please forgive me. Forgive me.*

Sleep didn't erase the emotional pain, and I bit my lip as I slid my phone back in to my bag.

"Hey, what's in that bag?" I asked Adrian, noting a paper gift bag on top of my suitcase.

Adrian shrugged, "Bo said it's yours—that you never opened the card. If you want me to take it—"

"No," I interrupted, "I'll just open it..." I hesitated as I ran my thumb under the seal.

The square card held a CD. I gestured to Adrian to put the CD in his player as I read the note Bo wrote:

November Blue,

You've given me the most perfect ten days that anyone could ever dream of having. I love you more each day, and plan to love you more for however many days I have left on this Earth.

The note slipped through my hands and hit the floor of the car as the music started, and familiar voices filled the space around us,

"Don't know what time it is, I've been up for way too long and I'm too tired to sleep..."

"That's me...and Monica...and Bo, from the first night we sang together at Finnegan's. It was the first night I met him. It's *The Wailin' Jenny's*—Josh must have recorded it..." I pushed Adrian's hand out of the way when he tried to turn off the music. "Don't...we sounded awesome." I managed a grin as I leaned in to the headrest and watched Concord fly past my window.

"...then maybe I'll walk a while, and feel the earth beneath..."

The song slapped me across the face as I heard Bo's voice join mine, a cappella, through the speakers. I reached for the card on the floor and opened the composition book to slide it in. As I opened the front cover, I noticed there was writing on the left side, opposite Bo's transcription of the lullaby:

"There is the kiss of welcome and of parting, the long, lingering, loving, present one; the stolen, or the mutual one; the kiss of love, of joy, and of sorrow; the seal of promise and receipt of fulfillment."

~Thomas C. Haliburton

I didn't feel Adrian pull the car over, but I knew we were stopped. My face was buried in his chest; his embrace tried to hush my body-quaking sobs right there on the side of the road.

My soul felt more battered than my body, but it begged me to stay; to find Bo and try to understand just one more time. My mind, however, couldn't process anymore hurt—any more lies. I handed my soul to Bo Cavanaugh, and was given bloodied knees and a busted face in return. I was broken. For the first time in my life I was broken, and it was at the hands of the cruel temptress "Reckless Abandon." Our souls had gone out ahead of us and made plans they couldn't promise they'd keep, and I was left in a sobbing heap.

"Shh," Adrian whispered in to the top of my head. "It's going to be alright."

"What if it's not? I loved him, Adrian. What am I supposed to do?" I had no strength to pull my head from his chest—I kept sobbing.

Adrian rested his chin on the top of my head, and I felt him shrug. There weren't any words that could resuscitate my soul—not today.

Somewhere, in between my incoherent wails and whispers of reassurance from Adrian, loneliness let herself in and swallowed my soul.

ACKNOWLEDGMENTS

First and foremost, I have to thank my husband, Scott, for fully supporting my dream. Thank you for putting up with a dirty house, lots of take-out dinners, sometimes sleeping alone when I stayed up way too late to write, and my attitude the next day. Thank you for helping me schedule time to get out of the house to spend hours writing, reading, editing, and editing, and editing. I love you.

Thank you to my parents for always encouraging my writing, and showing excitement over reading this book. Dad, I *really* hope you didn't read Chapter Six. Mom, don't let dad read Chapter Six. Please. Oh, Brian (my brother), if you happen to read this book, you also may not read Chapter Six.

Thank you to Ruth Moody of *The Wailin' Jenny's* for granting permission for me to use the lyrics to "Heaven When We're Home." Receiving your e-mail was one of the highest points of writing this story.

Evan Spinosa – Thank you for the gorgeous photograph and cover design.

Jessica – You read each chapter as I finished it. You read some righteous crap and loved it anyway. I loved hearing you beg me for more. I hope you read it again, I promise it got tons better.

Jennifer Roberts-Hall – Your editing wizardry left me in awe. Thank you for cleaning up this work, chatting with me about line and word choices, and being so gracious and selfless. I bow in your honor.

My Beta Readers: Michelle Pace, Michelle Mankin, and Melissa Perea – Every step of the way. On every step you helped me find words, colors, senses, and feelings. You were my personal cheering section online, on the phone, and on Skype. Your encouragement held my hand and my heart. **Mankin** – I love that you're a huge fangirl for Bo. Your encouragement and praise through the whole process has been humbling. **Pace** – Your Adrian love makes my heart smile. We must schedule time for my friends to meet yours in Jefferson Point. **Perea** – Thank you for helping me trickle angst through the rainbow of love. Keep reading, Pix, there's more.

Maggi Meyers, Leslie Fear, Melissa Brown, and Dave Newell – Late night chats, honest critiques, and the necessary videos and songs at 1:00am helped me stay just this side of sane. I wish absolute and stratospheric success for all of your novels – you deserve it.

Melissa Perea – Yea, you get two. I can't thank you enough for hours of late-night book banter, critiques, deep discussions, and a promise to never let each other publish anything less than our best. I hope this lives up to our pact.

The Indie Bookshelf – You ladies are amazing. It feels wonderful to be part of a group supporting independent arts. Thank you for your support, and the chocolate :). Check them out at www.theindiebookshelf.blogspot.com.

Starbucks – Thank you for the swanky office space, free wifi, delicious energy, and support for this book.

To all the Indie authors who have helped pave the way and are still keeping the streets clean – You are all rock stars to me. I want to specifically thank J. Sterling, Colleen Hoover, and Tarryn Fisher. Without you, and the road you paved with rainbows, butterflies, pumpkins, strength, and venom, this book wouldn't exist.

BA Ladies (and Fred) – Your unwavering support for Indie Lit. is encouraging; spread the love.

The Clapp Memorial Library in Belchertown, Massachusetts— Thank you for your teen book group when I was in high school, and your summer reading program. Your efforts poured the foundation for the will of this book.

Finally, to everyone with a dream and a will – If it scares you, you must do it.

ABOUT THE AUTHOR

Andrea Randall lives in Upstate New York with her husband and three children. She holds a B.S. in Development Sociology from Cornell University, which, she promises her parents, was put to good use in writing this novel.

Connect with her via **Facebook** at:
www.facebook.com/AuthorAndreaRandall
or on **Twitter**: ARandallAuthor

If you liked this book, write a review online.
Better yet, tell a friend!

ANDREA RANDALL

Read on for a sneak preview of

Reckless Abandon

Book 2 of
The November Blue Series

CHAPTER ONE

"Stop! Stop!" My voice sounds like record player static as I race toward Bo.

"November!"

The call stops me in my tracks. Bo is looking at me, but the voice is coming from behind me. I turn to see Adrian charging my way with bull-force; his arms waving me out of the way. I turn back just in time for the buttons on Bo's shirt to introduce themselves to my face, and I land head-first on the pavement.

They collide in a sonic boom of testosterone; neither seems concerned with the blood pouring from my head. A shadow blackens my view of the fight, and suddenly a bear paw of a hand is in front of my face.

"Come with me." The smoke of his voice encircles my senses, making my blood run cold and scared.

"Get away from me! Bo, Adrian, help me!" I'm a foot to the side of them but they don't see me, or *him*. They're battling to the death; my voice sounds further and further away in my head each time I scream.

"Get up." The paw snares my upper arm, yanking me with it.

"Adrian! Bo!" I'm trying to shake free, but the snare tightens and drags me away.

By the time they admit there would be no winner of this fight, it's too late. My screams are going unheard as I'm pulled into the darkness.

"Ember, wake up!" a voice beckons from above.

Suddenly I am graced with the peace that this is a dream. I let his voice pull me back to reality. My eyes flip open and in one motion I'm seated, trying to regulate my breathing.

"Sorry, did I wake you up?" I say, to prove I'm out of that hell in my subconscious.

"No, I haven't gone to bed yet. Another nightmare, huh?"

I glance at the clock; it reads 10:00 PM. I shake my head at the exhaustion I've been ignoring in favor of wallowing.

"Yea, another nightmare. Thank you for staying with me the last couple nights."

"Of course." He runs his thumb across my chin and disappears to the kitchen, returning with a glass of water that I feverishly accept.

"Thanks, Adrian," I manage after half of the water is gone.

He just smiles and walks quietly back to the living room, giving me time to collect myself.

I gulp the water in fury, hoping to flush the nightmares from my body; but the S.S. Cavanaugh appears unsinkable in the turbulent waters of my soul.

After a few moments and another deep breath, I head to the living room. Adrian sits, flipping through the channels on the TV, settling on ESPN. After driving my soulless body back from Concord, he's stayed here the past two nights; and hasn't gone far during the day. I asked my parents for some time after they insisted they come and stay with me; they obliged. For some reason I felt I couldn't burden Monica with my mess, but before I could tell her "no" when she assumed I'd stay with her, Adrian offered to stay with me until I felt safe and calm.

We haven't spoken much about what unfolded between McCarthy's and his hotel room, or between me and Bo. Frankly, we haven't spoken much at all. He's worked on his laptop in my living room most days, while I travel between my bed, bathroom, and kitchen. He's prepared at least two meals a day for me, and doesn't

2

scold me like a child when they go largely uneaten.

"You OK?" He catches me staring and puts down the footrest on the recliner.

"Yea."

I walk to him and stand for a moment, our knees touching. He sets the remote down and grips the arms of the chair, working me over with concerned eyes.

"Em . . ." His eyes beg me for something, anything.

In one long blink I curl myself onto his lap. His hands hesitate for a moment before finding rest around my waist. He breathes in my shampoo as I settle my head on his shoulder. My breath falters against the words brewing in my throat. Adrian notices.

"What's going on?" He nudges my shoulders, forcing me to sit up and look at him.

"You called me Blue, Adrian."

"I know." He swallows hard; this is the first time I've brought it up.

"Right there, on the beach, in front of Bo, you called me Blue like nothing had happened. Like no time had passed." I keep my voice quiet and calm, reliving the memory of his voice against the waves.

"I know."

"I hadn't seen you in four years and we were standing in front of my boyfriend," I chuckle for the first time in a lifetime, "and, right there, you just blurt it out."

"Were you mad?" A grin tugs caution away from his face.

"Furious."

"Ha. You don't look furious." He tucks his bottom lip behind his teeth.

I shrug. "I was mad that it still made me feel the way it always made me feel." Heaviness flexes in my chest.

"How's that?"

"Special. Yours." I yawn and set my head back on his shoulder as he rubs mine.

"You are," he whispers.

"Which one?" I ask as my eyelids close up shop.

If he has a response, I don't hear it before I drift off. There won't be any nightmares here.

21244663R00146

Made in the USA
Lexington, KY
04 March 2013